Get To Know Yourself And Transform Your Life With The Wisdom And Magical Power Of Stories

Get To Know Yourself And Transform Your Life With The Wisdom And Magical Power Of Stories

Pejman Aghasi

iUniverse, Inc.
New York Lincoln Shanghai

Get To Know Yourself And Transform Your Life With The Wisdom And Magical Power Of Stories

iUniverse, Inc.

For information address:
iUniverse, Inc.
2021 Pine Lake Road, Suite 100
Lincoln, NE 68512
www.iuniverse.com

ISBN: 0-595-29829-X

Contents

Acknowledgments

I would like to thank my family, specially my brother, Paiman who had supported me all the way and without his support I could not have finished this book. I would like to also thank the love of my life, Sepideh, whose emotional support and encouragement helped me to carry on the long hours of work, which was necessary to finish this book. Also I would like to thank my friends, Nicholas R Mitchell, Ahmad Zohadi, Debbie Papadakis and Nader Zohadi who have helped me and supported me during the process. Most of all, I would like to thank god, who has given me the opportunity to write and publish this book.

Foreword

It is both an honor and pleasure to contribute the forward of this impressive and inspiring book.

Pejman Aghasi is a person who has overcome his own challenges, by connecting with god and divine order.

He went through life traveling from place to place, meeting many well known spiritual healers and masters, and spending time in India, Tibet, Middle east and north America, searching for answers.
Little did he know that the answers where within himself. He found fulfillment, a sense of meaning and satisfaction through his inner connection with god, who presented himself as the "divine order".

"Transform your life, with the wisdom and power of stories" will help you to rediscover the human significance and the need for physical, emotional, mental and spiritual balance, in the journey through life.

This book is consisted of 52 short but inspiring spiritual stories from various cultures and religions, their 52 offerings of hidden wisdom, and 52 spiritual and mental exercises, one for every week of the year.

The stories were carefully made and selected, to point out to 52 kinds of major challenges that we may face in life, and offers 52 answers to all of these challenges. Also these, simple, yet powerful spiritual and mental exercises and techniques will help the readers to overcome their daily challenges. Furthermore it allows the reader to learn, grow and move foreword toward reaching enlightenment, self realization and god realization.
Pejman Aghasi, who was disabled and could not walk when I met him, became a source of inspiration for all of us, when I was teaching a hypnosis Certification program. Because I and 15 of my students, witnessed a miracle in the class room.

I would like to share the author's own story with all the readers.

Pejman had lost his ability to walk as a result of a chronic muscular disease. He had not walked for the past five years when I first met him.

The origins of pejman's rebirth began quite accidentally and innocently. It began actually, while in a kitchen during a break in hypnosis class, I overheard Pejman discussing his physical condition with one of the students. He suggested that he would some day walk again, but not in a near future.

Then I suggested that, we can regress you back to the time that this disease was first created in your body, and find the cause and see what can we do about it. Pejman agreed.

The actual miracle of rebirth of Pejman was in my hypnotherapy training class of sept 28,2001. The actual event was so memorable that it continues to reside as a vivid, permanent moment in my life, along with the 15 on looking students that also witnessed this within the class room, who were in absolute awe. The actual conversations that, unfolded was as follows:

Pejman volunteered to be in a demonstration for a fast hypnosis induction in the class. While in trance as a student has described, he had an expression on his face that was "god-like"

Debbie: Go back to the original cause of your inability to walk, what is causing it? When is the time?

Pejman: I am surrounded with lights, I have no body

Debbie: Where are you?

Pejman: In the light

Debbie: Why was the decision made for you to lose your legs?

Pejman: To bring me back to my proper cause, enlightenment.

Debbie: How do you get the information?

Pejman: divine order

Debbie:How can you see the divine order?

Pejman: Time is near, you just have to ask, and it shall be given

Debbie: What do you need to get your legs working again?

Pejman: One shall not be concerned with physical appearance in the higher planes there is no need for physical body one is directed by divine to devote life to bring, peace and universal love to all beings.

Debbie: Once you learn the lesson, will you be released from this problem?

Pejman: What you call problem, is a spiritual journey toward completion, If all could be learned anyway, If that is god's will, so it shall be, I cannot question god's will, I am embraced with god, all I find here is love and light, I fill bliss.

Debbie: is god willing you to teach without leg challenges?
Pejman: When you are drowning in the ocean of love, It is so elementary now.
Debbie: could we experience the same level of bliss that you are experiencing now?
Pejman: There is no you and me, just different levels of consciousness. I am just your higher self, The body you see is just a mental block, If you ask, you will be given, the same.
Debbie: Memorize the feeling and emerge whenever you are ready.

He emerged after 15 minutes, and announced that he will walk and even run. To every body's amazement he started running in the hallway, outside my class, we even video taped his running.
He was healed and transformed instantly. After that event, he had acquired incredible healing and channeling abilities.

This book is a combination of information from the divine order blended with the interpretation of his own personal knowledge and experience.

Debbie Papadakis, Director
Hypno-healing institute
Toronto, Canada

Wisdom and power of stories

Stories can heal and resolve many minor and major problems without offending the listener. By telling a story to number of people, each one of them can subjectively realize their problem, and at the same time find a solution to their problems in that story without even the story teller being aware of their problem. This will protect the listener against embarrassment, humiliation and criticism, which is the main cause of why many people refuse to open up and tell others what is bothering them, but they have no objection against listening to an impersonal and educational story.

Another, powerful characteristics of stories are that they are accepted easier than facts and theories, because they bypass our critical and analytical conscious mind, and stories are automatically picked up and accepted by our subconscious mind, and then subconscious mind processes these newly gathered information to all areas of our lives, and these new information sheds new light, insight and understanding to our lives.

Furthermore stories are memorized much faster than other specific dry and difficult facts and commandments and are also remembered for a longer period of time. Since our brain stores memory by organizing the information and saves any given information with its existing surroundings. But most of the times theories are too abstract and colorless to be remembered easily, because it simply doesn't meet the "fun and interesting or vital" criteria of our Subconscious mind. Because our brain accesses its memory only based on a need, be it for pleasure or survival. Furthermore facts and theories often written for the already intellectual and well educated and expert people. Therefore, usually the purpose and usefulness of the facts are not explained, or even if it is explained, it is too complex for most people to grasp it. And when we are facing a problem which is emotional in nature, we lack the necessary logical focus to understand the meaning of these abstract and complex theories and even if we do make the time it will take a lot of energy and time to find a solution and relief from the problem.

However since the root of the problem is emotional in nature, it cannot be resolved by logical reasoning, that is, you can't solve it, simply by gaining more knowledge, and piling up lots of information won't help, you need instead gain a new understanding and a new view point to see your problem from a different angle.

And for doing so you need to access the right side of your brain which is the creative and emotional part of our brain which corresponds with our inner subconscious mind which is nonjudgmental, fast and more connected with our feelings.

On the other hand stories have that color, excitement, adventures, mysteries and passion in them. Stories, by having these characteristics are easily stored and imprinted on our subconscious mind and gives almost an instant and effortless relief and insight to our problems.

The stories in this book have been selected carefully to address the most universal questions and problems that many of us may face, in our daily lives.

I have included 52 Stories from variety of cultures and religions.I wish the power and magic of stories will help you to enlighten and to solve many of the challenges that you may encounter in your everyday life.

The hidden wisdom behind the stories is explained in each story and its connection to our daily life is also noted, so we can learn more about ourselves and our experience. I believe more we see ourselves as closer to God, we become calmer and more peaceful, because we become satisfied and content with ourselves, since we have stared, the wonderful journey of the self-realization which will eventually lead to god-realization and the ultimate freedom from all material bondage and returning to our divine self.

I am certain that these stories can help all the readers, because it has helped and healed many of my problems and also has helped thousands of my students whom I have told these stories to them in between of my lectures and seminars.

This book consists of 52 short spiritual stories from various cultures and religions, their 52 offerings of hidden wisdom, and 52 spiritual and mental exercises, one for every week of the year.

I believe knowledge and wisdom are only useful when we use them and put them to practice in our daily lives.

I wish your life, to become the sweetest story of success, love, happiness, health growth and enlightenment.

1. We see only what we believe

Once upon a time in Mexico, a Shamanic master lived in a small village. One day he had a friend visiting from united states, his friend who was a writer was visiting the shaman on a regular basis, to learn from his expertise and powers, and was planning to publish a book based on his findings. Each time he visited the master, he would teach him a new shamanistic point of view and would teach and show this new way of looking at the world to him in action. That day the master told his friend that. Most of the western society thinks that we believe only what we see. However in reality mind works the other way around, meaning we see only what we believe. The writer asked but how can it be?, He said I will show you shortly. He told him that the villagers usually come to visit him and ask for his expertise and shamanic powers to locate herds of wild horses, and two of them are supposed to come to see him today. We should wait till they get here. Shortly after two villagers came to him at different times, to ask him for guidance and information about the location where these horses could be found. The master told both of them about the location where they could find these horses, but one was told that the herd had eight horses, and the other was told it had twenty-four. The master was talking about the same herd at the same location. So the villagers went to the valley, and end of the night they came back with what they had captured. The first man, since he was told he can capture only eight horses and believed it to be true because he trusted and viewed the master as a reliable man who would only tell him the truth. Therefore since he could not imagine owning more than eight horses, he could find only eight, on the other hand the second man was led to believe that he can capture twenty-four horses, and he could imagine having and owning twenty-four horses, therefore he could successfully find and capture twenty-four horses. The American writer was amazed with the result, and asked the master to elaborate more on what has transpired. The master smiled and said, we can see only what we have thought about and imagined internally.

Every event or circumstances that are happening in our physical life, is a direct reflection of our imagination, thoughts and beliefs. What we believe exists for us, and can be observed and experienced. Therefore if we want to achieve some goal,

we need to first achieve that goal in our mind and by imagination we need to see
that we have already accomplished that goal. What our mind believes as possible
and true it tends to find and experience in the world. Because in reality, and in
nature there is an absolute abundance of possibilities of wealth, health and happiness, we just need to believe and recognize that they are out there and we deserve
to have them, only then you will find them.

Therefore only focus and contemplate on the positive, infinite and spiritual
abundance, in that way you will have an infinite and positive belief about the
world and its possible blessings for you, and consequently you will find those
exact things in your life.

The wisdom of the story is that our beliefs may limit us, and that we can have
only as much as we can imagine ourselves having. Most spiritual schools of
thoughts and metaphysical experts agree now, about the importance of being able
to imagine your self in the very situations and conditions, that will bring you success.

This implies that the famous belief that "I will believe only if I see it", should
be replaced by its opposite "I will see it only if I believe it." This means if we want
to achieve any thing physically, we first need to be able to imagine it internally.
Furthermore we also need to see what we imagine as possible and attainable.
Once we can include that new goal and outcome within the scope of our inner
world and consciousness, then it will manifest in our physical world. This is one
of the mental laws that parapsychologists, Hypnotherapists and NLP practitioners use in their daily practices to resolve their clients' problems, which states
"Whatever you believe internally, you tend to realize and find externally," which
really implies, whatever you believe is true and nothing else. Our belief system
acts as a lens that controls the flow of divine creative force into our lives. It controls and dictates what we can see, feel and experience in our lives. More negative
and limited our beliefs about ourselves and our world, more limiting is our lives.
Therefore we should decide to expand our horizons, and replace our limiting,
negative and destructive habits and beliefs, with the positive, progressive and
empowering beliefs. Only if we expand our beliefs and way of thinking, we can
expand and enrich our lives. Which will become full of love, happiness, success,
health and creativity. This book with its various wisdom and exercises is designed
to expand our horizons, and by reshaping our belief system will help us to get to
know ourselves and transform our lives.

1. We see only what we believe

Exercise: This week keep this story in mind and make a firm decision that you wish to change for better and improve your life in every aspect. You will do that by evaluating your belief systems and if you find any negative, outdated and limiting beliefs, you will replace them with a more positive and constructive ones.

Before doing so, for our purposes we need to first define change. What is a change? Change is a process wherein a situation is transformed from an undesired one to a desired one. In order for this change to happen, the situation that you no longer desire should clearly be identified and the plan and specific steps toward transforming it mapped out. The change that, we desire, can be really considered as a goal, and the obstacles that exist between you and your goal are considered as problems. Which in this case are our wrong habits and beliefs. There are four main components for any successful transformation and change, which are Inner commitment to change, agreement of all aspects of our being, surrender and effortless concentration, and finally taking action. Therefore before starting the book, you need to check and make sure to see if you are ready to commit yourself to improve your life in every aspect?, Do you want more wealth and success in your life? Do you want to have the best loving relationship with your loved ones? Do you want to have a healthy body and life style? Do you want to have lots of happiness and love in your life?

Do you want to grow spiritually and become closer to the god and his blessings?

If your answer is yes to all these questions, means you are committed and also all aspects of your beings, which are your physical, emotional, intellectual and spiritual aspects are in agreement with the positive change you are pursuing.

Next you need to lay out a plan to achieve what you are wishing for, determine its steps and finally take action based on your plans to get them.

The first step should be providing a work book, in which you will record all your spiritual, mental, emotional and physical experiences when you are doing your exercises, it will help you to evaluate your rate and quality of success and improvement as you move along. It can also be used as a future reference, for your decision making processes. This workbook will represent all your inner beliefs in all aspects of your life, and it will uncover many of your subconscious beliefs and habits, and by recording them you will become conscious of them. This will help you to clearly identify the wrong and limiting beliefs and behavioral patterns, and by using the stories, wisdom and exercises that are given throughout the book, you can easily replace these negative patterns and beliefs

with the more positive and empowering beliefs, which will consequently transform your life.

   And by doing so, we will discover a lot of information and knowledge about
our wrong habits and beliefs, and by changing them we free ourselves from the
chains of these limiting beliefs and habits. As Jesus has said, truth shall set you
free. Once we know what kind of negative and evil beliefs and habits are controlling and limiting our soul and our lives, then we can make a firm commitment to
change our beliefs, and in doing so become the free men and women whom we
were once.

2. Treasure is within us

Once upon a time, a very rich man was passing a busy street, he noticed a drunk beggar lying down in the sidewalk, so he approached him and wanted to give him some money, but to his greatest surprise he recognized the beggar. He was his best friend from high school, and he was shocked to meet him in this condition 20 years later. Anyway they talked for a while and then the rich man said here is some money, but the beggar refused to accept the cash, but he said if you want to do me a favor, you can buy a bottle of whiskey and we can drink together for the old times sake. After arguing a little, the rich man accepted and soon he was back with the bottle, so they started drinking and it went on and on for few hours, it started getting dark so the rich man decided to go home, but his friend was already passed out from over drinking. The rich man didn't know what to do because he couldn't stay, and he couldn't take him to his house, because it wasn't appropriate for his wife and children to know that he had such a best friend. So finally the rich man who owned a jewelry store, made a decision to leave something very valuable "a big diamond" in his friend's pocket so when he wakes up he would find it and by selling it, his life will be transformed for better. He figured this diamond's value is more than three hundred thousands so he will be all right. Having this in mind, he left his friend. Being a very busy man the rich man forgot all about his beggar friend, until one day, about a year later, again he was passing from the same street corner, and to his wildest astonishment he found his friend lying in the same street corner. He approached him, appearing very shocked and frustrated asked his beggar friend why are you still here? The beggar replied in a sarcastic tone, where would you think I be? You just took off the last time we met, without even saying good-byes let alone helping me. The rich man said but what about the big diamond that I put in your jacket's pocket.

The beggar put his hand in his pocket and in disbelief and astonishment found the diamond. And he started crying and saying all these times I had this in my pocket but I was still suffering. He thanked his rich friend and from that point his life was transformed, not only financially but he was also empowered character vice.

Because he realized that he already has what it takes to take back the control over his life, the only thing he has to do is to look for solutions and better ways of life within himself.

The wisdom of the story is that all of us have a hidden treasure within us, which we may not even be aware of it, which is our great creative force which has been given to us as a free gift by god. Our duty is to find out our unique ability and passion and purpose in our life and work on them to manifest those abilities into the real world so all others can enjoy that gift. Therefore when life becomes really challenging, instead of getting depressed or seek shelter by using drugs or alcohol, one should look within himself because god has given each and every one of us an unlimited source of wealth, all we have to do is to be positive and search for the better ways to solve our challenges. By asking the right questions from ourselves, our soul which has access to infinite universal information and resources, will help us to get what we want. Whenever we are faced with a great challenge, instead of asking why all these terrible things are happening to me, we should ask our soul, how can I reverse the situation to make it advantageous? What can I learn from this experience? What kind of resources do I have that will help me to get over the challenge that I am facing? We should have absolute faith that we will succeed if we truly want and ask whole heartedly from the god within us, because we are the beloved children of god and he will provide and protect us any time we ask him to. As Jesus said "Ask and you shall be given," therefore remember that god has given every thing to you, all you need to do is to look within, and ask for what you want, and then you will be directed toward your goal in a harmonious and mysterious manner.

Exercise: This week, I would like you to keep this story in mind as we create an appreciation list. In this list we will include every thing we can think of, that god has given us. Write down every little things, no matter how un intelligent it may seem to you.

Start the list with the big and obvious blessings and belongings that you have then move to things that you may value less. Here a sample list is provided, but feel free to add to the list as much as you want. Longer the list better and more empowered you will feel. Start the sentence with the following sentence. Dear Lord I am very fortunate and happy to have: a healthy body, good family, a place to call home, wonderful friends, nice job, good sense of humor, two beautiful eyes that I can see the beautiful and amazing world, two ears to hear the wonderful sounds of nature and hearing the voices of my loved ones, thank you god for giving me the power of speech and reasoning, ability to love and be loved, ability to learn, ability to eat and enjoy various delicious foods, ability to make new friends, availability of all kinds of knowledge that will empower and enrich my life, thanks for the every little and big things that you gave me my lord, absolutely free of charge!

It is very important to verbally and consciously appreciate what we have, because our subconscious mind will get rid of whatever we are not using. I am sure you have heard the saying: "You will lose what you don't use."

Whatever we are not focusing on mentally, our subconscious mind will assume it to be unnecessary, and therefore will get rid of it, and furthermore we move toward the direction of our dominant thoughts, so by focusing on all the good things that we enjoy, our subconscious mind will attune us with these types of pleasant circumstances and we are automatically driven toward these and more desired situations.

It is best to repeat this list and read it loudly as many time as possible, during the day, but if not feasible do it once before going to bed at night, and once when you get up. Read it effortlessly and in a relaxed fashion, because our soul and subconscious mind does not respond to force, and resists it.

And when you are reading the appreciation list visualize yourself as if you are enjoying and using all those blessings at this moment, feel it inside, live it and enjoy it, because after all it is all yours, and is included in your journey.

This simple exercise will transform your life forever, you will become more positive, motivated, energetic, compassionate and happier, and soon these positive moods and emotions will drive you toward taking more constructive and creative actions, which in turn will change your life. As Jesus said, "Ask and you shall be given." But most of us have forgotten this simple principle that god loves us and will give us any thing we ask him for.

3. Moderation

Once upon a time, Buddha, who was a prince and was not allowed to leave the castle by his father, because the king did not want his son to see the real world outside which was full of poverty, illnesses, crimes and other ugly things. But one day he decided to leave the castle to find out and explore what was going on out of his father's glamorous castle, that day he hid himself in a caravan that was about to leave the castle. When he saw the reality of life in the outside world, which was full of poverty, illness and death, he refused to go back to the castle until he finds a cure to all of human sufferings and short comings. Anyway he went to an isolated jungle where few monks were meditating, he sat there for almost eight years without moving, the other monks provided food and water for him. After eight years of meditation and leading a solitary life, he still had not found the answer to all of the worlds misery, all of a sudden he heard a fisherman passing by with his son who was playing a harp, the father told the son who was playing the harp very harshly to slow down, then the son started playing the harp but this time very mildly so no sound could be heard. Then the father said apply a moderate force to the strings so it will have a pleasant sound. At this point Buddha got up, all other monks were surprised and asked him what happened? He replied the key to calmness and understanding in this physical world is moderation, by sitting down and contemplations alone I cannot bring enlightenment to this world I have to also start actively teach to others what I have gathered through contemplation and meditation.

The wisdom of the story is that we have to apply moderation in all aspects of our lives if we want to achieve a well-balanced life. For instance neither overworking nor laziness is proper. Moderation will keep us harmonized with the nature and also attune us with god-consciousness. Moderation will keep the inner positive and negative forces in balance, and will allow our body, mind to function properly both singularly and collectively, moderation in our thoughts, speech, behaviors and actions balances, our masculine and feminine sides, our dark and bright aspects, our under activity and hyper activity, our inflow and outflow of energy, love and service, and our negative and positive side.

Most eastern religions believe that moderation which they refer to as "The middle path," is one of the needed attributes that one has to develop and apply to his life, before he can make progress toward enlightenment, because when our body and mind are balanced, then they become harmonized with every thing else in their surrounding nature and universe, and as a result our mind and body are in total harmony with the universe as a whole and this results in a constant and healthy energy flow into our mind and body, which will keep them in balance, and creates a perfect setting for our soul to use our body and mind to bring his goals and desires into manifestation.

In summary moderation balances the in flow and out flow of the cosmic energy and universal love, into our energy field or aura, which is necessary to keep our body, mind and soul in balance and harmony.

When our soul, mind and body are in total harmony, then we experience an inexplicable sense of peace, love, tranquility, wisdom and happiness, and these inner feelings will also affect our daily real life. Because once we are saturated with the positive and empowering feelings, we will be driven toward the similar circumstances and situations in life. Remember what we believe is true and focus on internally, we tend to realize, and experience externally in our lives.

Exercise: This week in your work book, draw a chart. This chart shows different aspects of your life.

It should include but not be limited to the following categories:

Physical, nutritional, sexual, emotional, relationship with relatives, relationship with friends, financial, intellectual, social, and spiritual aspects. Start evaluating and writing down what you may view as strong and weak points.

Check to see for example in your nutritional life, are you moderate, overeating or under eating. If you find out that it is not balanced in any way, make a reasonable plan to take immediate and feasible actions to rectify the problem. Use moderation also in choosing and applying the plan. It should neither be too stressful and difficult, nor a totally non-disciplinary plan. Start evaluating all aspects of yourselves. Because most of our habits and behavioral trends are in the form of subconscious habits, which are so fast and hidden that we are not even aware of having them. Therefore we need to uncover them first and bring it to the conscious level, and then almost magically the problem is resolved by itself and we feel relieved, as Jesus said, "Truth shall set you free".When you know you have a problem, and pinpoint that problem, the solution to that problem is usually evident within the problem itself. But if we don't investigate and be self-realized, then all those problematic habits and trends will remain operational and un touched. Remember the famous saying, nothing is fixed unless we fix it.

After you realized the problems and shortcomings in different aspects of your life, write down the solutions that you feel can resolve those imbalances, in front of its corresponding section in your chart. And say it to yourself loudly that you choose to change, and become balanced and harmonious, and you ask the help and support of god and holy spirit to be with you all the way through the process.

Again it is good to be always attentive to pinpoint and find the aspects and areas of your lives, which are out of balance and right it down, and set a plan to fix them. But if you didn't find enough time, go quickly over the list, end of the night, and once when you get up, it is best to do almost all of the exercises at these times, because your conscious and critical mind is tired and unfocused, so the new suggestions can enter your subconscious mind, which in turn will make the new insights and information as part of its routine programing.

That is, what is meant by self-realization, if you realize truly what behavioral attributes you carry, then you can see the problems and shortcomings in it, and then you will be able to fix it. And a self-realized person will be completely balanced and will eventually reach to higher levels of god realization and spiritual freedom that the great masters such as Buddha and Jesus enjoyed.

4. Divine help

Once upon a time there was a very religious man who was claiming that he trusts god so much that even if a flood comes to his area he would not leave his house, because he is sure that god will save him. One day he opened the radio and heard the flood warning saying that flood will hit the area in three days urging all residents to leave the area immediately, he of course did not listen and told to himself that god will help me, I don't need to escape like others, because I have prayed and obeyed god all my life thus he will protect me. The next day the neighbors came to his door and warned him to leave the house while there was time, but he refused again telling them god will save him. On the last day special police buses came to evacuate the area, and asked him to leave his house, he said no thanks, god will save me. Then the early morning of the flooding day when about 0.5 meters of water was in his house rescue boats came to get him, but again he refused to get on the boat, telling them boldly that god will help me, no need to escape. In the afternoon when his house was full of water, he went to the roof, where a helicopter came for rescuing, again he refused to get on it, shouting god will save me, I am a religious man. Anyway finally he was taken by the flood and drowned to death. On the other side his soul was brought against god, he asked god in a very disappointed tone, that dear lord I had served you whole heartedly all my life, I never committed any sin, and I trusted you hundred percent, why didn't you help me from drowning?

God smiled and said I sent you all kinds of warning and help, radio, neighbors, a police bus, a rescue boat and even a helicopter! What else did you expect me to do? He said I was expecting a divine help, not a help by people. God replied, any kind of help you got in life was a form of divine help, and you had to learn to accept the help they were offering you, but your ego didn't let you, because you thought you are better than anyone else merely because you prayed, but you prayed to strengthen your ego by distinguishing and labeling yourself as a religious man, you did not pray because you loved me, because if you loved me you would love and accept all of my creations, because there is a part of me in everything ever created.

The wisdom of the story is that, we should have an open heart, and don't limit ourselves by asking god to give us only what we think is good for us, we have to trust god whole heartedly and accept and cherish what he is offering us at any given moment in our lives, because our happiness, survival and enlightenment may depend on it. We should not try to control every event and fight against the flow of life, because if we do so we are acting against the divine order and our suffering and termination will be eminent.

We must keep in mind that every thing is god and from god. We were lead to believe that we are a separate entity from god, but the reality is that we are like a drop from the ocean of mercy which we call god. There is a drop of god exist in each and every one of us, even in animals, plants and inanimate objects.

Therefore since every thing contains god within it, then any love, service or help rendered to anyone is actually an expression of our love and gratitude toward god. And by the same token whenever somebody offers us a helping hand, or gives us a gift, we must also accept, because in reality it is a gift from their soul which is the god within them, to your soul which is also the god within you. In reality we are all included in the web of power, which consists of various energy fields, and all is happening is the exchange of energies between these fields to make the whole balanced. Many philosophies and religions believe in this concept, like Buddhism, shamanism and Taoism. In summary, receive and give your love and service generously and happily because it is the gifts and love of the gods that you are exchanging. More you exchange and share your blessings, happiness and love, more peaceful, balanced and empowered you become. Remember together, with love, charity and cooperation we all win. And going alone no body wins and benefits from the other member's gifts and blessings.

Exercise: This week, try to open your heart and ask others for the support and help that you need to achieve your goals and projects faster and easier. First make a list of your goals, then prioritize them in order of importance and urgency. Then decide to proceed and take an initial action toward reaching that goal. Then write down the list of the people who may help you to get to your goal, and in front of each person's name write down the kind of help they can offer you without harming or negatively affecting them. And finally simply ask them for help. You will be amazed and surprised how helpful and useful people can be toward us, if we honestly and openly ask them. As Jesus has said," ask and you shall be given". When you as a soul and god's child ask another soul who is also a child of god, he will help you as long as your intentions are not evil or harmful to them. So this week, openly ask your loved ones and others for support, and be prepared to give them support and help as freely and easily as you ask for them. Because the nature operates based on the mutual exchange of energies, meaning life is give and take. You must be ready to give what you are expecting to receive. By doing this simple exercise you will see your life will grow through collective and harmonious cooperation, in all aspects.

5. Giant elephant and a tiny string

Once upon a time a western man was visiting India, one day when he was passing a street he noticed a tiny man is walking with a huge elephant, the tiny man decided to go to a store to do some shopping, so he simply took a small tiny stick which had a tiny string attach to it and then tied the string to one of the elephant's leg and then he went on to the shop for almost an hour. To the western man's outmost surprise, who was watching and following the elephant's movement, the giant elephant did not move at all for the whole time the man was in the store, even though the elephant was stationed under the torturing sun and a shaded area was just meters away, the elephant didn't even try to pull the string. Anyway the western man got very interested and curios to learn about the secret of how this elephant which is supposed to be a wild jungle habitant is trained to be disciplined at this unbelievable level. So he approached the Indian man who just got out of the store, and started a conversation by saying hi sir, you got a beautiful and huge elephant here, do you mind if I ask you a question?

The Indian man smiled and said sure!, The western man said I am very curious to learn, how did you train this huge wild animal to be so calm and wait for you for an hour without even trying to remove the stick which was tied only with such a tiny string? The Indian man smiled again and said that is simple, when the elephant was about 3-6 months old, whenever I took him any where I was tying him to a huge tree with a very thick rope, being a wild and young animal he would pull the string tirelessly trying to escape or walk around the area, after trying many times he would give up the fight, and stay calmly till I come back and untie him. After about 2-3 months he stops pulling the rope, because by that time through repetitions his mind has registered that whenever your leg is tied up to a stick by a string, you cannot go free no matter how many times and how hard you try, so in this way it becomes, an imprinted and unchangeable memory which command him automatically to stop wasting his energy by pulling the string, because the result is hacked in his mind, which order him: You don't have enough strength which is necessary to tear the string. The western man who was amazed by the level this man's intellect, thanked him and said good-byes. Then he started to realize that we human beings are also tied up and paralyzed by many of these type of subconscious commands and programming that we like the elephant even though we are capable of many feats and achievements, certain subconscious programs and habits are limiting and paralyzing us to take action and become successful in getting what we want.

The wisdom of this story is that there are some negative, regressive and debilitating programs and habits rooted deep in our subconscious mind of which we are mostly unaware of, which controls our actions and as a result our lives. And the problem with these programs is that we are not even aware of their existence, so if we do not know that there is a problem, we can't fix it. Therefore we remain in our limited format for almost all our lives, believing that it was our fate, but we can broaden our horizon by observing our actions, goals, dreams and ask ourselves how can I achieve my goals? There must be a different and better way. We must search within to find out what is the source of these programs, and finding those initial sources of the negative programs, we can delete and replace them with positive and empowering programs to get to our goals easily. The many good stories, wisdom and exercises in this book can help you with achieving this transformation. I have also written a book called 'Stop pulling the trigger on yourself' in which I have pinpointed about one hundred of such negative and limiting programs and also have offered a way to delete and finally to reprogram your mind with the positive and empowering subconscious programs.

Exercise: This week, make a note of the habits that you have developed throughout your life. Find out and write down the negative, limiting and wrong habits that you have. It can be over drinking, laziness, over eating, smoking, using coarse language or any other bad habits. Then find a quiet place where you would not be bothered for 15-20 minutes. Then close your eyes, relax and allow your mind to settle down by taking five deep breath, when you feel relax and calm, ask yourself, where, how and when did you develop these habits? You first come up with obvious reasons that you are usually conscious of them. Write them down, and then ask your subconscious mind which is the store house of your memories and habits that what is the real emotional reason that even though you know those habits are harmful to your life, you still indulge with them?

Usually there is, what psychologists call a secondary gain for our subconscious mind that it decides to hold on to this wrong habits. For example if you are a smoker, if you go back to your youth, you can see that all your friends were smokers, and in order not to be excluded from the group you had started smoking. Even though in the beginning you might have hated the smell and taste of the poisonous tobacco, but the pain of being excluded from the cool and popular group of friends were more painful for you when you were young. So in this example our subconscious secondary gain is being included and enjoying a sense of security, which was way more powerful than the thought of dying of lung cancer or heart attack in the next fifty years. As we grow older, and friends disperse, even though consciously we do not need that sense of belonging ness and security anymore, but subconsciously that program and habit remain active. Because it is a mental law that a subconscious program or habit remains active, until it is changed by another program. That is why we fail when we try consciously through our will power quit smoking.

Because our habits are recorded at subconscious level with strong emotional secondary gains. Thus when you are in a relaxed state ask your subconscious mind, to take you back to the first time you started applying these wrong habits, and also ask what were the benefits of acquiring those habits?. The answer may pop up instantly, but some times it comes few hours, days or weeks later. The answer may even be given to you in a dream state. Do not push yourself to get the answer, because then your subconscious mind will resist. When you finally got the answer, write the secondary gains down. And again find a quiet place to relax, and convince your subconscious mind by telling it, that these behavioral traits and habits are no longer necessary, and are even harmful. Thank your subconscious mind for its protectiveness and caring, and ask it to apply the new healthy habits that you wish to have instead of these harmful habits. And repeat the new program five times a day in a relaxed state, so it will be picked up and applied by your subconscious mind.

6. Opposing Forces Within

Once upon a time, a merchant was passing by a small village in mountains near Siberia, he stopped there to get some rest and look for some food, but since there was no shop or restaurant he knocked the door of one of the houses which was relatively bigger than the other houses. An old man opened the door and said how can I help you? The merchant said he needs some food and a place to stay for that night and in return he can give him some money, or some of his art crafts, anyway the old man agreed and let him stay, and invited him to the backyard where he had already been cooking some meat on the fire. While they both ate their food, the merchant noticed the old man's two dogs which were very wild and vicious and he was keeping them in a big fenced area.One of the dogs was totally white and the other one was totally black but they were almost the same size. The old man threw a big piece of meat in the fence, so the dogs started to fight viciously and after about half an hour the black dog gave up and accepted the defeat, so the white dog took the meat and walked to a corner and ate it quickly. The merchant asked which one usually wins the fight?. Old man who seemed to be enjoying the scene said, these two dogs are similar to our opposing nature within. Lets say for the argument sake the white dog is our good, positive and godly nature and the black dog is our bad, negative and evil nature, they are also fighting like these two dogs constantly, and now we come to the answer to your question, similar to our inner forces of positive and negative, whichever dog I feed more for that day is stronger, so he would defeat the other one. Similarly more we feed by focusing on either part of our being good or bad will defeat the other one and we act based on the traits of the winner.

The wisdom of the story is that we have to be aware that there are these two opposing forces within us, which one of them is good, positive, constructive, motivating, optimistic and divine, and the other one is bad, negative, destructive, depressing, pessimistic and evil. These two opposing forces are recorded in our habits and subconscious thought patterns, and whichever we focus on will win the fight and as a result will dominate our thought process and forces us to take action in accordance with their need. Thus one should cultivate and focus on good thoughts, good speech, good deeds which are by the way the main and only commandments of the ancient religion of Zoroastrianism whose prophet Zoroaster lived in Persia about 2600 years ago, because by doing so we feed only the positive side and as a result the negative side remains weak and disabled. Because for any thought to be effective and for it to be able to manifest into an action, needs to be, the most dominant thought. And the only way, that a thought becomes dominant, is when we are focusing on it, on a regular basis.

Exercise; This week keep this story in mind and decide to only focus on the positive, empowering, divine and progressive aspects of life. Our mind has been trained and programmed to judge things and differentiate and compare them in order to learn about physical, emotional and mental subjects. Without this faculty, it cannot perceive, record nor process any information. Our mind works by judging every thing based on their negative and positive aspects. For example if we continually tell ourselves that we love sunny days, and you don't like rainy days as much as the sunny days. Therefore it arranges our feelings, and moods based on this belief, that mean on a sunny day, we feel better than on rainy days. Our subconscious mind has automatically and subconsciously picked up many of these complex set of programming which we are not even aware of. Thus as we can see one simple program, can create inner duality in our mind and create the opposing forces within. Due to the dual nature of our mind, we are constantly bombarded by these kinds of comparative and dividing programming which consequently adding to our inner division every day. But the good news is that we as souls can decide consciously as which one of these forces will win. We can focus on the negative and by doing so feed our dark and negative side, which many orthodox religions call evil, or focus on the positive and by doing so feed our divine and positive side, which many religions call holy spirit or our godly aspect. It is wiser to focus on god and his attributes, and in doing so we are merging and attuning to these qualities, we come to have and enjoy them in our lives. As a result our life will be full of happiness, love, health, abundance and creativity.

Find a quiet place, where you will not be disturbed for 10-15 minutes. Lie down or sit in an upright position. Close your eyes, take five deep breath, attend to your breathing for 2-3 minutes, that will allow your mind and body to relax. This state of relaxation, will make your subconscious mind more responsive and receptive to your self-suggestions. Imagine yourself on your mental screen, which is located between your eye brows, and is called the third eye, which is our inner eye. On the screen imagine seeing yourself as a soul, which is a being surrounded by a vibrant white and golden energy field, which is called the aura. Next start chanting some positive and divine attributes of god, you can use the following list, but feel free to add any other positive attributes that you can think of and feel comfortable with. Tell yourself in a chanting and rhythmic style that you choose to allow only love, abundance, health, happiness, success, growth, harmony, peace, creativity, positiveness and godly powers and blessings to enter your energy field. All other negative and undesired thoughts and beliefs will not be allowed to enter your energy field. Make a golden shield around your energy field or aura, and imagine that the positive attributes are freely entering your aura, but the negative ones are bounced back to the outer universe. Tell yourself that you will have this shield activated at all times, and this shield which are built by divine energies will block any negative thoughts, beliefs or intentions from entering into your energy field. Next start allowing those good attributes to enter your energy field, you do that by simply attuning to that characteristic, and the word it self.

For instance, imagine that the word "love, is approaching your energy field from every angle, and as is passing through your golden shield, imagine and feel the warmth and pleasure of feeling loved, you can also imagine and visualize the image of your loved one(s) as the word enters into your field, and visualize that this word, "love" enters to your heart and becomes an inseparable part of you. Next you send this love back to the universe, which will help you to perpetuate the flow of mutual love with the universe and all its souls. You continue this process for all the other attributes, and when you are finished thank your soul, god and the whole universe for allowing this positive transformation to happen. Then start counting calmly from one to three, and at the count of three open your eyes feeling empowered, happy and full of love. Do this exercise once a day, for minimum of 15 minutes. And it is very useful to repeat and contemplate on these positive words and suggestions any time you get a free time. More you repeat, faster and more effective, your new positive aspects will become the dominant thoughts. In this way by feeding the divine part of us, we become a divine person also. And this is one of the sure ways to start your road toward spiritual unfoldment. Because as Sai baba an Indian saint has said, "Only pure and clean minds can acquire divine wisdom and enlightenment."

7. It was all included

Once upon a time around 1880's an Italian family moved to united states, and ever since they moved there, the father was constantly saying one day we will go back and visit our relatives and village again, many years passed but due to financial hardship neither he nor any of his family members could afford to go back to Italy, but one of his daughters kept promising to herself that she will visit his hometown and long lost relatives one more time, almost 50 years passed when she was about 65 years old, his parents and brothers had all passed away, she decided that she will make the trip, so she used all of her saved money to buy a ticket, and soon she was on her way to Italy on a passenger ship. After about 10 days she arrived to her village, she met her cousins and she lived through her memory lines, but after two months she realized that she has spent almost all of her life in united states and she was so used to it, it was impossible for her to conform herself to this kind of lifestyle in Italy, plus she had two daughters in united states, so it was time to go back, but she only had a little money left, so she had to work for a while, because she was shy to ask for money from relatives she hadn't seen for half a century. So after about three weeks she had just enough money to buy the ticket back to united states, but she only had money to buy food for two days of her 10-day trip. Feeling helpless she decided to go anyway, she figured that she can stay alive by eating very little each day. But she was wrong after the fifth day, her food was finished and she was very hungry, so at day six, she went near the ship's restaurant, looking from the window outside, she saw everybody dressed up eating and drinking all kind of tasty food, hopelessly she went back to her seat and stayed hungry for another day, then for the next two days she would go and watch everybody eat in the restaurant, but being shy and proud she never begged for food, so finally in day nine she gave in to the powerful force of hunger so she decided to go to the restaurant and eat and later she thought she would offer work in the kitchen in return for the food she ate. So she walked in shaking from embarrassment and hunger approached the self service area and she ate and ate and ate, finally she was full, then the feeling of guilt and shame hit her, she started feeling the butterfly in her stomach, she saw everybody is leaving and the restaurant is becoming empty, until she was the last one, when a polite waiter came to her table and said, is there any thing else we can do for you? She replied in a shaking tone that I am sorry I ate lots of food but I don't have any money to pay for it, so if you show me the kitchen I am ready to work and pay for what I just ate. The waiter smiled and said there is no need for it, "it is all included in the ticket," she was relieved and cried out of happiness.

The wisdom of the story is that in the journey of life our kind and generous god has included a lot more blessings and wealth than we ever realize. Just by opening up our heart and horizons we can realize how many better things life has to offer us. It also shows that by believing in yourself and god and by taking risk you can move beyond your life's limitations which has been created by your own limited thinking, that is Accomplished by believing that your self-worth is much more than you perceive it to be (because we are all part of god, so we can experience any thing we wish for) then you can move beyond your present situation. What we internally believe about our lives and ourselves tend to be manifested and realized in our external lives. So believe that since you are one of god's beloved children, you are entitled and you deserve to have everything you need, and just watch how your world starts to change for better, because remember we become what we think about and what we say to ourselves. Therefore ask and think about only the good and positive things.

Exercise: This week, keep this story in mind, and make a list of the things that you wish to have in your life. Don't be shy or too logical about it, regardless of how far or impossible it may seem to your logical mind write them down. Because god's way are usually mysterious and incredible to our conscious and logical mind. After completing your list which may contain wishes like having a beautiful house, a loving relationship, a cure for a so called incurable disease, a new job, entrance to a school, writing a book or whatever else it maybe. Find a quiet place where you would not be disturbed for 15-20 minutes, lie down or sit down in an upright position, close your eyes, take five deep breath, attend to your breathing for 2-3 minutes that allows your body and mind to relax and settle down, this makes your subconscious mind more responsive to your suggestions and imaginations. Visualize and imagine yourself being at one of the beautiful gardens of heaven, which is full of colorful flowers, beautiful trees full of fresh and colorful fruits, calm streams are seen at every direction, beautiful rainbows with their vivid and pleasant colors in the blue sky. Imagine that an angel is there to waiting for you to greet you, and give you a tour of this beautiful garden in the paradise. Imagine that the angel is directing you to a little but beautiful square room in the middle of the garden. He tells you that "this is called the "The wish temple," and only the children of god can enter to this room, you can ask god for any thing you wish for, be it health, happiness, success, growth, love and/or abundance. As long as your wish is in harmony with the universe, and is not intended to harm others, your wish will be fulfilled. And since you are one of the god's beloved children you can enter the wish temple any time you desire, and be certain that you will be given what you wish for. The only catch is you have to visualize what you want and see it as already happened the angel added.

He also says that, god loves believer not hopers. So believe and visualize specifically and with a complete mental expectancy of its fulfilment, but ask and visualize effortlessly.

And as Jesus Christ has said, "When you ask you shall be given, because you are the blessed child of god, and deserve any thing you want as long as your intentions are divine and positive."

Then imagine yourself entering the wish temple, where you find a room full of divine lights and sound, allow your imagination to create the image of the wish temple by itself, and when you feel ready visualize your wish or goal, and ask god for whatever you need, be honest and sincere, and after you are done, thank god and your guardian angel and also your soul which has allowed you to visit the wish temple. As you are about to leave the beautiful garden, your guardian angel tells you in a reassuring and lovely tone, that you can come to this garden and visit the wish temple any time you wish, all you have to do is to focus effortlessly and mention the word "wish temple." Thank him again and say good bye, and start counting from one to three whenever you feel like opening your eyes, at the count of three open your eyes feeling wonderful, happy and energized. Do this exercise once a day this week, and you can even do it when you have some extra time, waiting on line in a super market or at a bus stop. As you progress, you will not need to close your eyes or spend 15 minutes for this process, you can quickly and as effectively visit the wish temple, make your wish by visualizing and feeling it internally, and believing it as if it has already happened, thanking god and your guardian angel and return. This exercise will help you to improve your communication with god and higher levels of consciousness, which in turn will transform your beliefs about yourself and your self worth. Once you develop an inner core belief that since you are the beloved child of god, and he is always there to take care of you, then you will start to believe that you deserve to have all the good things in life that may be lacking now. This new, empowered belief will lead you to have and enjoy a better, healthier, happier, richer and lovelier life.

Remember whatever we focus on and believe we become, so choose to think about the blessings and positive gifts and attributes of god, and soon you will find them in your life. With the same token negative and destructive beliefs, habits and usage of language should be absolutely avoided, because they will have devastating and destructive effects on you and your life.

8. *The importance of intention*

Once upon a time in India, in a busy street a prostitute lived in a small home, even though she hated selling herself but she had no other way, the abusive husband had left her, she had three children. And it was very hard for a woman to get a normal job that could pay for the cost of their living, and right in front of her house a very famous pious monk had a temple and was living there. At the end of her work, every night she was crying and praying to god and wishing that she wasn't a prostitute and didn't have this bad reputation, so she could go visit the holy monk and ask for forgiveness from her sins, deep down she really wanted a cleaner and more proper way of living, and for that she was always praying. On the other side of the street, the famous monk was also praying every night to god and he wished that he wasn't a famous holy monk so heI could go like all other ordinary men and visit the beautiful prostitute across the street. Anyway years passed by and a flood overtook their city and incidentally both the monk and the prostitute were killed the same day. At the other side both woke up beside each other standing and waiting for a carriage to get them, finally an angel arrived and they started their journey, after a short while their vehicle came to a stop, they both looked outside, it was the gate of hell, so the prostitute got ready to get off, where the monk was sitting graciously and had a victorious smile on his face, but the angel said no to the prostitute, you are going to heaven, the monk should get off here. Both the monk and the prostitute were shocked. After few brief seconds the monk asked crying, but why? I worked and worshiped all my life for god and his people, and this filthy woman chose the easiest and worst way of living, and now god is sending me to hell, and sending her to heaven!, The angel replied, this lady when she was at the darkest conditions, she was praying to reach light and god, her intention was god even though life had forced her to do evil things, but you, the so called holy man when you were given an opportunity to be in the brightest and holiest conditions, you were praying to reach darkness and evil, even though life put you to a godly position, your focus and intention was to satisfy the lust and the evil side of your self. And since god is aware of all our thought and intention. Therefore, this is the only fair sentence, that is for you to go to hell and for her to go to heaven, because deep down what both of you were praying for all your lives. And god is very fair, kind and impartial so he is giving you what you wanted.

The wisdom of the story is that we cannot fool anybody specially ourselves and god. Therefore we have to choose the right way and be kind, compassionate and pious within. Because god is always aware of our intentions and we will be judged both in this world and in the other, and are rewarded or punished according to our intentions. As the Moslem saint Ali has said "The intentions of a pious man are more important than his actions." Mental and spiritual energies always follow intentions. Therefore Before taking any action we should make sure that all aspects of our being are satisfied and happy with the change. Since we are a multifaceted being, made of many parts like our physical, emotional, intellectual or mental, and our spiritual selves. Usually if the goals that we are setting do not match the needs, desires and goals of any of our aspects, then that part will become imbalanced and sabotage our success. More importantly this disparity and disharmony will create inner divisions and conflicts. Most of our daily self-talks and doubts are created because our intentions are not the same as our goals and behaviors. As we all have heard the phrase "one should walk his talk, and talk his walk," meaning we should say and do only what we really intend and believe, and we should also believe in what we are saying or doing. If it is not this way, then our inner turmoil and division will continue to grow, and eventually it will affect us negatively not only in this life, but also in the next. Therefore one should evaluate his inner motives and intentions for all his actions, and organize them in a way that, it is harmonious and in accordance with high values and is also collectively harmonious.

Exercise; This week, keep this story and make a decision to examine and identify your intentions behind every thing you do in life. Some times we are doing wrong and destructive things for wrong reasons or even unknown reasons. This happens because some times our motives are subconscious and belong to our past emotional experiences. These motives are so hidden and habitual that we seldom think about them. Our subconscious mind may have created a habitual lifestyle for us, which causes us to act in a certain way, based on our values and beliefs at earlier times, however most often as every thing else changes in life, our goals, desires and priorities also change over time. However unfortunately our subconscious mind is not designed nor able to adjust our priorities, motives and goals, hence it continues to force us to act in the same old manners. However we can make a decision and replace those previous goals, motives and priorities with new ones that are more applicable to our present goals and priorities in our lives. Because it is next to impossible to succeed when we have conflicting goals inside. Our subconscious mind continues to search for all of the goals whether little or big, from our early childhood to the present moment, and it will not stop the process, until we give a direct order that we no longer wish to pursue those goals. If we imagine for the argument sake that if our subconscious mind has a hundred units of energy that can be used to help us to reach our goals, and if we had 49 unfulfilled wishes from the past, then whenever we decide consciously to pursue a new goal, this will be added on top of the other 49 goals, in this way our subconscious mind divides its energy among all these 50 goals, meaning only 2% of our total mental energy is focused for achieving our goal, and consequently we are only successful by 2%. Thus, before starting any goal, we should evaluate our motives. And more importantly we must delete and stop the processing of our previous subconscious goals if we are to get to our goals. Because if we don't, it is as if we get on a taxi, and give the driver 50 addresses and tell him to take us to the most proper location, of course the cab driver will get frustrated, confused and most likely will stop and would tell us make up your mind, then I will take you. Most often this phenomenon happens to us, we start a new project, we are very excited and motivated but all of sudden, our mind stops, and lose its focus and dedication. The reason is the same, our subconscious mind is confused and lacks the enough mental energy to focus.

This week, decide to make a list of all the goals that you may have had since you were a child. In your work book make a list of all your previous dreams, goals, wishes, projects and fantasies that you have not fulfilled them. No matter how elementary or unintelligent they may seem, write them down, because our subconscious mind is not concern about the time or location of that goal, it simply remembers and continues to process any memory that has given us pleasure or pain. After you wrote down the list of your previous plan and wishes, which may be some thing like that, I wished to be a superman, I want to fly, I wish to open an ice cream shop so I can eat ice cream all day, I want to be a brain surgeon and so on. For this exercise you need to find a quiet place where you would not be disturbed for 15-20 minutes, lie down, close your eyes, take five deep breaths, attend to your breathing for 2-3 minutes, that will allow your mind and body to relax, then imagine yourself as a soul and sitting in a court room, notice that you are actually the judge of that court. Next visualize your conscious mind and subconscious minds are present in your court room to settle their differences, no body is guilty. You can visualize your subconscious mind as looking like you when you were 12 years old, and you can visualize your conscious mind as looking like your present age. Next read all the goals one by one, starting from the first one, which is the oldest. Then as your conscious mind presenting them to the judge, which is your soul also visualize and listen to what your subconscious mind or the child within you is telling you. After thorough examination the judge makes a final decision to whether hold on to this goal or not. If any of the goals are outdated and are no longer productive is dismissed, and you visualize the judge banging his hammer firmly twice, indicating his order of dismissal. This sends a clear and symbolic signal to your subconscious mind to drop that goal from his database and memory bank. After you are done, evaluating all the goals, thank your soul, your conscious mind and your subconscious mind for allowing this transformation to happen. When you are ready in the count of three open your eyes, feeling lighter, happier and energized. You should do this exercise every now and then, because it is necessary to review and evaluate our motives, goals as we grow and change in your life, this will free you from the bondage of previous limiting beliefs.

For example, maybe once you believed making just enough money to pay your bills was perfect, if you don't change that old and limiting program, even if you make ten times more than what you made then, your subconscious mind creates circumstances to validate your belief, meaning you will have to spend all your income on your bills. So recycle and throw away your old, unnecessary and harmful beliefs and goals, just like you are throwing away your unnecessary items on a regular basis.

9. Vicious cycle of wishes

Once upon a time, there was a young boy who lived in a small town in Ohio, where his father who was a fisherman would take him for fishing every day, his dad wished for his son to also become a fisherman and follow their family tradition, since his own father was also a fisherman, but the young boy had a different dream, ever since he saw the small planes which were traveling above the lake that they were fishing, he had wished and made up his mind to become a pilot, because he found fishing to be boring and it lacked excitement, so when he grew up, after lots of argument he convinced his dad to send him to an aviation college, where he graduated and became a certified pilot for small planes. In the beginning he was very happy and excited about it, but after few years of flying, whenever he was passing from the lake that he used to fish, he was wishing for a day that he would be retired sooner so he could go fishing with his dad. Because he found the flying job to be very stressful, because it needed a high level of alertness and discipline. Looking back at his life. He realized that he has missed the chance of enjoying himself when he was a young child, by not being present in that moment, and wishing for some thing better and more satisfying in the future, and now he is following the same mental trend, that is he is missing the chance of enjoying and exploring himself by not being in the present moment, and wishing for some thing from the past. That was a great moment of realization for him, when he realized that he should always live and be happy with what he is doing in the present moment, because wishing about future, or wishing of past events, would only entrap him in the vicious cycle of mental wishes which will not allow him to enjoy the present moment, because always his attention is fixed and focused on some thing and somewhere else. So he decided to start enjoying his flying that day and every day. And as a result his level of peace and happiness increased dramatically.

The wisdom of the story is that by having many wishes all the time, and by not being content with where we are at the present moment, we miss the chance to enjoy life at the present moment, and the present moment is all we have, because in reality we cannot physically live neither in past nor in future. So by having wishes this young man always dreamed of flying when he was fishing, therefore he couldn't enjoy fishing and he was unhappy and disappointed with himself for being forced to do some thing he didn't want to do. And when he became a pilot and he was flying. He wished to be fishing, so he couldn't enjoy flying because he felt again unhappy and disappointed with himself for being forced to do some thing he didn't want to do.

Therefore having many out of reach wishes does not allow you to enjoy the present moment, and in turn stops you from enjoying life, because we can only live, in the present moment, but wishing is living in future, and unfulfilled wishes lead us to regret, and, regretting is living in the past. Having wishes is like, drinking salty water, more you drink more you have to drink. Thus one should enjoy what life and god has given him today, so he can enjoy life in the future too, because future is just another present moment then. When contentment and self-satisfaction becomes a trend, it will continue to remain that way.

Exercise: This week, keep this story in mind, and evaluate your goals and desires in life. Most of us get too busy with our daily responsibilities that we don't get a chance to sit down and really ask ourselves, why are we running around day after day, week after week, month after month, year after year without enjoying our lives or achieving any real goals in our lives? We have been programed by advertisers to buy and buy the things that we really don't need, we keep working longer hours to pay for our credit card bills. We have set too many unnecessary goals and desires in our lives, too many so called big things. But attaining these goals requires energy, money and most importantly time. We lose most of our times to work and run around to fulfil our self-created yet unnecessary responsibilities and burdens. Instead of being a slave of material desires, we can focus on our real purpose in life as children of god. We have been sent to this planet to experience and enjoy life, we have been sent here to learn, to grow, to love one another and experience different states of being. Real wealth is being able to enjoy life with your loved one, and growing in all dimensions physically, emotionally, mentally and spiritually. We need to start re prioritizing our life. We need to have a balance life style which takes care of all of our real needs. But we are programmed to neglect our soul and body for our mental wishes and fantasies. Our wondering mind will not stop wishing and running us around, we are the one who should choose to stop the vicious cycle of material needs. Because we know that the real treasure of happiness is within not without.

Decide to take control of your time and your life, use what you possess to enjoy life, instead of allowing what you possess to control your time and life. We are the only one who can make this choice, and nature and god is in no hurry to change us. What we refuse to learn through wisdom, we must learn through pain. Do not wait till you are too old to enjoy life. This week, make a plan to do the things your heart and soul and the child within you wants to do, become more playful. Do what is necessary to obtain a happy home, do your responsibilities as a family member, but do not equate your life with responsibilities. You are a soul, and a child of god and you have to discover your mission, passion and purpose in life, which is more than merely repeating your daily responsibilities over and over like a machine. As the Chinese proverb states," a man dies when he is thirty, but they will burry him when he is sixty". Because most of us in the high pace society stop learning and growing, and become habitual machines, This week contemplate about your life, and search within yourself for your mission, passion and purpose in life. And when you really want to have a purpose and mission in life, the divine hand will direct you to your path, maybe by meeting a master or being introduced to a book. Have faith in yourself and follow the path of light, and you will start living again and will be joyful, vibrant and happy as you were during your youth.

10. Never underestimate anyone

Once upon a time, a farmer couple from Mid west, who were in their 50's went to Harvard University to visit the dean, because they had a son who always wished to study and graduate from Harvard, now that he was dead in an accident they wanted to build something in his memorandum inside the Harvard campus and in turn get an honorary degree for their son. But when they reached Harvard, the secretary said: the dean is very busy and can't see you now, you have to wait two hours, so they waited, the secretary who didn't take them seriously had even forgot to tell the dean that they want to visit him, dean felt un necessary to meet them and told the secretary to tell them to write a letter to him, but they refused and said we will wait, because we have traveled so far and we won't leave until we meet him, so eventually the dean reluctantly gave in to their demand. So finally they were in his room, they explained the situation of their son, and demanded the permission to build a campus or library in their son's name, Dean looked at the old couple, who looked very poor and said I appreciate your interest, but I don't think you can afford to even build a statue here in Harvard let alone a campus!, A campus will cost you $200.000 dollars which were a lot of money in early 1800's, the couple smiled and said if all it takes is two hundred thousands of dollars we can do it ourselves and they left Harvard's dean office.

The last name of those old-couples was Stanford. Who built a university almost as big and as prestigiously as Harvard. And they named the university after their son.

The wisdom of the story is that we have to respect and appreciate all human beings, and never underestimate their effectiveness and capabilities, because after all god has given each of us a unique gift and we all have access to the divine resources which are will power, dedication, discipline, faith, concentration and love. So whenever you need help or information, don't prejudge any possible source based on their appearance, because help may very well come from an unexcepted source. Respect and love all. Because what you send out, you receive back. If you continually discredit and dismiss other people's abilities, and as a result you will also be dismissed and discredited by others.

Exercise: This week, keep this story in mind, and be more attentive to the people around you. Take time to listen to everybody who is trying to tell you some thing. Even if he or she is your child, a lay person, cab driver or anyone that you ordinarily dismiss or ignore. Because god's messages can come from any source, and since his ways are always mysterious, we usually miss out on lots of opportunities and insights that we may receive from an unexpected source.

This week be more open to everybody that you encounter, you can make a list of your daily concerns and challenges that you may be facing in life, and then ask at least 10 people for advice and help, and pick these 10 people from all different walks of life, rich, poor, healthy, ill, disabled, a child, a teenager,

A lay person, scientists, women, man more categories you cover, better feed back you get. And later when you come home write down your feed backs in your work book, and see collectively what these feed backs and messages are trying to tell you, in this way you get a collective solution which represents all aspects of life.

This exercise makes us humble, because we learn to respect everyone even before they have manifested a social status, and in doing so we see them as equal. And that is the reality anyway because we are all children of god, and he loves us all equally regardless of our social status. Our faith and good thoughts and deeds are what matters in the eyes of god, and many times people whom we neglect because of their lower social status possess great wisdom and compassion. And by neglecting them we deprive ourselves from the blessings and insights that they have to offer us. Because after all, material gifts are not the only kind of gift that are available in this world, the less financially privileged may have more valuable spiritual gifts for us, which will come to us as a smile or an uplifting word that will uplift us spiritually and transforms our lives.

11. See only god in every thing

Once upon a time Jesus Christ and some of his followers were to pass by a village where he wanted to meet with people and spread the word and love of god. His opponents and enemies decided to sabotage his visit. They knew that Jesus would not be stopped by their usual type of antagonism, which was throwing stones at him, and using coarse language toward him, because they had tried it before and they had witnessed that Jesus was very dedicated to spread the word of god, and nothing seemed to offend or bother him. Even when they attacked him in the past he would respond by a loving smile, and would wave his hand at them as a gesture of sending them love and divine blessing. They decided to kill a dog few days before Jesus was supposed to arrive, then they dropped the dead body of the dog in one of the narrow alleys of the village. The day came and when Jesus and his followers arrived to the alley, there was the dog which looked terrible and smelled very strongly, it seemed to have died about a weak ago. So his followers tried to block Jesus' view so he wouldn't see this ugly scene. But Jesus with a calm and smiling manor said let me see the dog, I want you all to look at god's power, look at its teeth how white and healthy it is. Then he grabbed the dead and rotten dog, and asked his follower to find a spot for its burial, and as they finished he prayed for the dog's soul and he continued his journey toward the village center as if nothing extraordinary has happened. Once again his enemies failed.

The wisdom of the story is that we have to see the positive in every situation, no matter how dark it may seem from the outside, surely there is a positive side to any experience. Because by focusing on the positive our mind becomes trained to see and comprehend only the positive and godly things, and will simply ignore and not noticing the evil and negative things. Jesus was so immersed and focused in the ocean of divine love that he could see only god in everything, and for him there was no room for evil, ugliness and negative situations, so among all the negative things about that dog's dead scene, he was noticing and seeing only the positive thing which was the dog's healthy white teeth. But most of us unfortunately are the other way around that is when in a given situation in our life we have nine good things and one bad thing, we underscore those nine good and positive points and only nags about and focus on the one thing that is not going our way, so life takes us where our focus is. If we are trained to focus on negative things, life will take us there. Therefore we need to be like Jesus Christ and focus only on the positive things in any given experience and instead of evil see god in every thing.

Exercise: This week, whenever you find yourself complaining or criticizing, someone or some condition, remember this story and instead of asking why all these horrible things are happening to me and others, ask your self this question, what can I learn from this experience or condition? What are the positive and beneficial aspects of this experience? Write down both your initial mood and attitude which were focused on the negative side of the experience, and also write your later attitude which was focused on the positive side of the same experience. Usually we cannot control many of the events in our lives, but we can control the way we are reacting to those events. Remember you always have a choice, And our choice is to which way to put our attention, if we focus on the good, positive, health, abundance, wealth, peace and love our mind which moves us toward the direction of our dominant thoughts will take us to the similar positive states and circumstances in real life. And similarly if you focus on negative, sickness, poverty, war and hate your mind will direct you and your life toward those negative states and circumstances. So this week, be very attentive and catch yourself whenever you are talking about something negative. As soon as you realize you are doing so, stop the negative sentence, and correct it by talking about a positive aspect of the experience. If an experience is too horrible like death of a child, and you do not find any thing good to say, remain quiet and just pray for his soul to be embraced by the compassionate god who is the ocean of mercy. Just by doing this exercise routinely your life will change in all aspects for the better. In short we become what we think and focus about, so focus on godly and holy things instead of evil and destructive things.

12. God's rules are impartial

Once upon a time in India, a baby died of an unexplained disease, her mother who felt strong emotional bonds to her baby refused to accept his death and believed that she can find a doctor or someone to bring her baby back to life. Even after all the doctors and healers in town told her that nothing could be done to revive the baby, she refused to burry his son. After a week the baby's body started to rot and a rotten smell spread to the whole neighborhood, so the neighbors started to complain to her, but she refused to let the child to be buried, so finally an old man approached her and said I know a man who can maybe revive your baby, if anybody can do it, it is him. So she was so happy and crying from joy asked the old man, where can I find this man? The old man said I will tell you but under one condition that if even this holy man couldn't heal your baby, you will agree to burry him. She agreed. She was directed to where this holy man who was Buddha sitting under a tree. Without hesitation she grabbed the baby and ran to the hillside which was about 20 kilometers away, she ran tirelessly till she arrived and noticed a man who was glowing from a distance, she was relieved and happy and she was so excited that she couldn't talk, after few seconds she started explaining the baby's death and that she heard, Buddha can bring her baby back to life. Buddha smiled and told the mother, okay I can bring him back to life, but I need you to do two things before I can do that. Women said restlessly anything, and you just name it! Buddha said first you need to bring me a sesame seed, she was relieved because it was the sesame season and it could be found easily every where so she ran quickly to a nearby village and got a sesame seed from a farmer and returned to where Buddha was, Buddha said great and secondly you need to find a household who has not suffered from any death in their family in the past 20 years. Again she ran to the village she started knocking the doors, the first house she knocked they had lost their daughter two years ago, the second house had lost their father, third house had lost their son and so after tirelessly trying about 30 houses, some thing hit her, a glimpse of divine insight, that what had happened to her that is loss of a loved baby, is nothing limited and special for her only, and it is a reality of life that everyone else has to experience it, she had no reason to feel that she should be excluded from the divine law of death. So she was completely relieved and a beautiful sense of calmness overtook all her being, and in a very accepting and happy manor she came back to where she left the baby beside Buddha. And thanked Buddha. Buddha didn't say a word, just smiled in a loving way, and put his hands in a prayer format together.

The wisdom of the story is that whenever something goes wrong or a terrible thing happens to us, we should not feel like a victim and act irrationally, we have to whole heartedly accept our own and our loved ones' divine fate. We do not have to beat ourselves up, nor try to suppress our feelings by enduring and pouring all of our sorrows and sadness inside. Instead of feeling paranoid, frustrated and over whelmed, we should accept the impartial and fair divine rules of justice. Divine rules are far more complex than what human consciousness can conceive of. For instance, divine rules include all of our past lives and previous existence in this planet. If we view this life as a university, different students need different number of years and credits to graduate from the university, some need only two credits which require them to attend the university for only three months because they have previously taken the other credits in the previous lives. Yet others need more credits, because they are new students. Similarly different souls have different level of purification, some need only little experience to be purified and be freed from this physical body so they may die and ascend to higher level of consciousness at a very young age, yet others may live 80 years because they need to learn and purify themselves more.

But what is certain is that god loves us, and we have all come from god in the form of soul and we must and will go back to him. We are like the drops of water that have evaporated from ocean, and are momentarily separated from the ocean, but we will be returned by rain to our origin which is the ocean. Similarly, we have momentarily moved away from the ocean of mercy which is god, and our souls have chosen different places to experience different states of being, but sooner or later and when our lessons are completed we will return to god, physical death is simply similar to the process of rain, which simply brings back and frees the soul from wondering around and hardships in the body and back to the ocean of mercy, love and freedom. So when somebody that we love passes away, we need to be certain that god loves all his children and is merciful enough to make sure that every soul is directed to a higher level of consciousness in order to enjoy god's blessing more than the previous state. So we are all ascending and progressing toward god all the time, and death simply is the end of a semester. Which means one has successfully completed his lessons. Therefore we should pray for the departed soul, and ask god to bless and protect him in his future journeys and lives. When you accept some thing wholeheartedly, you are immediately relieved. As Jesus has said, truth should set you free.

Exercise: This week, keep this story in mind, and think of the things or people whom you have lost in the past. It may be a job, friendship, a love relationship or losing a loved one. Write down the feelings that you immediately experience, when you think about each experience. What you most likely will find out is that you still have the same negative, sad and depressing emotions attached to those memories and experiences. Our subconscious mind records all the memories and information with great details, specially those with high emotional charge.

These negative memories had remained active and are continually affecting your moods, behaviors and as a result your life.

As noted before it is a mental law that a habit, memory or mental programs remain active, until we consciously decide to change it. Of course we cannot change history, and cannot change what happened to us, but we can change the way we react and remember our past memories. This technique is used in NLP and hypnotherapy to help the clients to relieve the past, and detach the negative emotional charges that are attached to that experience. In this way the subconscious and hidden emotional blockage is released and the client feels lighter and relieved. You need to find a quiet place, close our eyes and think about a time when you felt a loss of loved one, ask your mind to take you back to that time, and ask for it to allow you feel the same feeling you felt, it maybe a little overwhelming in the beginning but tell your subconscious mind that you choose not to have these feelings in regard to this experience anymore. Because with the new insights that you have gained by this story, you know that your loved one is in safe hands, and is protected by god, who will be by his side and help him in every step of the way to take to him to his next station in his existence. And order your subconscious mind, that from now on you will trust in the justice and divine orders of god, and you will accept gracefully any loss you may encounter in life. Because now you know that god always knows the best and takes care of things in the best possible way. Similarly if you lose a job, instead of feeling horrible and blaming everybody and everything including yourself. Close your eyes, relax allow your emotions and thoughts to settle down, and then ask your higher self to help you and guide you toward a better job, have faith that every loss we experience in life, is a necessary end to a repetitive cycle, and was needed for our spiritual growth, and believe that a better and more exciting job will be offered to you soon, or you may even open a new business for yourself. Since beliefs are developed by self-suggestion or the suggestions that others give you. Focus and develop the positive beliefs by using affirmative, positive self-suggestions which are always positive, constructive and empowering, and stay away from negative sources of suggestions. Remember we become what we or others constantly tell us, if we believe those suggestions to be true, then our subconscious mind drives us toward becoming exactly what we say and think about ourselves. Our inner self-image creates our outer destiny. So decide to entertain only the positive, godly and empowering emotions, values, beliefs and thoughts in your mind. As the famous saying states," As a man thinks he becomes."

13. Life takes care of itself

Once upon a time when a truck driver from Arizona was driving home, noticed a small little green plant is stuck to his shoe, he decided to take care of the little plant, but he didn't want to take it home, because his wife didn't like plants so every day he would cuddle and play with this little plant which he had it planted in a little pot. He became so attached to this little plant that he had to spend at least one hour at his car with the plant before going home. This made the wife very suspicious, she nagged and complained, and asked him: Why are you late? Where have you been? So finally he confessed and explained the situation with the plant, But his wife did not accept it and thought he was hiding something from her and probably he is cheating on her. Anyway he showed her the plant, but still she wasn't convinced and said it is un acceptable for you to be late one hour every day for a stupid plant, so he was forced to get rid of the plant, he decided to plant it in a half-shaded place about half a mile away from his house. After that he got so busy at work that he was always away on the road, so he forgot about this little plant, and one day about six months later, he remembered about the plant, so he ran quickly to the site where he had planted the plant, to his surprise it was still alive and it had grown so big, he couldn't believe it, even though it hardly rained for the past six months, the plant managed to stay alive, it seemed that life can and will take care of itself.

The wisdom of the story is that we should not think that we are solely responsible for every thing that goes around us. Some times we become overprotective and worrisome about our loved ones specially our children. We feel overwhelmed and stressed out by always trying so hard to give them the best we can. Which is of course a great thing to give your children all you can, however some time we fall into the trap of believing and assuming that they belong to us, and we are the only one that can protect and train them in their lives. We over push ourselves and the children, and selfishly try to force or convince them to choose the way that we think is right for them. And in doing so we get frustrated because most of the time the child wants to pursuit his own unique goals and desires. Then we think that we have failed to raise them correctly and end up blaming ourselves.

However we should keep in mind that first, we don't own our children, we were just chosen by god to facilitate the descending of the child's soul to this physical world. We have a partial responsibility to raise and protect the child, but we should allow the independent development of our child's character. Because god is the real protector not us, and he will protect and guide every soul. So in order not be overwhelmed with parental responsibility or any other form of responsibility, we should try our best and leave the rest to god.

We may not realize, but almost for all of our lives we have been embraced and protected by god.

Whenever you face a condition that you feel is beyond your ability, simply ask god to help you and stand beside you every step of the way. He will guide you and takes care of you and your life as he has always done. But his ways are different from ours. We may choose a solution to our problem, in a very certain way which is limited to our learned experiences and knowledge. However god chooses the best possible way that we may not even have thought about it.

Exercise: This week, keep this story in mind, and be attentive and examine your relationship with others. Check also to see how you are viewing relationships in general. Are you always trying to control the situation, by imposing and applying certain rules when you are interacting with others? Or are you flexible and spontaneous? Make a list of the immediate people who are in your life on a regular basis, in front of their name write down the type of relationship that you have with them, and also write the quality of your relationship with them. If you find that you are trying too hard to be in charge, better, or controlling, or to be too perfect, decide to change it to a more spontaneous, compassionate and flowing relationship. Because being always right, and acting the same way, even though may be socially acceptable and intellectually appealing, however it is emotionally dry and boring, and it is suffocating for the soul. Our soul hates being controlled, pushed or disciplined by others, on the other hand it likes equal, loving, sharing and spontaneous relationships. After reevaluating your relationships, you can check your other goals such as your financial goals, write a list of your goals and challenges, and in front of each of them write the way you approach and view the situation. Do you feel that you are the only person in charge? Or does your success depend on th input of others? How trusting and optimistic are you toward outside help? How much are you concerned about the end result? Are you pushing yourself by being worrisome all the time? Or do you trust that god will provide you with the best solution? Answering these questions will help you reveal your subconscious beliefs, values and priorities, it also reveals your hidden fears and worries toward life in general. The main reason that we worry and fear from any thing in life, is because of our wrong and limited belief that we have to fix every thing physically and mentally ourselves, and on the other hand we also have an opposing belief which is that we have limited resources and abilities, therefore nothing can be done unless we really push ourselves, This creates a constant sense of responsibility and inner suspicion about whether we succeed or not? When we attach too much importance on the result and we try to get things only the way we think is the right way, we often get disappointed since our mind is limited only to our own experience, we usually limit our expectation to what we believe internally, however our soul sees the big picture and has access to the infinite resources and blessings of the invisible world, may decide to provide you with what you want but in a better way that will serve your whole being as oppose to only one aspect of your self.

For example you may wish for some extra money in order to go for vacation. You really want to go because you feel emotionally and physically exhausted, so you may make a plan to work over time for three months in order to provide the ticket and other travel costs.

Your mind pushes you to work, but your soul which sees the big picture doesn't let you, because by over working for three more months you may have a serious physical or emotional break down, in this way your soul which is omniscience can foresee the future, and know that what you are doing to yourself is not good for you, it is even destructive. So it makes plans differently. For instance, when you ask for over time, your employer will refuse to give over time, as a result you may get upset, because you may think that it is over now. And you won't be able to go to your vacation. But your soul which has access to infinite resources will help you mysteriously to get you what you want, for instance you may receive a call or an e-mail from a travel agency that they have a special promotion for a fraction of the cost. In this way, when we trust our soul and god, it will get us what we want in the best way. But the catch is that we must believe that we are a soul, hence part of god. And being a connected part of god, we have access to the invisible web of power, which connects every thing in the universe together. In this way we view ourselves as one with god, then we are like a drop in the ocean, as oppose to viewing ourselves as separate which then makes us a drop in the desert. When you are one with god, like the drop in the ocean that enjoys all the peace and blessings of ocean we can also enjoy the blessing of god which is ocean of love, mercy and infinite blessings. But remember a drop can't force the ocean to act in a certain way, but by trusting the infinite and kind ocean, it will take him wherever it wishes. In summary, one should set his goal, Repeat his goals and effortlessly visualize it as if it happened (see other sections), then release it to the universe and god, believing whole heartedly for it to happen. Once it is effortlessly released, this shows our trust in our soul and god, and since we are not limiting the way of its manifestation, our soul has variety of mysterious ways to bring us what we want. Therefore one should always do his best, and leave the rest to god. We are his beloved children, and he knows what is best for our spiritual growth and unfoldment, and every thing is already taken care of.

14. Sharing your gifts with others

Once upon a time in south America the Indian god or great spirit decided to create the animal kingdom, and after doing so he decided to give each animal one special gift. He gave the control of rain to the frog, powers to rule the jungle to the lion, the gift of strength to the elephant, the gift of beauty to the peacock, the gift of patience to the turtle, astuteness to the fox, the gift of freedom to eagle and so on, and at the end he gave the gift of controlling the daylight to the seagull thus he set the rules and left the animal kingdom, because he believed that now they collectively have every thing they need to sustain their life and live happily beside each other. All the animals were excited to have their unique and special gifts, they all shared their gifts the first day, they were happy, until the night arrived and after 10 hours still the sun wouldn't come out, so they checked among themselves to see who had the gift of sun light, they found out it was the seagull, they went to see it, but it refused to show them the sun, which it was holding under her wings and it said that only I can enjoy the brightness, because god has given this gift for my personal use. All the animals begged the seagull to give up her stubbornness because it was getting really cold and they were not prepared to live in the dark all the time. Anyway three days passed without sun light, so finally the animals gathered to find a solution to this vital problem, the fox offered that we can distract the seagull, and the worm can stick a torn in the seagull's leg, and that would force her to let go of the sun, in order to take the torn out. So they did as the fox suggested but the seagull still didn't let go, so it had to stand on one leg for two more days, by that time it was dying of thirst, hunger and pain it asked for help but no body wanted to share their gifts and resources with the seagull, so he realized what was happening and agreed to share the daylight in return for food, water and help to get the torn out of it's leg, and from then on the seagull learned to share his gift and in return enjoy all the special gifts the others had to offer, and they lived happily and harmoniously ever after.

The wisdom of the story is that we have to learn to share all the gifts that god has given us, whether it is wealth, kindness, health, happiness, a smile, and our available time with others. Because in this way we obey the law of god and nature, which is, more you give more you receive, and as a result we all benefit and grow stronger. Since we are social beings and can enjoy good things more when we share them that is when you share happiness it multiplies, and as a result of being a helpful member of the society you can also openly ask for help, and any sorrow shared by others is divided and becomes easily bearable.

Exercise: This week, keep this story in mind, and decide to share your gifts and happiness with others. Make a list of your loved ones, coworkers, friends, or you can even go one step further and decide to give some thing to whoever you meet this week. Be reminded that giving is not limited to material gifts. You can give a smile, a pat on the shoulder, encouragement, your time, caring and love. You do not even need to tell the other person if you find it socially inappropriate. You can simply wish them health, happiness and success in your heart and simply smile at everybody. Before any meeting or gathering visualize the people that you are expecting to visit, view them as shiny bright souls because that is what really we all are, then send them love, respect and caring and imagine a cord of golden light travels from your heart to their heart, and imagine them smile and send a golden ray full of love back to you. You will be amazed how good, light and positive you will feel, and also your relationships will improve miraculously. Because other souls receive your love, and what you send out you receive. And if what you are sending is love, then you will receive love many folds. This week or every week for that matter, love all of god's creation. Because god is love, and when we love others, we show our respect and love for god, and in return he embraces and protects us with his endless love, which will bring us a joyful peace, abundance and happiness which irreplaceable and incomparable with any thing else in the universe.

15. How horrible is it to experience death?

Once upon a time Napoleon's army was ambushed by the Russians and almost all of his soldiers were slaughtered, but he managed to escape to a small village, where he entered to a farmer's stable, he asked the farmer to hide him, and also told him that if the Russian came and looked for him, tell them that he has not seen him, and if the French back up army units came, then show them where he was hiding. Then he hid himself under a stack of hays. Shortly after the Russian army arrived, asking very violently, did any French officer came here? The farmer spankingly replied no, they stuck barnetts and spears, to where the hays were, and the farmer said to himself, oh my god Napoleon will scream now, and the Russians will kill him too for lying to them, and even if the Russian doesn't find him and he dies then the French army will kill him, because they won't believe the story, anyway Russians also searched his house and couldn't find any thing and they left immediately because their messenger let them now that the French army is approaching. The farmer didn't dare to look under the hay, but shortly after the French arrived and all of sudden Napoleon got out of the hay stacks and stood up, he looked very seriously at his French general and told him what took you so long? The farmer didn't know what to say but was relieved that he is not dead, moreover he was sure that he will be well rewarded for saving Napoleon's life. So he gathered his nerves and courage and asked Napoleon with a smile in his face, How horrible was it to experience death? All of sudden Napoleon got so angry and replied, how can you dare to speak to me in this tone, you stupid peasant?! And he ordered the troops to close his eyes, tie his hands and legs, and shoot him to death. He started crying and begging and saying please, I saved your life have some mercy on me, it is not fair. But he did not listen, so they made him walk for about one kilometer, while he was terrified, speechless, and couldn't breathe, he was sweating but his body was cold and shaking, he couldn't cry but felt so helpless, finally they arrived and Napoleon ordered to the shooters to get ready to fire! The farmer said his final prayers and calmly waited for the inevitable, but all of sudden somebody opened his eyes, it was Napoleon, and he said laughing very loudly, now you know how it feels to be so close to death, and walked away while ordering his troops to untie him and reward him generously for saving his life.

The wisdom of the story is that it is very difficult to fully understand what the other person is going through, so when we face a friend or anyone who is acting in an unusual manner, we should not automatically condemn them and should not judge or label them as bad people, because probably we would act in a similar fashion if we were put into that same position.

Therefore instead of prejudging and labeling anyone for their behaviors, ask yourself how would I react if I was faced with the same situation? This usually helps you to understand the person's behavior more realistically. Furthermore we should keep in mind that we always act according to the best knowledge and capabilities that are available to us. Therefore even if someone acts in a way that seems limited to us, we should realize that maybe the person does not or did not have access to the resources that you may have, plus in tough and challenging times in life, one is usually over excited, frightened, or depressed, therefore cannot react in the most proper way. Remember more you respect and protect others, the more they will respect and protect you when you need it. And by the same token, more critical and judgmental you are about others, more they will be critical and judgmental about you. What you send out, comes back to you. So instead of criticizing and labeling others for their actions, send them love, and support them to get over their problem.

Exercise: This week, keep this story in mind and be attentive when you catch yourself becoming upset with someone, or when you are talking behind some body's back, or criticizing someone or passing a judgement on them. Usually we don't realize but we have a double standard, when we do some thing wrong, like being rude to someone in an argument, we feel justified because we feel we were going through a difficult time that is why we acted inappropriately, and we feel it is not a big deal and others should understand us and forget about the incidence. But we unfairly react when someone else does exactly what we did, we never think they were justified or they had a right to act that way because they were going through a though time, we label them as rude, inconsiderate and unbearable persons, and then we start sabotaging their image by talking behind their backs to other common acquaintances. In our own case we separate a behavior from ourselves, and about others we equate their one time behavior with their characters. This week keep in mind to separate people's behaviors from their real beings. The real being of everyone is their soul, which is part of god and is always kind and positive. And whenever we encounter someone who is not pleasant to us, do not attack nor try to retaliate, because you know the other person does not really mean you harm, and he is only going through a though time and it will pass, instead of retaliation offer help and support. Love and caring will always win over anger and hate. So this week try to think as if you are in the shoes of the person who is attacking you, then you may understand him better and not react and instead offer help, love and support to diffuse the tension.

Similarly if you find you are attacking or humiliating someone who is weaker than you and is dependent on you like your children or employees, step back and put yourself in their shoes and see how would you feel, if you were treated the same way you are treating them. By doing this exercise you will become humble, understanding and loving, and as result your relationships will also be lovely and healthy. Remember we receive what we send out, so send love and receive love. And as Jesus, said, act the same way with your neighbors that you want them to act toward you.

16. We believe only what we see, but is it right?

Once upon a time a frog from Oceanside was very thirsty, and there was no drinking water around, except a well he found near a house, the frog almost dying from thirst decided to dive into the well, even though he knew he may never come out of that well, but he figured it is better than dying. So he jumped and after enjoying the fresh water and drinking a lot from it, all of sudden a feeling of entrapment overtook him, he wanted to get out, but as he predicted there was no way out, because the walls of the well were very slippery and it was almost 20 meters deep. As he was thinking and calculating how to get out, he heard a beautiful female frog talking to him, he looked around and there she was, the most beautiful frog he had ever seen. She said welcome to my house, have you come to live here? If so there is a plenty of room for both of us, because my house is the biggest house in the world. The ocean frog thanked her but he explained to her that he has to go, because he is used to ocean which is much bigger than this well, and he will be very bored if he would stay here. The female frog who seemed to be offended by the idea that there is a more beautiful and better place than her well, told him it is impossible, your ocean may be big but is probably this big, she swam about a quarter of the well's length, but he said no it is bigger, then she swam half way through, and looked at him questioningly, he said no bigger, she continued to swim to three quarters of the length, again he said no bigger, she swam to the other end of the well and in a sarcastic way said it may me this big, but cannot possibly be any bigger than this, because this is the biggest thing I have ever seen. But he explained to her that she was living in a well, and there are many vast and big habitats exist out of this well. Since he was attracted to the female frog, told her maybe you want to come with me, so I can show you my world. She said I don't know about this, even though my well may be smaller than other places but it is safe and I like it, I am afraid of living somewhere where I don't have any control over my surroundings, anyway at this moment a bucket was thrown to the well, the ocean frog which was used to freedom, despite all of its dangers decided to jump to the bucket and escape, and asked the female frog for the last time to join him, and told her : You have nothing to lose you can jump back to the well if you don't like it outside, at last moment she, having liked him jumped to the bucket, so they both got out of the well, she was shocked to see the vastness of the horizon and the ocean nearby, now she was to make a decision to go back to the secured well with no dangers but no room for new experience, or to go to this wonderful unknown world which was also full of danger. She decided to give it a chance, and at the end she was very happy she did so.

The wisdom of the story is that whenever we feel stuck in a situation in life, we need to search for new ways by asking for the advice, expertise and help of others. We should tell ourselves that there should be another better way of dealing with my challenges. Tell yourself that you are certain that there have been other people in the past that have experienced the similar difficulties and challenge in their lives, and they have successfully found a solution that has helped them to get over their hard times and challenge and become victorious. Whatever we believe inside we tend to realize outside in our real life. If we believe what we know is all there is out there in the world, and if what we already know is not enough to offer a solution for our problems of life, then no matter how hard we consciously try our mind set and beliefs will not allow us to, over come our problems. Because solutions come from our minds thinking faculties. However if we believe that there is a solution somewhere out there that you may not yet know about it. You will have an open mind and open heart, and your mind and soul will lead you to the necessary information that will eventually help you to solve your problem. The help may come as a book, unexpected cash, a job offer, a cure for your illness or any other ways. Remember god loves us and will help us, but we need to do our share, which is to ask him with an open heart, and have faith that there is an answer to our challenge.

Exercise: This week, keep this story in mind, and make a note of the situations or goals that you may have in your mind. And specifically write down the goals that you feel are or have been very difficult and almost impossible for you to achieve them. Then in front of each goal and project write down the possible sources that may help you to achieve your goals. It can be your family, friends, coworker, financial institutions or any other source. After you finish doing that, find a quiet place that you usually do your mental and spiritual exercises, and close your eyes and take five deep breath, and allow your mind to settle down, when it is clear of any thought, imagine and visualize the holiest person you can think of like Jesus, Buddha, Mohammad, Moses, your higher self or whoever you believe in. On your mental screen where your third eye or your inner eye which is located between your eye brows visualize that holy figure is standing in front of you, simply ask him to give the solution to your problem, ask him to guide you toward your goal, at the proper pace without harming anyone including yourself. Have faith and visualize and act as if what you wish is already happened. This is thinking from the end, when your soul and subconscious mind believe something has happened to you inwardly, it will find ways to be manifested outwardly here in your life. Because it is a mental law, what you believe internally, you tend to realize outwardly. So instead of feeling helpless and believing there is no solution, choose to believe that there is a solution and you will find it, And remind yourself that you are a precious child of god, and he will be by your side, help you and protect you all the way, as long as you keep your attention on him. So always think of the possible positive solution to your problem, that will create a positive mental expectancy that will certainly lead to an answer, and at the same time have your effortless attention on god and holy spirit that can guide you to get to what you want in a faster, safer and happier way. Again like other exercises do not push or rush the process, allow your soul which is part of god and is almighty and omniscience to give the solution as it sees proper.

Because some times if not always, what we are going through and considering as hard times, is necessary for our spiritual unfoldment and growth in all other aspects of our lives. When you get the answer that may come as a flashing thought, or as a dream, or in a book, or you may get it from another person, write them down in your work book. When you have the solution, contemplate effortlessly on the solution, and ask your self and your higher self, what should your initial step be? Where, when and how should you start? Then listen to your inner voice and start taking persistent actions until you get to what you want, and be certain that god will be by your side and will help you every step of the way.

17. It all depends on how hard you want it

Once upon a time a young who wanted to be enlightened and reach god-realization went to the nearby mountains where he heard an enlightened master lives. After few days of search he found the master sitting by a river. He approached him and told him that he wants to be enlightened, and asked him: What should I do?

The master very calmly said, no problem we can get you there now!, So the young man was excited and said how do we start?, The master showed him a buckle he had, and told him to fill this bucket with water from the river and than we can start. The young man agreed and ran to the riverside and soon he was back with the full bucket of water. He asked the master unctuously what next?, Then the master asked him, are you sure you want this? He said yes, please. So the master said ok you have to follow my instructions flawlessly and without any resistance. Young man nodded his head as a sign of approval. Master said ok, then he asked him to put his head in the bucket of water, so he did, then the master grabbed his neck and held his head completely under water, the young man did not resist because he trusted the master and also thought he is testing him to see how obedience he is, 20 seconds passed, he pushed himself upward as a sign that he is getting out of breath, but the master didn't let go and pushed his head even harder into the bucket, another 20 seconds passed he was really breathless so he gently hit the master's leg to please let go, but the master didn't and pushed his head even harder, another 20 second passed the young man felt he is dying, so he hit the master's leg very hard, but he Wouldn't let go, so the young man gave all he had to escape death, and pushed the master back, and started hitting him, But the master was laughing. The young man was so shocked and upset and told the master, you are not a master, you are crazy, you almost killed me there, why did you do it? The master very calmly said, you can reach enlightenment and god realization only if you want it as hard as you wanted to stay alive, you gave every thing you had to survive, you didn't think whether it was appropriate to hit me or not, your spirit took over and saved you. So you need to give everything you got to be enlightened, let me know when you are ready, and he left.

The wisdom of the story is that we must first evaluate our goals and new projects, before taking any actions. Our goals should satisfy and benefit all different parts of our beings. Which are our physical, emotional, intellectual and spiritual selves. Furthermore each of our aspects have their own subdivisions. For example our physical parts contain various dimensions with their specific needs, for instance, our sexual, physical comfort, physical health, beauty and so on. As oppose to a general view that we are one individual, in reality we are consisted of many different parts, of which each and every one of them have their own peculiar and specific needs, goals and desires. In this way, if we view our selves as a multifaceted being, we are then similar to a community. As it is in the outside world that democracy is the best type of government, same is true when we want to arrange and govern our inner collective being. Because if we oppress or neglect a group or part of the whole, that part will not cooperate as it should, and as a result the final outcome will not be satisfactory. Therefore it is very important to know exactly what we want in pursuing this new goal?, And in doing so we need to take into consideration, and ask ourselves the following questions, how will this goal affect my physical aspect? How will this goal affect my emotional self? How will this goal affect my intellectual self? How will this goal affect my spiritual self? You should even extend your questions to include any other aspects that you may think of, for instance how will this goal affect my sexual, financial aspects? If you find that all of your aspects are satisfied and are benefitting from the new purposed goal, then you are ready to start taking action. But if one part of you is not happy, then you need to adjust your plans and goals, to accommodate that part also. Remember just like a healthy society, which works best when everybody is happy, satisfied and has its voice heard, our being as a collective being operates best when all parts of our beings are harmoniously benefitting from a change. This is what is meant when we talk about how hard do you really want some thing? When all parts of you being agreed on getting some thing, they will cooperate a hundred percent, and the harmony of their collective force drives us toward taking the proper action in the quickest and most proper way. But if one or some parts of us, is not really satisfied with the change, then it means we as a collective being do not really want that change to happen, so we meet obstacles and inner resistance, which will slow our progress toward our goal by sabotaging our efforts. Remember more unified you are within, more solid and focused your mind and actions will be, and more focused, organized and persistent your actions and thoughts, the faster and more efficiently you will reach your goals. For some thing to be an ideal goal for us to follow, it should serve our general and main purpose, passion and mission in life. This is what Buddha called "dharma". Therefore it will help you a lot, and save you a lot of money, energy and time to choose the right goal, before taking an action. One should search within his soul, to find his mission, purpose and passion in life, and he should live and strive for only the goals and objectives that are in harmony with his dharma. Because without any of these components, one will not have the necessary stamina to carry through the extensive works that are some times needed to achieve their new goals in life. In simple terms, you must love and passion your new goal, you should find it purposeful and being some thing worthy for a bigger cause like enlightenment, And you should also feel an inner responsibility that this is your mission because it will not only serve you individually, but also when you improve, you will help and improve the well-being of the whole society also and in this way you are doing some thing noble and spiritually valuable.

Exercise: This week, keep this story in mind and decide to lay out a fundamental plan for your life as a collective being. This means determine and decide what is your dharma in life. Find a goal, or a change that will lead you to be a person who lives with a passion, mission and purpose, as oppose to a person who is simply living a repetitive and dull life, paying bills and simply getting by. Remember if you choose the first option, which is living with passion, mission and purpose you are "living," on the other hand if you chose the second option, even though you are alive physically but spiritually you are not living. That is the phenomenon that the Taoist masters refer to which states "A man dies when he is 30, but they, burry him when he is 60", because they rightfully believe when a person stops learning and growing spiritually he is dead. Because in reality, our real self is our soul.Therefore we must start and decide to set a goal that serves our soul, mind and body in a harmonious manner, and is also progressive and positive in nature. Our goal should include spiritual values, such as love, compassion, charity, wisdom, cooperation, harmony and spiritual unfoldment, it should also have some mental values and characteristics such as organization, discipline, social integrity and intellectual development, and it should also serve and benefit our physical values, which means, it should help us to improve our health, comfort, nutrition and even our sexual life. Since it is very important to pick the right goal, you should not rush the process of goal setting, and even when you have picked your goal, you have to be flexible to adjust your goals as you change yourself in life. In your work book, make a chart to include all aspects of your being, and then examine and find out what exactly each aspect of your being needs, in order to be balanced and happy, you can use the information gathered from other parts of this book, as well as your previous experiences to complete this chart. After you are finished with the preparation of the list, make a goal which is collectively and democratically accepted by all parts and aspects of you. Then make a plan to take the first step, then take action. Check the results that you get, if it took you even a tiny bit closer to your goal, keep going, if you see it doesn't feel right, be flexible and adjust your approach until you get to your goal.

Being flexible is the key, just like the nature, when heavy storms break the thickest trees because they fail to bend, but little tiny grasses withstand the biggest storm because it bends during the storm knowing it can return to its original straight position once the storm pass. Similarly we should be flexible in hard times, and adjust our plans and courses of action as we go on. Also remember life is not a straight journey, it is like a journey on the boat, the captain has his goal which is reaching a certain destination in mind, but he makes thousands of minor and major shifts in direction because of waves or storms, but he is not worried, because he knows that these minor changes are necessary for him to get to where he wants to go.

18. How many lives should I wait for enlightenment

Once upon a time in a jungle in India, a very care free young man, was singing and walking around, when he saw a Buddhist monk sitting beside a tree, he approached him and said hi, The monk looked at him in contempt and in a very harsh manor, and told him to be quiet, because he said the angel of reincarnation and enlightenment who visits earth once for every thousand years, and today is the day he will come and I am waiting for him, in fact he said I have waited for this moment my whole life, and I have been sitting here for the past 30 years, just praying and meditating. The young man apologized, and was about to leave, that a thunder hit right between him and the monk. And the angel of liberation from the material world appeared in front of their eyes. So the monk got up, and was getting ready to receive the gift of enlightenment from the angel, but the angel said you need to live few more lives to be enlightened, he got so angry but kept himself from saying any thing rude, then asked the angel, how many lives? The angel pointed to a broken tree branch, and said you have to come back and live for as many times as there are leaves on that broken branch. He ran to the branch and there were eight leaves on it, he couldn't keep himself, and started saying bad words to the angel and complaining that it is not fair, he has prayed and done good things all his life.

The angel was about to leave, the young man asked him laughingly how many lives do I have to come back to be enlightened? The angel pointed the jungle with his hand, and said you have to come back for as many times as there are leaves. The young started jumping and singing in happiness and said out loud, oh thank you god, so there is a chance for me to be enlightened one day. The angel looked at the young man and said you are already rewarded with enlightenment, because of your open, joyful, honest and simple spirit.

The wisdom of the story is that we never know how close we are to god's realization and spiritual freedom. Because in reality, we have never been separate from god to begin with. This is an illusion that our mind, religions and society have created. In reality we are all part of god and from god. If we compare god to an ocean of mercy, our soul is a drop which is inside and is from that ocean. We as souls have temporarily acquired and put on this physical body, in order to experience and manifest in this physical world. Because our soul cannot tolerate the harsh and low vibrations of this physical world. Just like we put a jacket on when it gets really cold.

However over time we have forgotten that we are actually a soul and we are all connected with invisible energy cords of love, and our mind has tricked us to believe that we are separate entities from our creator.

We are lead to mistakenly believe that our true self is our physical body, and we think we are a physical being that some times having a spiritual experience when we meditate or pray for example. But in reality it is the other way around, we are spirits and souls that some times having a physical experience. Therefore, since we already have part of god within us in the form of soul. All the heavenly knowledge and godly attributes already exist within us. Spirituality is not a field that we should search outside ourselves or wait a life time to be enlightened. Spirituality is a field of recognition. You will be enlightened and reach god realization, when you recognize that god is within your heart. When you develop the belief of the possibility that you as a soul and son of god are worthy of possessing godly attributes you will be enlightened. The time that it takes, for reaching enlightenment, and spiritual freedom, does not depend on social and/or religious ceremonies, or how long you have mentally tried to become enlightened. Since enlightenment is a spiritual phenomenon, you can only reach there by your soul, and that requires dismantling of the social mind and having an open heart full of love, playfulness of a child, and humbleness. Your ego will not allow to achieve spiritual growth, if you solely meditate and pray to impress others and present yourself as a pious person to get recognition and credit from others. Your intentions are more important than your actions, when you are dealing with spiritual matters.

Exercise: This week, keep this story in mind, and find a quiet place where you will not be disturbed for 15-20 minutes, close your eyes and let your mind to settle down and relax, then visualize yourself as a bright and radiant being which is surrounded in an egg-shaped energy field. This energy field is called the aura. Visualize yourself as getting brighter and brighter. Start sending love and good will to others, first start with your immediate family and loved one, and imagine a golden or shiny white ray of energy which carries your love, is spreading from all angles toward the various people that you love, as you send them love invite them inside your energy field or aura in order for them to feel your love even more. Next start sending love to your friends, coworkers, neighbors and other people that you know. Imagine the rush of golden rays of love that are traveling from your heart to every single person you know, and also invite them to come inside your aura to enjoy your love and presence. Next send love to all your country man, and invite them all to your energy field. And go even further and send love to all of the human population, regardless of their nationality, race, ethnicity or religion background, and invite all of them into your energy field. Imagine the whole world is smiling back at you and embracing your love, next include all of god's creation and send your love to all animals, plants and even the inanimate objects, and invite them into your energy field.

And finally send love to the whole existence, all galaxies, and include them in your energy field. And finally invite god into your energy field and send him your love.

This exercise will uplift you in all aspects of your life.

Because when you love all, every thing and everyone in life will love you back, a sense of harmony, unification, peace and happiness will spread all over your world of relations. Love is the greatest unifying force in the universe and can heal and overcome any difficulty and illness. More impartial and more universal the love is, the more powerful it becomes. So love all and serve all selflessly and impartially, and I promise you, you will be on your way to enlightenment in the quickest and most proper way.

19. Should I be careful or trust god for protection?

Once upon a time in Arabia, a merchant who was a very pious man was going to travel through the desert, and he almost always trusted god for protection of his jewelry store when he was in his hometown, he would leave his store unlocked when he was going for daily prayers. But now he was going to travel through the deadly hot desert, and his only way of transportation was his camel, it was impossible to travel through the desert without a camel. So he was puzzled in what to do. That is, should he tie his camel?, to be on the safe side, or should he trust god to protect him by not letting the camel to escape and not to tie his camel. So he decided to ask a holy man who was always in the mosque, he explained to him his dilemma and asked him: Should I tie my camel or should I trust god for its protection? The holy man smiled and said do both, tie your camel and also trust god for its protection.

He continued by saying that god has given us the intellectual faculty, so we can use it for our protection, so you have to use your mind and experience for the parts that you can handle it by yourself and is in your hands, but for greater matters which one has no control over, then one should ask god for protection, but in any case it is good to both trust god and use your mind for protection and help.

The wisdom of the story is that we shouldn't simply become careless and irresponsible in our life, and assume that god will take care of our duties as a human being, because these responsibilities and activeness are necessary for our self-development and spiritual unfoldment. So we should use all our faculties, our experiences, our physical, mental and spiritual assets that we have gained throughout our lives to deal with the challenge that we may face. However at the same time we need to always trust that there is higher force looking above our shoulders and will help us whenever he sees that we are giving our best to overcome a situation. As the Moslem saint Ali has said, "Divine help comes as much as your effort, dedication and persistence in any given situation."

Exercise: This week keep this story in mind, and decide to always use a combination of both individual efforts and faithfulness to god for every thing that you do. If we are to view life as a road that we walk on, from birth to the time of death. God has created the road, created the sceneries and infinite possibilities, he has also given us all the tools, like our body, mind, soul and all other blessings like health, material gifts, food, water, love and most importantly he has given us the freedom to choose our own path in life. God has created many impartial and universal rules, whereas there is no exceptions, short cuts or favoritism. Every soul is free to act within the boundaries of the physical and mental rules set by god, in order to maintain a universal arena, which is equally fair for all.

In the game of life, laws of nature, laws of mind and body are the rules of the game. However we are free to experience in this road of life any how we desire.

Having this in mind, find a quiet place where you would not be disturbed for 15-20 minutes, lie down, close your eyes, take five deep breath, attend to your breathing for 2-3 minutes, this will allow your body and mind to be relaxed, and will make your subconscious mind more responsive to your imaginations and suggestions. Next think about a goal or project that, you may have, imagine that you are walking on a golden road, which has beautiful trees and colorful flowers in both side of it, visualize and see your goal at some point ahead of you down the road, you can see it but you need to walk on the road to reach there, next notice that somebody is waving his hand at you, a little ahead, as you approach him, you see a very vibrant and holy being, he introduces himself to you as your guardian angel. He also tells you that he was sent by god, to help you whenever you need him any where and any time while traveling on this road. He also tells you that he has some instructions and guideline directly from god, which instruct him not to carry you on his shoulder, or fly you to your goals. However god has permitted him to help you when you fall, or when you need a little push or a break from hardships. God has also told me to help you only when you have tried and gave your best efforts. Imagine the angel is also telling you in a reassuring way that he will always walk beside you and help you out throughout your journey, however he cannot walk for you. You must walk for yourself, because that is how you learn, when you interact and deal with daily challenges. Next visualize yourself walking the road toward your goal, and also feel, the angel beside you, and see yourself reaching your goal, and thanking your angel and god for allowing your wish to come true. Whenever you are ready, on the count of three open your eyes, feeling motivated, happy and full of energy. You should develop a positive attitude about life and its challenges, always try your best, and leave the rest to god, and be certain that when you have god on your side and in your heart you can achieve any thing you believe.

20. Instead of changing the world, change yourself

Once upon a time in India lived a king, who all of sudden was stricken with severe and unbearable headaches, he tried all the doctors and healers throughout his kingdom, and he offered very generous rewards for whomever that could cure him from his debilitating headaches, but nobody could. Finally he heard about a monk who lived nearby his palace beside a river, so he ordered his soldiers to bring this man to his palace. The king, who was becoming really helpless and frustrated with these headaches, told the monk that he would give any thing he wishes if he would heal him, the monk said I don't want any thing but I can heal you. The monk told the king to provide a green curtain and hang it in front of his bed or seat, and instructed him to gaze into this green curtain in an effortless and relaxed manner for about 30 minutes, three times daily, until his headaches would fade away, the king got really happy and thanked the monk from the bottom of his heart. The king's headache was completely healed in just two days. The king was so relieved and happy by his healing that he ordered his soldiers to paint all the walls in green color, he also ordered new green carpets, furniture, and soon he changed the whole palace to a green color, he also wore only green and visitors were authorized to enter the palace only if they were wearing a green clothing. He never suffered from those headaches for years. One day the monk was passing by the king's palace and he remembered the king's headache so he decided to check on him to see if he was doing fine, so as he wanted to enter the palace, the guard told him that no one can enter the palace unless they wear green clothing, he asked why is that? The guard told him about the king's headache and he said that a monk has ordered him to view green colors to be relieved from the excruciating headaches, The monk laughed loudly and told the guard that he was the man who healed the king, so after asking the king's permission they let the monk in the palace to see the king. The king was very happy to see the monk,and his healer. He again offered the monk any thing he wished, but when the monk refused, the king asked him then what brings you here?, The monk said nothing in particular, I just wanted to check on your headaches and see if you need any help. The king said thanks but I have not had any headaches for years, thanks to your advice and remedy, and as you can see I have ordered for every thing to be changed to a green color, so everything will give me relaxation, and avoids my headaches. The monk laughed at him, and said why not instead of painting the whole palace to green, you could just put a green glass on your eyes, so you could view everything in green, without going through this much trouble.

The wisdom of the story is that we don't have to change the world to fit it to our likings, it is much easier and practical to change our inner perspective and our view of the world to make it more agreeable and plausible with realities of life.Because in most cases we can't control our outer world circumstances which are beyond the scope of our control, but we can manage and control our inner states of feelings and perceptions. In this way we can change and control the way we react to those circumstances. It is now a widely accepted phenomenon by the metaphysician and para psychologists that "We only see what we believe", as opposed to the older slogan, which stated "We only believe in what we see," therefore by changing our beliefs and the way we are looking at any event in our lives, we will meet only what we believe in our lives. But in order to do so one has to develop an inner discipline, which is based on divine, positive and progressive belief system that will allow him only to experience and be affected by the divine, positive and progressive situations and circumstances.

Exercise: This week, keep this story in mind, and be attentive and catch your self when you find yourself automatically reacting or complaining about a situation or circumstance. Immediately stop your negative and critical words and reverse it to some thing positive which will empower you. Because whenever we show reaction to some negative circumstances like raining, traffic, political conflicts on the news and so on, we absorb all those information that we believe are destructive. And what we entertain in our mind whether it is meant as a critical and undesired situation, our subconscious mind will record it as some thing we desire to focus on and believe in. And as we learned earlier what we believe and mentally focus on will become part of us. Because our mental programming, directly controls and affects our behaviors, and as a result we would be subconsciously driven toward those negative circumstances. Because our subconscious mind which can't take a joke or indirect conversation will figure that we want o experience these states of being that is the reason why we are constantly talking about them and putting our attentions on them. Therefore we can see that when we respond to a negative experience, we actually focus on it and lose control and as a result that situation over takes us, and we will be doomed to merge with those undesired conditions and feelings and eventually experience them.

But we can choose not to respond, and to redefine our beliefs and values, or simply redefine the way we respond to any bad or negative circumstances. For example when we hear in the news that a serial killer had killed 20 people. Instead of focusing on that news all day and talk about with whomever we meet, we can choose to change the channel, and not to talk about it. You should just pray for the victims soul, and believe and be certain that god's justice system is flawless and more powerful than any of us, and he will punish the murderer in the most appropriate way. And also ask god and holy spirit to protect yourself, your family and the whole humanity from these circumstances. In these cases or less extreme cases, do what you think you can to protect yourself, but leave the rest in the hands of god who can easily take care of it.

Of course this was just an example, you can use many similar approaches and techniques to change your point of view and reaction to the events you encounter in your life.

Because in most cases it is impossible to change the world and what goes in and around it, but we can choose not to be defeated by their destructive and evil effect, and not to get entangled with them, instead we choose to move beyond it and look at the event in a dissociated manner, and choose not to give any power to it, and by praying and meditating and using positive words and blessings we actually reverse the effect of that incident. Remember nothing has a power, unless the power you mentally give to it yourself.

21. If we help each other god will help us too

Once upon a time in Egypt, Moses, the Jewish prophet who was actually talking to god in mount Sinai, one day god told him to gather his pious followers and believers, and to take them to the higher mountains because there would be a flood in two days which will cause the river of Niles to flood and destroy and kill everybody in the city, god said I am sending this flood to punish the nonbelievers and destroy the oppressors. So Moses went down to the city and asked all of his followers to move to the mountains to avoid drowning, so thousands of them escaped and left the town.

The rest of the population which didn't believe in Moses' god and were none-believers stayed in the city, however being afraid of the possible flood they started building shelters and store food, water, medication and all other necessities, they also helped the old, women and children, they cooperated selflessly and collectively, and awaited their possible doomed faith. But they made a decision to help each other and stick together to the end, no matter what happens. The stated two days passed but no flood, on the third day Moses went near a mountain where he could see the city beside the river bank, but to his surprise nothing had happened, god had done everything he told him up until then, he went to talk to him again, and told him: Dear Lord, I followed your exact instruction, why isn't the flood coming to kill the nonbelievers? I forced a lot of people out of their house to the wild and harsh mountains with little food and water, and they are already restless and angry, they have started fighting among themselves for food, water and shelter. Dear lord, please tell me what to do. God told him that there will be no flood. Moses asked why? Lord replied, those people helped each other during their worst moments of facing destruction and death, they selflessly helped the elderly, women, children and disabled to the safe area that is why, When I saw that they are acting in a selfless and kind manner and they are willing to put their own life at risk for saving others, then I decided that I will also help them and they shall not suffer, they are loved and protected by me. On the other hand these people gathered around this mountain, even though they are completely safe, and on the verge of reaching a new free and empowered life, are fighting and hating each other. One who cannot love his fellow man cannot love god neither.

The wisdom of the story is that we need to love, support and help our loved ones, friends, co-workers and be cooperative to all of our fellow men if we are to be helped and blessed by god. Because god exists in the heart of all human beings and other beings. If we respect and help our fellow men, we are actually serving the god within them. Because every person is actually a soul regardless of his or her background, ethnicity, race and religion, and thus is protected and loved by god. If we cannot love others, how should we expect others including god to love and protect us. It is a divine and universal law, that what you send out you receive. So give love and support and receive the same in many folds in return.

Exercise: This week, keep this story in mind, and catch yourself whenever you find yourself talking behind some body's back or spreading rumors. Catch yourself when you are intentionally blocking some body's success because you feel threatened that he or she may get ahead of you in a job. Catch yourself when you want to buy your way through in a job interview or wherever there is a competition. We all know deep in our heart that what our true intentions and motives are in regard to any decision and action. And we know which one is moral and which one isn't. But in order to become aware of them write these incidents down if any. They do not have to be necessarily this drastic in measure. Write it down when you realize that you are subconsciously and habitually are trying to sabotage somebody's success, stop and decide to reverse your action. That is support and help him to get what he wants. If you continually and selflessly help others, sooner or later you will touch the persons' heart and soul, and also you will win the support and help of everybody else that sees your good intentions.

As the Persian saying, puts it beautifully, "Do good to others, because if you pick up a person who has fallen to the ground, then the hundred people that see you doing that, when you fall in the future, you will have a hundred people eager to get you up and help you, and don't do bad to others, because if you kick somebody who has fallen to the ground, and a hundred people see it, when you fall in the future, you will have a hundred people eager to kick you."

So do good to others this week and watch your life grow in every direction. You will have harmonious, cooperative, peaceful, productive, compassionate and progressive interpersonal relationship. Furthermore god will love, help and protect you because of your love, help and caring toward others.

22. Who is my real friend?

Once upon a time in India lived a very rich merchant, who had become so upset over time, because he felt that all of his old friends, co-workers and even his family did not love him for himself. He thought that they were nice to him only because he was helping them and giving them money. They never visited him for the sake of seeing him alone to have fun, but only when they needed something. So he became so suspicious from everybody and got so attached to his belongings and he was led to believe that his true friends are his belonging and his wealth. But he still missed his friends and family. This duality was causing him a lot of frustration and sadness, he wished that he was not so rich so he would have a healthier relationship with everybody, so he will be happy.

One day he heard that a famous wise man a guru is in town, so he decided to go and see him, and ask for a solution to his dilemma. So he went to a monastery where the monk was staying for few days, and he approached him and explained his problem and asked him. Wise man who is my true friend?

The wise man smiled and said we all have three kinds of friends in this world.

First kind is our belongings and wealth, which if we die they don't even accompany us until the door step. The second kind, is our family and friends which can and will follow us until the grave but they can't accompany us any further. And the third kind of friend is the wisdom, love, compassion, and self-realization that we have gained and gathered in our heart, and this kind of friend can accompany us for ever. So your most valuable friends are your inner wisdom, love, understanding that you store within yourself before death, those inner resources will give you eternal peace and happiness in both this life and after your death in other side.

The wisdom of the story is that we should mainly focus on the wisdom, love and self-realization. Because these are the only things that we can take with us after our death. When we leave the physical world, nothing of this world including all our material possessions and our loved ones, can accompany us. We have to leave them behind. God has descended each and every soul alone when he is born to this world, and it will also ascend him back alone at the time of his death.

Certainly our money and material things are the least valuable to us when we die, because we cannot even take a penny with us to the other world. As the Persian saying states, our body bag has no pocket. Even if we could take our monies to the other side, it won't be useful for us. Because in the spiritual worlds of god, matter and money, does not exist. Next type of assets and friends that we enjoy in this life are our family, friends and loved ones, they also can play a very limited role when we die. They can accompany us to the grave side, but they cannot accompany us even if they want to. Because their time has not come yet, and their soul has still more time to spend in their bodies and in this physical world. But what remains are your good deeds, thoughts and words. These are our best friends, because they will be accompanying us forever, no matter in which world or level of existence we are.

The level of inner peace, love, humility, wisdom, understanding, self and god realization that we have acquired and stored during our life time, will be kept and used to choose our next destination after death. Our good deeds will also cause others to remember us and pray for our soul. And prayers of others that we have touched their heart by our kindness, love and charity will help our soul in the other worlds. Because prayers are spiritual and nonmaterial in nature, and only spiritual vibrations can reach spiritual worlds where the soul is.

Exercise: This week keep this story in mind, and decide to dedicate some time for spiritual activities every day. This can include visiting holy places, attending prayers, or reading spiritual scriptures based on your belief. You can also do some selfless activities, like doing some voluntary works or visit the orphanage houses, senior houses, mentally challenged, disabled or any other charitable organization. Buy them some gift, or take some of the stuff that you have in your closet and storage room that you rarely use. Even if you do not have a material gift to give, just visit them and show your love and compassion. Or you can simply help a family member, or a friend in any project they may have, without expecting any thing in return. Make others laugh, listen to them if they need someone to talk to. Most of the time just being there beside someone who is going through tough and challenging times, is enough. Because you make him/her to feel secure and not alone, and your invisible force of love and support will help him/her to over-come any challenge. And when you are by yourself, pray for the well being and prosperity of others and humanity as a whole. More you develop and send out these feelings of love and selfless giving, more you will receive from the universe in thousands folds. And since you are not expecting any material or social rewards in returns, you will be rewarded spiritually by developing all those attributes that you are focusing on. You put the seed of humbleness, love, charity and wisdom in your mind, and once they become part of you, they are yours to keep, and they will help you enjoy both in this life, because more you give more you receive, even if your intention is not getting back any thing in return, And these spiritual attributes will accompany and put you at a higher level of consciousness and blessing after you depart from this physical body.

23. When am I ready for enlightenment?

Once upon a time in Persia a young rich man decided to give up every thing he had to go and find a master living in high mountains in order to be enlightened, he just kept enough money to pay for two of his servants to carry him through the rough mountains and valleys, and also to buy the necessary food, drinks, blanket, tents and horses. After a long search of almost one year he reached the site where the master was sitting at the gate of a cave, he had just finished his food, water and he had given the horses to the servants as an extra payment, because their journey took longer than expected, So after a brief rest the servants left the young man and headed back toward their town. The young man who was now middle of no where, all there was in his eye sight, were very tall mountains reaching the clouds, but he was happy that he had made it, so he ran toward to the master who was facing the cave sitting in meditation format with closed eyes. Young man told him that he was a rich man and gave up all his worldly possessions to become spiritually liberated and enlightened, he said that he has shown his dedication and he is ready to start right away. But the master without even opening his eyes or turning his back, told him that you are not ready yet! The young man was shocked, disappointed even scared, because there was no turning back he had no money, no food. He asked the master when will I be ready? The master pointed to a very tall mountain range which was stretching over the horizon, and said you will be ready when you cross all those mountains and then I will meet you on the other side and you will only be ready then. So the young man helplessly started his journey, but since he didn't have any money, for the first time in his life he experienced hunger and thirst, since he lost his blanket and tent, he experienced coldness and being without the protection of a shelter for the first time, in his long journey which took another year he had to do all kind of harsh and degrading works which he wouldn't even dream of doing before, he washed people's toilet, cleaned shoes, carried heavy stuff for merchants, he literally changed to a person who didn't have the slightest resemblance to his old self, he had been transformed to a poor, homeless man with no sense of social identity. After all those hardships he arrived to where he was supposed to meet the master, even though he had started to doubt whether the master will really be there, because the master was very old and looking at his physical appearance it seemed impossible for him to make the trip. Moreover he thought it would be impossible for the old man to know the exact time of his arrival, but to his surprise as he came down from the last mountain he found the master sitting at a river's bank, smiling at him. Master got up in very fast and agile fashion even though he looked more than 100 years old, and told him, you are ready now, the young man was shocked, because the old man had not even looked at him about a year ago at the cave!, So he asked the old man in a calm and non unctuous way that, why did you put me through all these difficulties, a year of physical, emotional, and mental hardship, I went through hunger, thirst, cold, hot, I was attacked by wild animals, I was beaten by thugs, I was forced to do all kind of low paying jobs and in short I did whatever I thought I would never do. The master smiled and said you were not ready then, because your ego and social identity was polluting your soul and impeding your path. Your ego was as big as those mountains, he pointed with his finger, you had to take your ego away from your heart, so you could be self-realized and enlightened, similar to these humongous mountains. Young man said but I already had traveled for a year to meet you for the first time, why was the second trip necessary? Because in the first trip your ego was not touched a bit, you traveled with servants, riding on a horse, eating and drinking your usual food, and sleeping in a safe and guarded tent. Your initial intention was to add enlightenment as a new thing to your ego, but enlightenment is achieved when you give up your ego and social identity. So the second trip forced you to only depend on god and your soul, your past identity and ego couldn't provide you with food, water and shelter, thus your past, social identity and your ego fell piece by piece as you passed these mountains. In order to be enlightened you must become selfless and ego-less only then you can find the inner master which is your soul, and only your soul can take you to god-realization.

The wisdom of the story is that our ego is often the obstacle to our spiritual development. Our egotism and selfishness also effects our relationship with others. A selfish person, often disregard and/or neglects other people's need and concerns, and is focused only on taking advantage of others for his own benefits. But these type of selfish behavior which is based on a wrong archetypal belief that I am better than anyone else, and since I am the center of the universe, everybody else should pay extra attention to me, and to sacrifice their own, time, energy and resources to accommodate me and my needs. This belief will not be successful and beneficial for anyone who adheres to it, because it is against the natural and divine rules. Every thing in nature is created and made of energies with various vibrations. These energies are the divine energies that give life and causes movement and manifestation in this world, if these energies are not flowing properly, it will cause a blockage in the circuit, it will be similar to a bended water hose, which cannot remain blocked for a long time, without causing the person who is blocking it, a great deal of harm. Love, charity, wisdom and service should be in constant flow, meaning you should give as well as you receive, if you try to hold on to all the love, service and knowledge that you are receiving from your surroundings and not giving back any thing in return, these blessings will actually become heavy burdens on your shoulders. Love and service when it is inter changeably flowing, among people is refreshing and life giving like a flowing river, but when one or some people decide to take more than they give, that extra stored energy will become heavy and stagnated like the dead water of the swamps. Remember life is flowing and moving, any thing that does not flow, is not natural. And any thing which is not natural will cause energy blocks in our energy field or aura. And these energy blocks will manifest in our life later, by causing various forms of physical and emotional illnesses.

In the eastern cultures, it is believed that all the diseases have their underlying cause in our inability to give or receive love and divine energy. Our selfishness, and lack of harmony acts like a big rock, that is blocking the natural flow of a river. And it makes us imbalanced. We must decide to take this rock out of the way of our soul, so once again we can enjoy the purity, simpleness, playfulness and sense of peace and harmony that we once enjoyed as a child. As Jesus has said, you must once again become innocent and pure like a child in order to get to the heaven. And by giving your love and service freely and happily, you will receive the same in many folds. Because it is a divine law, what you send out comes back to you.

Exercise: This week, keep this story in mind, and make a decision to review and examine your beliefs about yourself in relation to others, also review your behaviors toward others in your relationships. Make a list of the people whom you usually meet during the week in a regular basis, and also add a category which includes the strangers that you may meet occasionally like the bus driver, cashier in the super market, parking lot attendant and so on. In front of their name write down the way you have been acting toward them, rate it from zero to ten, where ten being a perfect attitude, which is polite, loving, giving, caring and respectful, and the zero being a very negative and showing unacceptable attitude, such as impolite, rude and aggressive. Rate your behaviors toward others, then see where your low scores are. Then make a plan to compensate and balance your relationship.

Do every thing from heart, meaning really want to change, before taking any action. And for a real change of heart, and change of attitudes we need to change our existing belief system if it is limited. We need to replace the self-centered belief that "I am the best person on the earth, and I am better than anyone else, so I don't need to respect anyone, since they are inferior to me," we need to install a new and right belief that is "I love all, respect all and serve all, because they are all as good as I am, since we are all children of god, we are all like brothers and sisters, and we are all equally loved and protected by god." This belief of seeing everyone as a soul, and equal will transform your relationships and also your inner state of being. Because once you stop to focus on taking only, then the flow of divine energies will increase into your life, which will lead you to enjoy a happier, healthier and more creative life.

24. How can you treat the beautiful and ugly the same?

Once upon a time a Russian man was passing from a jungle in northern China, he was so tired and he had finished his food and water, as he was talking to himself and wishing to find somebody or some thing to eat he came across to a small river, there was a middle-aged Chinese man sitting by the river, he approached him and asked him if he could offer him some water, food and a place to stay, in return for some beautiful Russian art crafts and knives, the Chinese man agreed and got up, they walked for about twenty minutes in thick jungle until they arrived to his house, two women greeted them, and he introduced them to him, to the Russian man's surprise they were both his wives, one of the woman was so beautiful and attractive but didn't smile at all and was very impolite to his husband, the other lady who was not so beautiful, and as a matter of fact looked very ugly and masculine was very kind, full of life and very polite and caring to her husband. Russian man spent two days there, and he was constantly paying attention to see why is this Chinese man treating both of his wives the same?, Because one of them looked like a goddess, and the other one was a normal lady with no feminine attributes, but he didn't dare to ask. But when he was about to leave the house he couldn't resist his curiosity, so he asked the Chinese man, how do you manage to act impartially and in the same way toward both of your wives? One is so beautiful and one is so ugly. The Chinese man smiled and said it is easy, because my beautiful wife has very beautiful appearance outside, but her inside is so ugly and disturbed that balances out and neutralizes her beauty so I view her as a normal woman not a beautiful woman, on the other hand my other wife who seems ugly by appearance, her outside ugliness is balanced and neutralized by her inner beauty, kindness and spirit, so her other ugliness is balanced by her beautiful inside, so I see her as a normal woman not an ugly woman. As a result I treat both of them the same, because the inside is as important if not more, than the outside of everyone.

The wisdom of the story is that we should not judge people merely based on their appearances and physical looks. Like books that cannot be judged by its cover, similarly we should not pass a judgement or discriminate someone, only because of their physical features like their beauty, color, race, health condition and so on. Because we human beings are multi dimensional beings and we have many different aspects. For example a disabled person, may be very intelligent, kind, knowledgeable and spiritually developed. Or a blind man can be the best musician. We must also remember that physical beauty even though is an asset and blessing, but it is not a prerequisite for being a nice person. Furthermore one must realize that our physical beauty is like autumn leaves, which will leave us as we grow older, but the true beauty which is always with us, is the beauty of our souls. A kind, compassionate, caring, and loving soul is always beautiful, regardless of age, race, physical look, ethnicity and backgrounds. So we should value, respect and love all human beings equally, because deep down they all have a beautiful soul, which is actually a part of god. And any thing that comes from god is beautiful and blissful.

Exercise: This week keep this story in mind, and be attentive to catch yourself whenever you passing a negative judgement or comment about some one based on their physical look, race, color or ethnicity. And decide that starting this week you will stop all forms of prejudice that you may have against any specific group. Because now you know that we are all equally loved, respected and protected by god. God has created all of us with a soul at our core. Instead of focusing on our differences, we should focus on our commonalities. And our main common thing is our souls. Our souls are all interconnected by webs of invisible energies of divine energies which allow us to communicate. The main component and building block of these energies is love. Therefore more you develop the love toward others and yourself, the better your connection and integration would become to the whole.

Even though we are all physically different, we should focus on our common unifying aspect which is our soul.

That is what Hindus call unity in diversity. This week you should do the following exercise to help your subconscious mind to focus on our commonalities with others instead of our differences. Find a quiet place where you won't be disturbed by anyone for 15-20 minutes, close your eyes, take five deep breaths and attend to your breathing for 2-3 minutes to allow your mind to also relax like your body. Then visualize yourself on your mental screen. Imagine and view yourself as a soul which is surrounded by a golden and white energy field. Then visualize that you receive and give currents of bright lights and energies from and to your heart. After you become successful in visualizing yourself clearly as a soul, then start visualizing your family members, your partner, your friends as souls also. Imagine you are exchanging energies and love by your invisible chords of love which flows directly from your hearts to one another. Fill yourself with that great feeling of love, compassion and security that your connection with others brings you. Tell yourself that you choose to decide to only see others as souls and children of god, and only send and receive love in order to feel the same good, positive, empowering and loving emotions that you are experiencing now. Then imagine that more people you send love to, the brighter and bigger your energy field becomes, and decide to send love to all the people, animals and even plants, and imagine as you send them love their energy fields become brighter and bigger too and they also send you back their love and blessing from their heart. Visualize yourself receiving those loves and blessings in your heart. Next imagine that this love and bonding become so strong that all of your energy fields merge and become one, and all of the existence becomes one. That huge and infinite energy field is god. Once you love all and serve all you are accepted and welcomed to the kingdom of god.

Because only those who can see heaven and truth internally can be admitted to heavenly places. And developing universal love, and seeing everybody as souls, which are connected together, will help us to overcome our old, wrong and materialistic view that we are separate beings, instead we come to believe that we are all one but different aspect of god, then we truly understand the meaning of unity in diversity. Remember the only thing that can lead you to heaven is love, and the best way to cultivate love is by sharing, and giving of your love, blessings and service. So serve all and love all equally and for sure you will be on your way to heaven, both in this life and in the next.

25. Should we sacrifice and neglect our physical body for wealth and power?

Once upon a time in Persia lived a wise spiritual king who had no children, and as he was getting old, he decided to find a successor for his crown, so he invited all of his top commanders and advisors, so he would choose the best man among the candidates. Everybody knew that the king respected and held onto, spiritual values and righteousness and also believed in sacrifice for the greater cause and for common good. Having that in mind all of them who really wanted to become the next king for personal reasons, they were ready to do anything to get appointed. So the day came and king chose five of the candidates which had the best credentials and personal background of great service to the kingdom, and he also invited his spiritual advisor and friend to witness the election process. So he welcomed all of the five men, and told them that he will test their level of loyalty to their duty, by checking to see how much would they be ready to sacrifice for the kingdom, and then he will choose the best candidate to become the next king after his death. They agreed and silently waited to be called. The first man was called to be tested and questioned, the king asked him would you be ready to be killed for the empire? He said yes, king said very well, and pointed to the second man to approach him, he asked him would you be ready to lose both of your legs to save the empire? He said surely I will do, king said very well, and pointed to the third person to approach for questioning, he asked him would you be ready to lose one leg for empire? He said yes, from bottom of my heart I would do it, king said very well, pointed to the fourth man, and asked him would you cut one of your hands for the empire? He said yes my majesty, of course I would. King said okay very well, and finally he pointed to the last man and said would you give your small finger for the empire? He said surely I will do it. He said very well. Then he looked at his spiritual friend and jokingly said let me ask my friend here too, would you agree to be slapped or lose limb or die for empire? The spiritual man started laughing and said no way, Ii won't even let anyone touch and pull a single beard off my face. The king smiled and said I have chosen the next king, he looked at the five candidates and told them none of you are fit to protect the empire, the next king will be my spiritual friend. They all started to complain, saying but our majesty we are ready to give our life, our limbs, we are ready to sacrifice our physical body for you and your kingdom, but this man doesn't want to sacrifice anything, he doesn't even want to lose a piece of hair from his face for you, and you are choosing him over us. The king smiled again and said that is exactly why I chose him, because all five of you can't even take care and protect your own bodies, you are all so clouded and manipulated by your desire to get to power for personal reasons, and as a result you are blinded to other people's need and welfare, that is if you sacrifice and neglect your own body, it is clear what you will do to the people of this kingdom, because an empire is like a live being, the king is the head and its people is his body, if he is not one with his body and doesn't take care of his body it is doomed to death and disaster.

So if you can't take care of your body, how can you take care of the empire. On the other my friend here, is a wise and spiritual man, and he knows that one should not neglect or sacrifice his body, which is his vehicle and means of living and which he depends on it for survival and learning divine values, for personal egoistic mental desires. And he knows that if mind goes against the body, the body will fail to function properly and as a result it will make the mind suffer too, so since he knows that our mind and body are interconnected, therefore he doesn't allow any damage to his body. So since he cares and protects the least valuable part of his body, a piece of beard, he will be able to protect the empire, because he would care for every nameless and lay persons in the empire, and in doing so everybody would love and respect him. As a result there will be inner harmony and unity in the kingdom and nothing will be able to destroy it. Even though the king is the head of the empire, but people are the neck of the empire and can decide which way the head turns, so you should respect and protect all parts of yourself and empire.

The wisdom of the story is that we should take care of our body, and do not neglect and sacrifice our body for our financial and material goals and fantasies. Most of the time we do not appreciate what god has given us for free. And we only value them when we lose them. Health is one of those undetectable and often unappreciated gifts that god has given us, and the other is security and safety. Yet we often neglect our health and safety by over working ourselves, and not sleeping enough and properly. We justify our attitude by telling ourselves and others that we have more important priorities and responsibilities than resting

and exercising properly. So we get caught up in daily activities and our ever growing greed to work harder than ever to buy more things we don't really need.
Please don't think that I am against material expansion and wealth, in the contrary I believe being wealthy is a great blessing and should be attained and
enjoyed by all. However I believe you should approach life in a balanced way
without neglecting or sacrificing any aspects of your being. You must respect, be
attentive and take care of all aspects of your being, which are your physical body,
emotions, intellectuality, social self, finances and your spiritual self. Because
whatever you don't focus on and don't use, you will lose it. This is a mental law,
whatever we don't focus on, our subconscious mind will assume that we don't
need it, and it will stop its proper maintenance of that aspect of our lives. For
example if exercise, healthy diet and rest are the number ten in your priority list,
then you subconscious mind will give its attention and care only at the minimal
level and soon your health will start to deteriorate. Being wealthy means not just
what we have, it more correctly means how much and at what quality we enjoy
what we have. Because what is the use of millions of dollars if you don't have
time to sleep, exercise or eat right?. What is the use if your body aches all over and
you always have headaches?

So as we learned earlier moderation is the best solution, But remember if we
compare life with a river, our body is the only boat we have to make the long
journey with, and the quality and length of our journey depend on how we take
care of our body.

Because if we have an unhealthy body, it will simultaneously affect all other
aspects of our being. Our emotions, relationships, jobs, success and overall life
depends directly on the level of our health.

So do not give up your basics, which are proper diet, proper exercise, proper
rest and comfort for any so called big mental goals and fantasy. Because it is
impossible to enjoy life without taking a good care of your basics.

Exercise: This week and always keep this story in mind, and decide to make a
practical personal plan for yourself. Find a quiet place and write down a diet plan,
an exercise plan and a resting plan for yourself.

If you feel, you don't have the necessary expertise to pick the right plan then
ask an expert. Fortunately the personal care industry is exploding these days as
more people find out the importance of vibrant health. Do, whatever is necessary
to put you back in track as soon as possible. Because sooner you start, sooner you
will start enjoying life millions of times more than ever before. If you need an
exercise buddy, find it. If you need to see a nutritionist, a physician or a gym

instructor to get you started, do it. Start reading and focusing on health, diet and exercise issues, this will make your subconscious mind focused on these subjects and as a result it will drive you toward these types of healthy activities. Also spend more time in nature, parks, and beaches if possible. Spend relaxed times with family and loved ones. Do meditation and prayers and visualize yourself, relaxing and feeling happy and refreshed. Because our mind has direct psychosomatic effect on our body. Also do some mindless activity for at least 30 minutes a day that will also make you vibrant.

26. Father, have I become a good king?

Once upon a time there was an old king in Turkey, since he was getting really old he wanted to prepare his son to become the next king, so he taught him all he knew about the kingdom. His kingdom was consisted of many states and he had appointed 10 kings to rule in each of his 10 states and he was considered the king of the kings at the head of the ottoman's empire. So when the young prince was ready, he appointed him as a king for one of the states who had recently lost its king due to illness. So the prince, who was very ambitious and rough by nature, started to rule in that state which was the farthest state from his father's palace in the west of the empire. King intentionally sent him there so he can depend only on himself and learn to make though and necessary decisions by himself. He also told his son: When the time comes, I will choose between one of the ten kings, and you will not be automatically appointed as a next king, because I want to choose my successor to be the most competent person, because the empire is more important than my own personal preferences, but since I love you, I am giving you a chance to claim the crown. The prince having this precondition in mind started to really work and achieve positive and revolutionary changes in his state, he built a very big army, and provided the best weaponry and training available any where, soon he started to attack the neighboring states and as a matter of fact he invaded and captured five countries, and now the size of his state was as big as the rest of the empire. He soon became the most powerful person in the western part of the empire, and he almost completely discontinued consulting and receiving orders from his father, and as a matter of fact all other neighboring states respected and feared him more than his father. One day king decided to finally step down due to severe sickness and old age, so he sent his messenger to all the ten kings including his son, that king will visit all the ten states of the kingdom, and at the end of his journey, based on the achievement and progress of each king, he will choose his successor. The prince now in his thirties, started preparing a big welcome for his father, who were to visit him the last, because he was on the opposite end of the empire. And he was sure that he would be elected as the next king, because first of all he was his son, secondly he was respected and was actually more powerful than his father, and finally he had made greatest amount of progress in compare with other kings. The day came. And the king arrived to his son's palace, the guards and people greeted the king who was loved and respected by people, he made his way through the newly built palace, He was surprised and impressed by the appearance of the city and his palace, every thing was so glamorous, all of the building was covered with gold, silver and precious stones designed by the most beautiful paintings and statues. The suiting sound of music and nice fragrances of beautiful flowers were coming from every where, he was expecting to see his son who he had not seen for 15 years at the gate of the town to greet his father, but he passed the whole city and he was no where to be found, as he was approaching the palace a deep feeling of sadness and disappointment Overtook him, he was talking to himself saying "it can't be, my son for sure has missed me and respects me more than this, why didn't he come to greet me" then his sad feeling changed to being worried that maybe his son is sick or even dead that is why he hasn't come to greet him. He was in the middle of his inner talk that he noticed that his caravan has arrived to the main hall of the palace, so he got prepared and got off his carriage which was being carried by eight horses. To his surprise lot of people where standing to greet him but his son wasn't there. He entered the main building of the palace and entered and he walked very long hallways until they reached the main big hall where his son was sitting on his seat at the opposite end of the hall, As the king entered the main hall everybody got up and greeted the king by bowing down to him as a gesture of respect. But his son didn't get up, and stayed seated. The father who was now very angry, frustrated and disappointed with his son, approached his son, still he didn't get up and he just ordered his advisors to direct his father to sit on a special chair which was near his right side, about 3 meters away, so he did.

Finally his son spoke, without any greeting he said, so father, what do you think? Have I become a good king?

The King looked at him in a disappointed way, and looked around and pointed his right hand to the palace and all the people in it and said of course you have become a good king, but the problem is you have forgotten something which is more important than being a good king, and that is being a good human being.

You have lost all of your values, your love and sense of respect as a human, in order to become a king.

But the problem is a nonhuman cannot be a good king either. That is why I will not choose you as my next successor, because if you act in this kind of non-

human and immoral way toward your own father, who is the person who gave
you life and also gave you every thing you have now. How will you act against the
others who are below you and are only average people. You may sacrifice and
undermine anyone or even the empire for fulfilling your ego. And as I told you in
the first day, the empire is more important of any one's personal ego.

The wisdom of the story is that regardless of how significant we become in our
social life, we need not to forget where we have come from, and don't have to
change the way we used to respect our parents, friends and others. Very often,
people who get promoted in a corporation, unfortunately change their attitude
and character almost over night toward their co-workers. Because immediately
they start to think that since they will have authority over their fellow co-workers
and have a higher position professionally, they are entitled to feel deservingly that
they are better than rest of the population. Subconsciously and automatically one
will start disrespecting and putting down others, knowing that they have no
choice to put up with him, because their job may depend on it. However we have
to keep in mind that regardless of our social, professional and financial statues, we
are all equal in the eyes of god, because we all have a soul which is a part of god
himself.

So we do not have to forget this fact that whenever we disrespect and humiliate someone else, we are actually offending and disrespecting god. And whatever
we send out in this universe, we will get back. What goes around, comes around.
So we need to respect all and love all. We may become the richest man on earth,
but if we disrespect our friends and loved ones, they will not be around you out
of love, but because of financial gain. And love is the most precious thing in life
that cannot be purchased by force or money. In this case all the riches in the
world will be useless, because you will be depriving yourself from true love.

Exercise: This week, keep this story in mind, and catch yourself whenever you
unintentionally or intentionally putting someone down, criticizing him, or
humiliating him because you feel superior to him financially or socially. Then
remind yourself that it is a wrong archetypal belief to believe that you are better
anyone else, since you have a better job, you are more educated, and have more
money, you are superior to others that are from a lower income group. Catch
yourself when you are trying to justify your actions, thoughts and words that you
are better. Remember we are all equal, and we are all children of god. It is not
right and we are not entitled to treat others with disrespect no matter what they
are doing in life, or who they are. Therefore this week make a plan to respect all

the people you meet, send the good wishes at least in your heart if it is not practical. Respect life and you will receive respect in return. Send hatred and sense of superiority, and you will be hated and disrespected. Practice to smile and treat everybody with respect and love, and watch your life grow to a richer, more harmonious, and happier life. Because respect creates love and bonding, and love is the essence of happy life. So decide to be respectful and loving to all of god's creation.

27. If you refuse a gift, it is returned to its giver

Once upon a time Buddha was visiting a remote village in the northern part of India to spread his word and help everybody to be enlightened, he was with many of his disciples and followers when they arrived to the village's center square, as he was getting ready to start his preaching about enlightenment, a young man approached him and started yelling and swearing at him, calling him a liar and untrustworthy man, a thief and saying so many other rude words to Buddha. So some of his loyal and fanatic followers wanted to attack this rude young man, or at least answer him back with their own yelling and bad words. But Buddha raised his right hand in a very peace full manners and ordered them to stop and to do nothing. One of his followers said but why?, Buddha smiled and said if somebody brings you a gift and if you don't accept it, then to whom does it belong? After a short pause, he answered himself, it would belong to its giver if no one wants to take it. And furthermore he added, everyone can give only what he has in his possession, this poor young man had no gift other than hatred ane vulgarness within him, so he has no choice about what he can offer me, because he has no other choice, in other hand I have a choice of whether I want to receive his gift or not, Receiving it means acknowledging and admitting the inner doubt that he maybe right and to start a strategy to defend against his accusation by reacting, if you do this then you have received the gift and that gift now becomes a part of you and in this way the attacker's purpose is served, however if you don't show reaction, his gift of hatred will be returned to himself, and you will remain unaffected. By the same token, I can also give this young man and to anyone else for that matter, only the gifts that I have available to me, which are limitless love and compassion, so I am giving him my love, but again it is his choice whether to accept it or not. Then he turned to the young man and expressed his love to him by a divine and compassionate smile and offered him to join his lectures to uplift his soul, so he can get rid of his frustration and anger toward life, he also offered him food and clothing if he needed it. The young man started crying and apologizing and he agreed to join to Buddha's path of enlightenment. Then Buddha turned to his followers and said smilingly that now this young man has accepted my gift and it is his to keep and he could even give it to others who may need it and accept to have it. And that gift is universal love and compassion for all beings.

The wisdom of the story is that whenever we hear or see some thing that we don't like, instead of reacting and allowing it to bother us, we must choose to not accept it. And what we refuse to accept is returned to its sender. Because lets say a person is trying intentionally to make you angry, or make you react in an irrational way in order to take a revenge or simply take an advantage of you, by making you angry in front of your friends and loved ones to point out your lack of control and as a result, humiliate you. Therefore not responding, and being indifferent both internally in your mind and externally in your actions, will protect you against the negative emotional effects of any verbal attacks and insults. If you do this you are victorious because you had maintained your control over your thoughts, emotions and actions, because his attempt to cause you act the way he wanted will fail. On the other hand if you respond you have failed, and the attacker has won, because he was successful to direct your behavior and take the control away from you. Remember a spiritual man is in full control of his emotions, thoughts and behaviors. That means he is active, and nothing outside himself can cause him to react. Since he knows and believes that he is a part of god, and he acts only based on god's higher and divine values, and will not react to any comments that will affect him negatively. He always remains calm and in control, because he sees no reason to protect himself or his beliefs. Because only the one who is doubtful about himself, his values and his beliefs will react to the outside comments.

Exercise: This week, keep this story in mind, and decide to be active and not reactive. Meaning choose not to respond to the negative, critical or hostile comments you may hear in your daily lives. When that happens calmly, tell yourself, first I will choose not to respond and remain calm because I know this unfortunate person has no better gift to give me, he has no choice but I do have a choice not to accept it, and I am not accepting it. Secondly send him love and peace, because this is the way each divine soul acts, meaning you choose not be defeated by badness and choose to defeat badness by goodness. Thirdly tell yourself that I chose not punish myself by reacting to him and absorbing his negative emotions, Because there is no reason for me to punish myself for the shortcomings of others. And finally if applicable offer him your help, to ease his tension and try to find out why he is frustrated. Because a spiritual man knows and believes that we are all from god, and cannot be evil people. And a spiritual man views and sees a person as separate entity from his behaviors. And knows that the person is probably going through a though time that is why he is acting this negatively. So instead of attacking him back, a spiritual man tries to help him get rid of his anger and frustration. And furthermore you need to also make sure not to attack or deal with others in an angry manner. Because what you send out, you will get back. So develop lots of love in your mind and heart. Because whatever we focus on will grow and become part of us, so instead of anger, hate, and frustration, focus and develop peace, love and happiness. And then give and share your divine gifts as much as you can, and watch your life become healthier, richer and happier.

28. The powerful effects of our spoken words

Once upon a time in America a young athletic man who was at his last year of high school was walking home in a cold rainy day in November. In his mind, he was planning his date that he just had met in his mind, and as he was completely preoccupied in talking to himself and trying to think of the best lines to impress her during their date that night, his attention was suddenly shifted when he heard three of his classmates who thought of themselves as cool and popular, were making fun of a boy who was not like them, he had a normal and out of fashion clothing with mismatching colors, he had clumsy and dirty hair and he was walking in a very insecure and a depressed mood. So he watched them for few second, he wasn't sure what to do, because those guys were his cool friends and he didn't want to jeopardize his friendship with them, because being friends with them who were all popular and football players, meant having the opportunity to meet the most attractive ladies in the school, and he was also late and he needed at least one hour to get ready for his date, and his date was exactly in one hour, so in the beginning he decided to ignore the situation and not to interfere. But his friends started calling this young man who was carrying lots of heavy books on a Friday to his home to study, "you geek, Don't you have a better thing to do on the weekend? We never take any book home on the weekend, we leave all of them at our locker." The poor young man was afraid to even look up, and he couldn't run because of his heavy books, so he just kept walking without saying anything. He was taking lots of insults and those guys refused to give up bothering him. One of them ran very fast from behind and jumped on top of this poor young man, and he shouted "touch down" and all of them started laughing, then suddenly the young man got mad and shouted at them to stop, so they all got pissed off and took his bag and threw all his books on the ground which was very wet because of the heavy rain, and they started hitting him from every angle. The young athletic man could no longer keep himself, so he ran to help this poor guy from those vicious beatings and he told them to stop, and being his friend they stopped, and he started by helping the boy to pick up his books, and his so call cool friends told him what are you doing? leave this geek alone. He told them to shut up and leave, so they told him okay you made your choice, we don't want you as a member of our group anymore. He said, I hate to be one of you guys anyway. So they left, he helped and gathered all of his books, and tried to cheer this boy up who was in a very down and depressed mood. He told him, oh my god you are a very strong person, because those books must be 200 pounds, and you carry them like a feather, but let me help you, I walk you to your house. And he told him that, I can help you to make minor changes in your appearance for example a modern haircut, few cool clothing and you would be all right, because you are very handsome and athletic, so any girl would be lucky to go out with a nice handsome guy like you.

You can start by not taking all of your books home, on Friday. Both of them cracked and laughed so hard that they couldn't continue walking for few minutes.

Thus they became good friends, and this young man soon was transformed, he became the best football player, graduated as number one in his class with highest marks and he was also very popular and loved by ladies. The end of the year came, being the best student he was chosen to represent his school to make a speech at the end of the year. So he went up the stage and started his speech, he started by thanking everybody that has given him the opportunity to become a successful and happy individual, he said "I would like to thank my teachers, my parents and most of all, a friend of mine who has not only changed my life but has also saved my life, and he turned his head toward his friend, and he said today I will share my story for the first time, one day I was so depressed and helpless, because of my boring life, no girl looked at me, I had no friends, no body wanted to talk to me, I felt like the loneliest person on the face of the earth and to make the matter worst many people made fun of me, and actually assaulted me, so one day I decided to end this, It was a Friday, I cleared my locker, because I didn't want my parents to come and get my stuff later on, but as I was going home I was attacked by some so called cool guys, and someone that I didn't personally know, for the first time in my life really cared to help me and defended me against those guys. He gave up his date that day to cheer me up, his very simple but kind words transformed my life and even caused me to change my mind about taking my life. Because I was going to kill myself that day. His words were, you are a nice handsome and strong guy and with few minor changes you gonna be all right. Those words gave me new hopes to stay alive and to transform myself. His friend who was shocked, never thought how important his words were at the date of that incident, which he had actually forgot about what he had said that day, started crying and ran to the stage and hugged his friend, and all the people in the hall including the teachers cried with them. Then he continued by saying to everybody that, please be aware of the importance of your spoken words, it can save a life or it may cause somebody to take his life.

The wisdom of the story is that our words have a very strong and real effects on others. However, it may be both positive or negative in nature. Some times a simple pat on the shoulder, or a positive and encouraging comment to a child or an adult can transform his life in a revolutionary and dramatic way. For instance a child who was a grade five student, failed his mathematics exam in the first semester, he was punished by his parents. He felt neglected and unloved, and viewed himself as a failure at the time. But one day his uncle offered to teach him mathematics, after about five minutes of practice, the uncle who was a very kind and wise man told the child, that "oh my god you are one of the smartest kids I have ever met," this comment alone changed his whole view, not only about mathematics, but also about his whole life. He got the highest mark in his mathematics class that year, and his overall grade average was second in the school.

He was transformed from a C-student, to an A+ student by one simple positive suggestion at the right time. This child grew up and went to university and later became a successful international author, instructor and speaker. This child was me. Therefore we can see that our words really matter, and we should use them responsibly.

Our words when used in a negative and hostile manners may be viewed as a wild animal like a tiger, if it is used negatively it can tear up and destroy both others and ourselves. And our words when used in a positive and a supportive manner may be viewed as guardian angels who can act as a savior and supporter of us and others. It is completely our choice as which one we use. Therefore, it is wiser to discipline ourselves in the use of our language and spoken words. As the ancient Persian prophet Zoroaster said, do not say any thing, if you don't find any thing good to say about someone or some thing. The basis of his teachings was very simple and based on these three simple principles: One must have good thoughts, use good words and act in a good and positive manner. Remember what we send out, we also receive. So by choosing to give encouraging and positive words to others, you will receive the same in many folds.

Exercise: This week, keep this story in mind, and decide to use positive and encouraging words and comments only, when you are communicating with others or even yourselves. Unfortunately the majority of the population, have developed a habit of being critical of others. It may be their look, their behaviors, and/or their ideologies. This stems from our wrong subconscious and archetypal belief that we are better than anyone else, so if anyone is not similar to us, we start to attack them either directly or indirectly. However we must realize that this belief is not right, and we are equally as good as others, because we all have a holy soul within, which is directly from god and of god. We were all created differently only in terms of mental and physical characteristics, to enrich and diversify our experiencing process which was necessary for our colorful and diverse spiritual unfoldment. That is what Hindus and Buddhist call unity in diversity. Constant criticism, also programs our subconscious minds to become critical of ourselves too. It does that by becoming comparative about our own attributes, meaning it automatically compares for example our look, education, or finance level with others who may be more successful than us, this creates an inner frustration toward the more positive people too. In this way we become entangled in an endless cycle of hatred and frustration toward both the people whom we consider as doing worse than us, and also the people whom we feel are doing better than us. This vicious cycle of negative thoughts and emotions, eventually leads to confusion and inner division and lack of self-worth and self-love.

Furthermore this beliefs and emotions will make our lives limited, because we tend to limit our social gatherings and communications with only the people who are like us, meaning with people who are also critical, judgmental and negative. In this way we can see being critical, negative and antagonistic about others, not only harm them, but it also affects us, many folds more.

Because they are only suffering temporarily from what you may have said to them. When they hear it, they can choose not to listen to you, or not to react, to whatever you are saying. But on the other hand, you will be affected negatively and suffer from your negative thoughts and words constantly, because your thoughts are always with you. And through self-talk you perpetuate these negative and limiting, beliefs and behavioral patterns, which eventually will drain your spiritual energy, from your energy field or aura.

That is totally observable, for example when a person is negatively preoccupied, or is angry you can see his face is becoming darker and lifeless. But as he smiles his face starts to be brightened and open.

Now that we know the significance of our words, we should decide from now on, to train and discipline ourselves to use only positive comments, that encourage, support, empower and makes others happier. We should also use positive and empowering language with ourselves during our everyday self-talks. Remember whatever we focus on internally, we tend to realize and meet in our lives, therefore focus on love and happiness, and also think about sharing your love and happiness with others by giving them your words of love, support and empowerment. As you do that you will also receive the similar positive words as feedback. Words are not simply words, they carry certain energies with them that directly affect our energy fields, our emotions, our moods and actions. The quality of these words, the tonality used in the expression of these words, and the intentions behind those words determines our reactions and therefore our moods, behaviors and course of actions. Positive comments when truly meant, contain divine and godly energies which enrich our lives with power, abundance, happiness, health, love and creativity, and the negative comments contain evil forces and energies which limit our lives and also limit our access to the blessings and protection of god, thus we may find poverty, illness, hatred, conflicts and many other negative circumstances in our lives, because it drains our energy field, and blocks our reception of divine universal energy, which is essential for our overall well being. So decide to make a habit of using positive, encouraging and supportive comments both toward others and yourselves.

29. Living while dying

Once upon a time in China, the great Taoist master Chuang Tzu was getting very old and since he was in contact with god or what Taoist call the way, he knew his time of death and departure from his physical body.

So one day, when he was in the monastery, he asked everybody to be gathered on the beautiful mountain top nearby the next week, and when they asked him what is the occasion? He said laughingly, I want to say goodbye to all of you, I am going to leave you. Everybody was sad and shocked, and they asked him where are you going? You haven't left this monastery and your hometown for the last 30 years. He laughed out loud almost falling to the ground looking at their sad and worried faces who were trying to convince him to stay, he said you don't understand I am going to die next week at that mountain top a little before dusk, he pointed with his index finger, and he added that he would meet them all there and said goodbye. All of his disciples, followers and general public got very sad, and they decided to give the best mourning ceremony before he dies, so they all prepared black clothing and banner of sad words, they also invited several singers and drummers to preform sad songs and mourning in order to honor their master and show their sadness and appreciations to him. So they decided to meet two hours before dusk at the gate of the town, so they can go to the mountain all together, so it would look more glamorous, and to meet their master for the last time. It was about one hour walk to the mountain, all of them cried and mourned as the singers were singing goodbye songs that they had specially made for the leaving master.

Finally they reached to the mountain top, where there was a single huge tree and they saw the master's shadow from far. They approached while some crying out loud and some even beating themselves from sadness and sorrow, but as they got closer, they were shocked as they noticed that Chuang Tzu was sitting upside down, on his head and laughing. Two of his senior disciples who were candidates to become the next spiritual leader after their master death. They thought that he has lost his mind and gone crazy. They approached him and told him quietly to stop, and sit straight, they told him lots of people would lose their faith about Taoism, an ideology that he has worked almost all his life to promote and teach.

He laughed again and remained in his up-side-down position, he said, Move aside, I want all my people to see me. They asked him but why master? He said I want everybody to see that I love and enjoy every moment of life, and I will live even when I am dying. Because being joyful, playful, happy and vibrant means being alive, and being sad and crying means being dead. So I am living even in my dying second. That is the way we all have to be and live.

The wisdom of the story is that we must enjoy and celebrate every single moment of life. Every second is a gift of god that is why it is called "The present". Because more we cultivate happiness, content and love in our life, more they will become part of our being as a whole, and even after dying we will carry our inner state of being with us. God loves happy people, because when you are happy you are actively showing that you are content and satisfied with whatever god has given you. On the other hand sad people are actively showing their discontent toward life. Being discontent means one feels that life and god has been unfair to him, and he indirectly questions the justice and fairness of god. But we have to come to believe that god loves us, and any thing that happen in our lives is for our benefit and spiritual unfoldment, even death of a loved one. We have to accept graciously the divine and impartial rules of god. And enjoy life to its fullest. Remember we all are born into this world, and we will all leave this physical body by death one day. Lets say we are born in one island called "birth", and a ship comes and takes us, and we all know that our destination is another island called "death". We do not have a choice about our origin and final destination.

However, we have a choice and we can choose how to live and spend our time while we are in the ship traveling between the two islands. Similarly we have a choice to be happy, vibrant and enjoying life by focusing on the beautiful things and being care free, child-like and spiritual. Or we have a choice to be up tight, depressed, egoistic and unhappy. One should not bound himself to his social masks. We all have subconsciously and consciously put many masks on our soul which is our true selves. As the word "persona" means mask in Latin language, our personality is a combination of various, social, religious, and other masks. Our soul is being suffocated under those masks. Because when we put on these masks, we act differently with each different group of individuals, depending on what we want to get from them. For example we act one way at work putting a responsible, serious and punctual mask, a different mask with our family which is kind, joking, a different mask with our loved one, jealous, controlling and so on. Putting these different masks even though helps us to get short term results on the surface, however it leads to inner division of our energies and character. That will make us imbalanced, up tight, worried and divided. Remember our true being is our soul, which is from god and is undivided and unified. More unified we are inside, meaning fewer social masks we have, happier and freer we become. One way to be unified is to be like a child, which is honest, playful and happy. He doesn't see the need to lie or change his character to get some thing, because he is content and happy by merely being at the present, when he plays he is in the arms of god and doesn't need any material thing to feel happy, so he is naturally happy. As Jesus said, the way of heaven is the way of children. So we as adults need to awaken the child within us and let him teach us how to be happy, loving, fearless, imaginative, creative, honest, sharp and playful again. More you focus on these attributes, happier you become, and happier and more content you are, the closer you are to god. And closer you are to god, more blessing, happiness and love will find its way into your life.

Exercise: This week, keep this story in mind, and decide to examine and uncover the social masks which are actually the different mental strategies that you may use in your daily lives. And decide to eliminate and replace them with a standard and unified character which would include and represent your true self. Your true self, is your soul which is divine and god like, so write down in your work book the divine attributes you wish to develop and enjoy having and using in your life. You can use the following list to get an idea, but feel free to add as many good attributes as you wish to add. And use the final list that you have provided. Next, find a quiet place where you would not be disturbed for 15-20 minutes, close your eyes, take five deep breaths, attend to your breathing for 2-3 minutes allowing your mind and body to relax, then calmly and confidently tell your self, from now on, I am happy, playful, honest, energetic, confident, active, loving, correct, imaginative, creative, care free and protected and loved by god. Keep repeating these attributes to yourself in a calm and effortless fashion, without rushing them. And during the day whenever you find free time repeat these attributes to yourself in the same way. You have to keep doing it, until your subconscious mind becomes saturated with these positive attributes, this leaves no room for previous wrong and limiting habits. And in less than six months you will be transformed to a being that can only say, think and do positive, energetic and creative things.

Furthermore you can also dedicate some time to be playful and carefree. Because if we want to be as care free and happy as children, we need to say, think and do what they are using in their lives. So some times do whatever you were doing when you were a child, it can be playing hide and seek, playing soccer, different games, watching a senseless funny movie or whatever is appealing to you. I know it may seem offensive and belittling to our intellect at first, but remember having fun means, being intellect free for that given moment. So for a short period at least let go of your social status and identity, and become a child, that will energize your whole being and it will also improve all your other aspects of our being including our intellectual faculty.

That is why playing games and talking with your children, or the children in the family will automatically energize you physically and at the same time clears your head from tiring thoughts about your daily challenges. Usually we find a solution to our problem, after spending some mindless and playful time with our children, because our subconscious mind is more responsive to our emotions than logic, and when it sees us having fun and enjoying ourselves, it focuses on happiness and joyful results and circumstances too, as a result the solution to our problem is given easier when we are happy and in a positive mood. In negative, exhausted and frustrated moods, subconscious mind also responds negatively and as a result the information that would lead to a solution will be blocked. So decide to be happy and playful every day of your life, no matter what.

30. Dying while living

Once upon a time in India lived a rich merchant who was traveling to Africa for business on a regular basis. He was exporting furniture to African countries and was importing African art crafts from Africa to India. In one of his trips when he was visiting a small town in Kenya which was in the middle of a jungle, he saw a man selling a beautiful parrot that he had just captured, the Indian merchant fell in love with that parrot so he bought it, and brought it back to India where he lived. He became so attached to this parrot, who could talk, sing and even make laughing sounds. He built a golden cage for it, he gave her the best seeds and foods from all over the world, he even made a special room for his parrot where he put its cage in it. In the beginning the parrot was happy and felt lucky that he was captured and sold to this kind man, because he was usually having a hard time to find good food in the jungle and he was very tiny and weak then, but now he was getting chubby and strong. But after few months he missed his freedom that jungle offered and he also missed his friends. But he found out that there is no way to escape, because this man was looking after him and protecting him like the most precious thing in his life. Few years passed, when the parrot had lost all of his hopes and had gotten used to the life in a golden cage. One day, the Indian man came to see him, he told the parrot that I am going to your homeland, to the same jungle that I bought you from. Is there any thing you want from there? I can get it for you, any thing even another parrot. The parrot who truly knew how painful it is to be locked up in a cage, he said, no. I don't want another parrot to live with me, I prefer to have my private space. But, can you just say hi to my parrot friends and tell them about my life, my cage and my situation here in your glamorous house and also ask them that what do they think about me and my life?. He agreed, so when he finished his business in the African town, he went to the same spot that he had found the parrot to talk to the parrots friends. After about two hours he was able to find a parrot which was not afraid to approach him and talk to him, so he started by saying: I am the owner of a parrot which was your friend, and I took him to my home in India. The parrot asked how is he doing? The man said he is doing wonderfully, he lives in a very beautiful and spacious golden cage, he eats the best foods, I have even made beautiful clothing for him to put on when we have guests. The parrot said very well what can I do for you or him? The rich man said nothing, he just asked me to tell you or any of his friends about his life, his cage and his situation in my house in India, and told me to ask you what you think about it? The Parrot who was sitting on a nearby branch without saying anything suddenly fell to ground, and remained motionless. The merchant grabbed the parrot and thought he is dead, he was shocked and sad for its sudden death, but he shrugged his shoulder and left the parrot which was pretending to be dead on the ground beside a tree and left.

When he returned to India, after seeing his family, he ran to his parrot's room. They talked for a while, then the man said by the way I paid a visit to one of your friends in the jungle. The parrot got excited and asked the man what did he say, when you asked him how he thinks about my life here in this cage, He became quiet and sad and after a long pause said I am sorry, Right after I asked him that question about your life, your friend just suddenly dropped dead. Right at this moment the parrot dropped himself to the cage's floor and remained motionless, The man got so worried, he rapidly and recklessly opened the cage to check on his beloved parrot's condition, as he opened the cage the parrot jumped out of the cage and escaped from the window, but before leaving he stopped to thank him for his caring and kindness all those years, but he explained to the man that he had to go back to the jungle where he belonged. The man who was surprised and shocked about what just happened in few seconds, he said no problem, you can go. I didn't know you were suffering here, other wise I would have freed you a long time ago. But please answer one question for me before you go, The parrot said sure go ahead. How did you figure out about this plan to escape?

The parrot laughed and said it is simple my friend showed you the way. The man said but the parrot didn't say anything about escape he just died. The parrot said that was exactly the point, the only way for me to escape from this cage was dying while living, because only then you would take me out of this cage because I wouldn't have any use for you. So the man thanked him for this precious lesson, because he realized that he is also entrapped in the cage of his physical desires such as greed and lust, and the only way to free his soul from this cage of physical needs and dependencies was to let go of them and live like the parrot as a free boundless being, and he learned that he shouldn't imprison his soul for the sake of food, shelter and any other thing, because even though being free may mean more efforts and risks, but it is well worth it.

The wisdom of the story is that some times we get so attached and used to our daily routines and habits, that our soul becomes the prisoner of our mind. We all have developed habits at different periods of our lives, which were developed because they made our life easier, more manageable and more comfortable. Without many of our subconscious and automatic habits, our lives would be almost impossible. However, our habitual lifestyles have its negative side also. But our mind has a tendency to make every thing easier and more comfortable for itself and the physical body. And our subconscious mind does not know where to stop. As we grow older, our life is converted to a set of repetitive habitual routines. This makes our lives dull and boring. Even though we may receive lots of benefits in physical and mental terms, however our spirit feels suffocated and imprisoned by the repetitive patterns and experiences of our lives. Because our soul had descended to this physical world to experience as many various situations and circumstances as possible, and since it relies and uses our mind and body to achieve his goals, it gives his command to the mind. The mind in turn makes all the necessary things to help us to get what we wished for. However our subconscious mind records the procedure, and it will replicate the same mental strategy and behavioral pattern, at a similar situation.

But since all life situations are different, we miss the joy and bless of the new experience, we also miss the imbedded lesson that we were supposed to learn from that experience. Our subconscious mind, which has many responsibilities and functions, tries to protect us from getting hurt, and helps us to gain pleasure. That is it tries to maximize our immediate physical comfort and pleasure, however it is not capable to judge what is best for us in spiritual terms. For our soul, the experience of diverse circumstances and situations, and learning and gaining new wisdom, taking risk and being unpredictable, being playful and simultaneous, being care free and happy, sharing and cooperating, loving and giving freely are far more rewarding and essential than mere repetition of certain habits, which really creates same emotions and results every single time. It is like reading a book for 200 times or more. Therefore in order for our soul to be freed from this mental web that entraps it, we need to break from our habitual patterns and symbolically destroy and kill our egoistic self which is created by our inner mental self-image. Only then we can free our soul, and be playful, loving, sharing, care free, brave, happy and creative being. We must trust our soul, and try to do things differently, because if we keep doing the same things, we keep getting the same results, and consequently we will not learn or grow in life, then what a waste of time and energy will be to merely stay alive, instead of living. Living means being in present. Being in present require us to be fully alert and detached from the past and future thoughts. And the only way to achieve that is to quiet the mind and break its habitual pattern, only then our soul can open its wings and fly freely and enjoy infinitely in this physical world. If we fail to free our soul, which is our true self, we are dead anyway, because we are not growing nor enjoying life. As the Chinese saying puts it beautifully, "Most men die when they are thirty, but they bury them when they are sixty," this saying refers to the same concept that most people stop changing and growing, because their character is firmly set by their habits and belief system, and there is a minimal chance for further spiritual unfoldment, and since the purpose of life, is spiritual unfoldment, therefore a person who stops learning and growing is dead. So decide to live and enjoy life to the fullest, let go of your worries and fears, they are merely mental illusions created by your subconscious mind to make you tied up to your existing habits and status quo. But be like a brave child again, which is already within you, start experimenting and experiencing life in different new ways, expand your horizons, start learning and growing again. Remember only if we do things differently, we will get different results, that is in order for things to change, we must change. And this change starts by changing beliefs, views and behavioral patterns.

Exercise: This week, keep this story in mind, and make some time to investigate and examine your existing possessions, habits, beliefs and even relationships. Keeping in mind that for any thing new to be created, we need to destroy the existing forms. It is like, when you buy new furniture for your apartment, you need to remove the old furniture, first of all because both of them may not fit, and more importantly they will not be harmonious and matching together. Similarly we need to get rid of our undesired, negative and harmful belongings.

First check and make a list of you possessions. That includes your clothing, books and any other things. See which ones you really do not need or use, and simply give them away to a person who may need them, or if you feel it is too old or damaged, simply throw it away. This will help you to clear the negative and unnecessary energies. We have invisible attachment to all of our belongings. Our belongings include whatever we call "mine." Let's imagine, that you have 1000 units of soul, or cosmic energy in your soul's energy field. Having too many, un useful and piled up possessions will send some of your energy units to these objects. Lets say you have 500 different things that you don't usually use, but for some secondary and illusionary gains, which our subconscious emotional attachments, we hold on to them. In this way lets say one unit, of our energy goes to each one of these objects, even if we are not aware of it. In this way half of our vital power is drained. Therefore decide to systematically let go of your un useful stuff. And also remember by giving them away, some thing better will take its place. For example if you opened your closet before and saw it was completely full, you wouldn't have the inspiration and desire to buy yourself a new T-shirt that you always wanted, because you figure you already have lots of stuff. But by getting ride of the unused and out of fashion clothes, you realize how little of your desired clothing you really have. This exercise also helps you in clearing your mind from its liming and out of date habits and beliefs, because our subconscious mind works symbolically, if it views that we are clearing, sorting out and removing undesired items, it will move to do the same thing.

The next exercise is making a note of your negative, limiting, outdated and harmful habits which are no longer needed. Our mind similar to a closet needs to be regularly cleaned and cleared of unnecessary thoughts, habits and beliefs. Start by making a note of the various negative and limiting habits you may have, like over drinking, smoking, being lazy, over watching TV, dishonesty, anger, prejudice and any other negative behavioral traits you may find. And next to each one of them write the opposite which is the empowering and positive behavioral trends. And each time you catch yourself acting automatically on these negative habits, stop and take the opposite approach which is its positive form. For instance whenever you catch yourself being dishonest, stop immediately and be honest and tell the truth, this will help you to break your negative behavioral patterns.

The next category of the things that you need to get rid of is your negative and limiting beliefs, you need to examine and uncover some of the wrong and limiting beliefs you may have. These beliefs may be originated and recorded from your childhood, and are outdated and no longer serving their initial purpose and function, so the same way we have thrown our clothing from 10 years ago, we should also throw away, these old and useless beliefs. Similarly make a list of your wrong beliefs in various areas of your life, which are the physical health, emotional, relationship, financial, intellectual and spiritual aspects. In front of each one write the positive and empowering belief, for instance if your previous wrong belief was "The world is a crazy place, you cannot trust anybody these days,"

The positive one would be "the world is still a beautiful and peaceful place to live, and people are generally honest and trustworthy."

The last but not the least are our existing relationships that we need to examine and evaluate their quality and also their impact on our lives. Many times we tend to hang onto a harmful and negative relationship which is draining both parties involved, only because we either feel guilty if we decided to end it, or because we are emotionally attached in a subconscious way. That is, our subconscious mind forces us to keep the relationship, in order to protect us from the possible emotional pain that we may experience if we lost this relationship.

However usually the subconscious mind's standards and reference points were made long time ago, mostly from childhood, which is not applicable and practical anymore. Similarly make a list of your relationships, weigh their positive and negative aspects of each relationship. If the negative aspects outweigh the positive ones dramatically, then maybe it is time to, either end the relationship, or make arrangements to limit your contacts.

These exercises will help you to get rid of your limiting and imprisoning habits, beliefs and relationships and by replacing them with positive and empowering ones you will create a new self which is happier, healthier and more successful in all of the categories of your life.

31. We receive exactly what we ask for

Once upon a time in Nazareth lived a priest who was one of Christ's loyal follow-ers and disciples. After Jesus Christ was crucified, his teachings were banned by the ruling dynasty of the time. But this brave priest like many others continued to spread and teach the words of Jesus, even though there was a death penalty, for whoever was involved in any way in Christ's teaching. Regardless of all these great dangers, he was preaching and helping other Christians to come together to not only keep the Christian faith alive, but also to over throw the cruel and unjust rulers who were oppressing all of the people who were mostly poor and were sus-pected of being Christians. He was not afraid at all, because he had miraculously escaped death many times during his preaching, and he deeply believed that whatever he asked for the almighty god, he would give it to him, and he was also teaching others the same thing, that a follower of Christ can ask any thing from god from the bottom of his heart and god will give it to him, exactly as Jesus had said "ask and you shall be given". Soon he became very famous and he started to gain a lot of supporters all over the country, of course this didn't please the rulers and the king of the dynasty, so the king ordered a warrant and death sentence for him, and offered a great reward for any person, who could bring the priest and hand him to royal authorities, dead or alive. After a short search he was ambushed and captured alive by soldiers. The king decided to make an example of Christ followers and to demonstrate to all people that Jesus's god cannot pro-tect even his most loyal followers and messenger, so people should not trust this god. He wanted discredit Christianity and the god it was worshiping and depending on. So they decided to hang him by dawn in the town's main square the next morning in front of all public.

At his prison cell, The priest was praying, meditating and asking god to please protect me from being hanged tomorrow, he kept asking god please don't let them hang me, he repeated this prayer more than a thousand times until the time they opened his cell's door. He was certain that god will not let him be hung. The guards pushed him violently toward the main square were there was a gallop pole on a high plateau in the middle of the town center square, and everybody, including the king were present for his execution. It was a very noisy day, some people were cheering, some people were mourning depending on their beliefs and stand points. The priest kept his composure and kept asking god please don't let them hang me. His inner contemplation was interrupted by the sound of trumpets, which meant that it was time for everybody to be silent, because the king would make a short speech and announce the priest's death sentence, and shortly after he would be hung.

The king started his speech by saying today we are all gathered here to see if his "so-called god" can protect him from agonizing death.

It will soon be clear to you that his god does not listen to his cries and will not help him, so you will see how useless it is to trust and worship a god that can't even protect his most loyal worshiper.

He asked the priest if he had any thing to say?, The priest said calmly that there is no way that you can hang me today, I am certain because god will not let you do it. The king smiled and said, who said that we gonna hang you, there is a slight change of plan, I decided it will be more fun to cut your head off, with my personal sword, because that will signify the king's power against your god's power, and it will be clear to everybody who is the real winner. At this moment, The priest lost his composure, a cold chill took all over his body, he couldn't breathe and for the first time he felt unprotected and scared. As he was experiencing these emotions, The king ordered them to put him in a kneeled position, and without any hesitation they cut his head off when the king dropped his right hand that he was holding up as a sign of order. So the priest died and being a loyal follower of the Christ he was immediately transferred to heaven. There, He met Jesus and the almighty god. He was shocked and asked Jesus what happened?, I did and followed exactly your teachings, you thought us all, that we should ask and we shall be given. Jesus smiled and said that is true, you asked not to be hanged and you were not hanged!

Your head was cut off!, He continued by saying that you have to ask god only what you want in a positive form, The proper request and prayer would have been to ask him to keep you alive, because gods' rules are universal and impartial in the physical worlds, and we exactly get what we want and ask from god, and there are no exceptions.

The wisdom of the story is that we need to be very careful about the language we use. The quality of our lives depends on the quality of our communications whether with others or ourselves. Our subconscious mind which is the most powerful part of our mind, creates mental patterns and habits, and then makes us to act only based on those habits. And if our habits happen to be limited, negative and harmful, then our actions which are directly dependent and derivatives of our habits and belief system, will also be limited and destructive. How did or do these negative and positive habits develop? It is created by verbal suggestions, these suggestions can have their origin from what others have told us, it can be a negative and limiting comment that your parents, teachers, relatives or friends have told you when you were a child, and you had believed that they were right about their view about life, so at some point we had decided to contemplate and think about what they had told us. And by focusing on these suggestions for a long consecutive period of time, these suggestions had entered into our subconscious mind's memory bank and as a result a behavioral trend and habit had been formed which is totally based on those negative suggestions, and it has become a permanent part of our being through time. These negative and limiting beliefs would later manifest in our lives through similar habitual trends, and would limit and negatively affect our lives.

For example many of us have a negative and pessimistic view about our lives, or about the world in general. For example we are programmed to state what we want to avoid, instead of what we really want. This creates serious problems, because as the psychologist and NLP researchers have stated the subconscious mind does not comprehend the negative verbs, because it needs to visualize the action to understand the communicated word, for example if I told you "do not think of your right toe, or try not thinking about an elephant, your subconscious mind will instantaneously focus on the toe, or elephant. And it will be next to impossible, not to think about those objects, because our subconscious mind is so fast and decisive, and works similarly to the internet search engine, it always acts based on the first command, and the second command is usually delayed until the first one is finished. But in most cases, all we have is one chance to do it, and if we fail the first time, we cannot get the results we had wanted. For example if someone is walking on a very icy and a slippery surface, if you tell him: Make sure you don't fall. What will really happen is that his mind will immediately respond to this command, but it understands it as make sure you fall, because it does not comprehend negative verbs. Our subconscious mind needs to first visualize some thing, in order to be able to perceive it, thus it cannot perceive some thing that has not happened on its mental screen yet. As a result of this received command which says fall, our subconscious mind sends a signal from our brain to our whole body to create the motion of falling, and immediately we start to slip, and in most cases we fall. Therefore we need to state only the positive outcome that we want. For example the proper command for a person, who is walking on an icy surface would be: "Walk with confident and firm gaits." In this way his mind will focus on the right image and he will not fall. In our real life we always have to use positive verbs, and always and only talk about, think or do the things which are positive and are what we truly desire to have in our lives. We should also replace our negative and limiting habits and beliefs that are limiting our way of thinking and as a result our lives. We can do that by the installation of new, empowering and progressive beliefs and habits.

And we will learn to do that by using the exercise below that will teach us how to use self-suggestion or autosuggestion to create any new and positive beliefs that we desire. And then our subconscious mind will use these new sets of positive beliefs and create new positive habits, which then automatically and effortlessly drive us to take action in a positive and constructive manner, which consequently will change our lives.

Exercise: This week keep this story in mind and make some time to examine your goals in life. Also examine how far you are from your goals. Then examine and find the negative language patterns that you have been using on a regular basis. These can include but not be limited to negative beliefs expressed by these type of negative words and phrases such as:"I always have bad luck, life is too hard and it is impossible to really make it in this competitive world, only cheaters win, honesty never pays, it is a crazy world and you cannot trust anyone these days, I am always late for work, I hate traffic, rain, my job, my boss or my life."

These types of comments when used regularly will create a permanent mental impression on our mind, which is called an imprint. These imprints then will form the lens that we view the world, and as a result our behaviors and results are limited and confined to these set of mental imprints and habits.

In this exercise you should catch yourself whenever you find yourself using a negative word or phrase, and immediately reverse to its opposite which is the positive and empowering comments. It is also very useful to right down these negative phrases in your work book and write the opposite and positive one in front of it. Every night, write down your negative and positive list, and after reading the positive ones ten times, and the negative ones only one time. Then tear the paper which contains the list of negative comments to pieces and throw it away. Our subconscious mind works symbolically and it will also do the similar action and get rid of our negative habits. However since most of these habits have been active for a very long time, it takes time and practice to fully replace them. Next you must saturate your daily conversations and communications with positive-

ness. More you focus on the positive, sooner your subconscious mind will pick
up the new positive trends. Remember our mind will drive us toward the conditions and circumstances that we dominantly think about and focus on. So we
should focus only on what we want, and only think and talk about those things.

And at the end of the night, after you have clearly made a list of your goals and
priorities, find a quiet place, lie down, close your eyes, take five deep breaths, and
attend to your breathing for 2-3 minutes, after your mind and body calm down,
gently but enthusiastically state what you want in your life, your suggestions,
should be, believable to yourself, attainable, short, positive and descriptive meaning it has to contain emotions. It is more useful if you imagine yourself already
having all the things you desire, and act as if you are viewing yourself at the final
stage where you have achieved your goal, add feelings of satisfaction, pride, happiness and peace to that image, and contemplate on this image when you simultaneously giving yourself the prepared self-suggestions. Combining different
senses, will make the process of habit forming and change faster and more permanent. It is important to remember that our subconscious mind does not respond
when we insist and push for the faster results. This is the law of reversed effect
which means more the conscious effort, less the subconscious response. Therefore
you should effortlessly concentrate on your goal, and leave the strategy of creating
your goals to your subconscious mind. In this way you show that you have faith
in your soul and mind that you deserve and can get to your desired goals, and
since our subconscious mind acts directly based on our existing beliefs, if he finds
you calm, and acting and believing similar a person who had already achieved this
goal, then your mind will create the circumstance you want. But if you push it, or
worry about its outcome, your subconscious mind acts based on your innermost
belief, which is that you doubt whether it is gonna happen or not. And whenever
there is a doubt and negative mental expectancy, our subconscious mind does not
allow us to access the necessary information, and as a result we fail. So in summary only think about what you really want, repeat it to yourself in an effortless
manner, and act as if you already have achieved your goal, and have a positive
mental expectancy.

32. Little things can't have bigger understanding

Once upon a time in China, an eagle landed at a riverside which was located near a town where the great Taoist master Lao Tzu was living, as the eagle was drinking some water from the river, a mosquito that was also drinking water started talking to the eagle, it said hey you big bird where are you coming from? The eagle said I live on the other side of the town, but I fly around all over, and I come here every day for hunting and drinking water. The mosquito laughed and told the eagle, you are a big liar, it is impossible to fly from one side of the town to the other side in one day, it is impossible it will take at least one month to do that. The eagle said it doesn't even take me one day, I do it in one hour. But the mosquito was getting really upset and frustrated with this big lying bird, and he said I don't believe you any ways, but I would have appreciated if you told me the truth, because I want to make the trip to meet my friends on the other side of town. The eagle which was also getting frustrated told the mosquito that if you don't believe me follow me and I will show you that it takes a lot shorter than one month to get across the town. But the mosquito refused the offer and said whatever! You are just a liar and I don't trust you anyway and left. The eagle got so mad and wanted to attack and kill the mosquito for his rudeness. But right at that moment he heard a human voice calling him, he looked behind him, it was Lao Tzu.

He told him to stop, and said, I heard every thing that you two said to each other, The eagle said in an angry tone that, then you would agree that I am right to kill this stupid and rude mosquito who is accusing me of lying to him, when all I wanted to do was to help him. Tell me old man who is right? Lao Tzu smiled and said you are both right to believe what you believe to be possible or not. He continued by saying "bigger things have bigger understanding, little things have little understanding, and little things can't have bigger understanding." He continued: This mosquito is simply not capable of believing in what you are viewing as being possible, because he has not or cannot even think that the possibility of such an action of flying all the way to the other side of the town in such a short time exists. As a result it is really impossible for him to do it. What you believe you tend to realize. And it is useless to try to convince him, because there is no way for him to grasp something which he does not believe even its existence is impossible.

The wisdom of the story is that we should be humble when we meet others, who have not yet developed our level of understanding and consciousness. We have to realize that there are as many levels of understanding and awareness as number of people living on this planet. We all have different genetic codes, and also we have been brought up in a different environmental setting, thus we all have different way of thinking, talking and behaving.

Therefore we should respect the other people's uniqueness, as we expect them to respect ours.

People always act based on their best inner ability at that given moment, therefore we cannot judge them as being ignorant. Even if we get verbally attacked by someone, we should not respond because then we will attune, to their level of understanding and harm and regresses our consciousness in the process. We should not punish ourselves for the shortcomings and immaturity of others. An enlightened person, never reacts nor responds to any verbal attacks, because he knows that if he does he has done exactly what the attacker wanted, instead he acts responsibly, by refraining from a hostile response, and instead offering his help to alleviate the attacker's problem and frustration. An enlightened man has the responsibility to help people with lower level of consciousness and he will never get offended by other people's comment. Because it is like a university professor getting upset when a grade five student calls him illiterate. Since the professor is confidently aware of his level of knowledge, he does not get upset, but simply smiles. Therefore we need to be patient and humble with whomever we meet, because no matter how intellectual we may be, we are still as equal as anyone else. Because in the eyes of god, we are viewed as souls. We are all the same, we are like people who are walking in a dark cave, where the light can be seen at the end of the tunnel, more enlightened ones are closer to the end of tunnel where the light is, The others are a little or a lot behind him, depending on their level of spiritual unfoldment. However all of us will eventually walk the same path, and go back to where we came from, which is to god.

Exercise: This week, keep this story in mind, and decide to be humble with whomever you meet that may have a lower level of intellectual development. Be attentive, and when you catch yourself being critical of someone, or belittling him for some thing he said, stop right there and reverse the process. Meaning try to help him, and teach him the right way, and help him raise his level of understanding and awareness, or if it is not appropriate, at least refrain from criticizing and belittling them. When you are faced with these type of situations, remind yourself by telling to yourself that we are all souls, and he just needs to expand his horizons a little bit, and since you have also been at that level of understanding before at some point, you understand him.

And if a person verbally attacks you and offends you, choose not to respond. In the beginning of this exercise, it may be very difficult not to be affected emotionally. By not responding, your thoughts may want to convey to you that what you did was wrong and you acted cowardly and so on. If you felt overwhelmed by these kinds of negative thoughts and emotions, try this exercise.

Whenever someone offends you verbally, or bothered you in anyway, try the following exercise. Get a piece of paper, and write down exactly what happened to you during that incident, include your feelings during and after the incident, also your physical posture and reactions during and after the incident. Write a descriptive and colorful explanation of the event. More the details, easier it will be to get rid of.

Next read what you have written out loud, then leave it alone, and put it in your closet. End of the night when you are about to sleep, read it one more time, then write and copy what you wrote, on another piece of paper, and tear the first one or burn it if possible. Then leave the new piece of paper in your closet and leave it alone, follow the same pattern for three to seven days. In about two days you will start to notice how ridiculous it is to hold on to these negative emotions, and since by repetition our mind becomes bored, It also loses its emotional sensitivity and attachment to the situation. Therefore we can see that writing down our feelings and thoughts, will allow our subconscious and automatic thoughts which are usually unmanageable and chaotic, to come out and be cleared on the paper, and when we become conscious of them, then we can deal with it logically. That is what Jesus meant, when he said "Truth shall set you free."

33. Motherly love

Once upon a time in Persia, a young man fell in love with the most beautiful woman in their town. He was chasing her all day long, and at nights he was dreaming and fantasizing only about her. But she didn't like him much, plus she had a lot of wealthy men around her, who would provide her with any thing she wished, so she did not want to get married and be entangled by one man with limited resources. But this young man who was from a middle income family did not lose hope, and every day he was writing love letters and singing love songs that he made for her, he was hoping and believing that his true and genuine love will overcome all difficulties, and will eventually win her heart regardless of the other richer competitors. Since his father died five years ago, he took over his father's carpentry business, and he was staying with his mother, who loved him so much. His mom started to get worried about his son, because he had lost his focus, he couldn't sleep and as a result couldn't get up on time to open the shop, his financial situation was also being affected, so she decided to talk to him about his emotional affair. She waited one day for him to get back home from work, after serving his dinner, she brought two cups of hot tea and sat down in front of him, and said: My son some thing is bothering you and I can sense it because I am your mother, I think we should talk about it. The son who, did not want to share his emotional problem with her mom, laughed and said no mom, there is nothing wrong. His mother said I know what it is anyway. It is about that beautiful woman. I know you are madly in love with her, but she is not a woman that can be trusted or depended on, for a long term, she is a wealth chaser and she doesn't care not only about you, nor the other men. She continued by saying that I know it is time for you to get married and to have a woman in your life, but she is not the right one, if you let me I can find the best wife for you who is clean, beautiful, loyal and kind. At this point the son got really mad and said please do not make decision about my life, and do not interfere with my personal life, I have already made my choice no matter what I will marry her, and if I couldn't I will never marry at all. Mom didn't say any thing more, just whispered all I want is for you to be happy and left the room. Few days later when he was going to work he saw the beautiful woman who was walking around the street alone, so he decided to propose to her, he gathered all his courage and walked to her, and said I need to talk to you, she said okay, go ahead.. What do you want?

He said I am in love with you, and I want you to be my wife. She laughed and said you cannot afford me, because my life style is very expensive. He said: don't worry, I will work day and night to support your wishes, she said sorry I don't think that will be enough, he said I will sell my lands and give you the money, she said sorry I have people who can give my weight in gold but I still refused them, the young man being really infatuated by this unbelievably attractive woman dropped to his knees and said I will do any thing just name it, what is that you want? She started getting frustrated with this man, and he didn't seem like he wants to let go. So she decided to tell him some thing that he couldn't do, and after a long pause told him, there is only one thing in this world that if you bring it for me, I will become your wife. The man got up, joyful and smiling, asked: Just name it, my goddess, and I will get it and bring it for you. She said I want you to kill your mother and bring me her heart, only then I will know for sure that you love me. He said but she is my mother, she has raised and cared for me all her life, I can't do that. She smiled and said I knew that, that's why I told you that it is impossible for me to be your wife, because you don't love me enough to sacrifice your dearest thing in life for me. Young man became quiet for a while and then suddenly said I will do it, I will meet you here this afternoon, and I will bring my mother's heart for you. She nodded her head in agreement and they both left. He immediately went back home, his mother was surprised to see him back to the house that early, and ask him what is wrong, did you forget any thing, my dear son? He said no, something happened today and I need to talk to you about it. And asked her mom, will you do anything to make me happy? She said of course I would even give my life for your well being and happiness.

He cried and explained to her what the woman has asked from him, she hugged his son and said I will happily give my life and heart to you, but I feel obligated to tell you again that she is not the right woman for you, and she cannot be trusted and she is just playing with your emotions. He said mom I cannot continue living without her, if I can't marry her I will kill my self today. So the mother said no, you can kill me instead, because if you kill yourself I will die of your sorrow, and you are the only reason that my heart is still beating, if I wouldn't have you beside me I won't need or want my heart or my life. So after long silence, he killed his mother by suffocating her, and grabbed a kitchen knife and pulled her heart out, it was still hot and beating, he ran while crying to the place that he was supposed to meet the woman, in the way his feet got stock when he hit his toe to a big stone, and he fell, his feet started bleeding. At the time the mother's heart started crying and talking to him, and told him: Oh my son I wish instead of your toe it was my heart that was bleeding, I wish that I was alive and could give my life to you once again so you wouldn't get hurt. The son started crying and kissing his mothers heart, and saying I am sorry mom, I love you. But her heart spoke again, and said go my son she is waiting for you now, your happiness is more important than my life. So he ran again and found her there talking to another man, he yelled I did it, I brought my mother's heart, and gave to her. She grabbed the heart in a very indifferent fashion and then threw it on the ground. The young man was shocked and angry, and told her, isn't that what you wanted? She said I was just testing you, I will not be the wife of a person who doesn't even respect and feel sorry for his mother who is the most precious being in any one's life, she had cared for you all her life and you responded her kindnesses by killing her for your lust and desires, now imagine what you will do to me, since I have not done any thing for you, if you find a more beautiful woman, and if she asks you to kill me, then you will kill me in a flash.

The young man dropped to the ground, and he realized what a big mistake he had made, he grabbed his mother's heart and went back home, he wanted to end his life, but his mother's heart spoke to him again, saying my son I will always love you no matter what, and if you are sorry and want me to be happy with you, you have to continue living and marry a nice lady who would be loyal and kind to you and your children. This way I would feel completely happy and satisfied because I would know that my son is not alone and unhappy.

The wisdom of the story is that we should constantly appreciate and love our mothers. Most of young people specially men, after getting married forget or neglect their mother. This story reminds us that our mother is our guardian angel that loves us no matter what, even if we are poor, crippled, mentally slow, shy, depressed or anyhow. It is a human trend that we love the people whom we give service more than those who give us service. But the motherly love is the closest love there is to divine love. Of course I do not want to underscore and undervalue the spouse love or any other kind of love, all I am trying to convey is that, appreciate and take great care of your mothers, because she has not only given you life, she is also ready without any hesitation to give her own life for your happiness and survival. A mother's love is clearly visible, it is flowing obviously and directly from her heart and embraces us wherever we are.

Exercise: This week, keep this story in mind, and make a plan to surprise your mom. You may buy her flowers, invite her for an outside dinner, take her to her favorite place, take her to a movie theater or give her a greeting card in which you express your deep gratitude for all she has done for you. Tell her that even though there is no way for you to repay what she has done for you, but you are willing to be by her side and never leave her alone for the rest of your lives. Tell her as often as you can that you love her. You will be amazed how much these simple words and actions would mean to her. Every week make some time to help your mom, with whatever she may need. Never rush to leave when you are around her, make her feel that you love and enjoy being around her. Always respect and acknowledge your mother in front friends, wife and strangers. No matter what, stand by your mom in hard times, because she would certainly do the same and more for you. And in the eyes of god, mothers are the front runners in the road to heaven, because the first prerequisite to enter heaven, is to selflessly give love and service to others without expecting any personal rewards, and mothers more than qualify to enter heaven. They have made our lives a heaven in this world, and in return, god will grant them the entrance to the heaven in the next life. The irony is that even if the mothers knew they would go to hell, if they loved their children they would still not stop loving them.

34. Should you be prejudice about whom you teach or help?

Once upon a time in India lived a Buddhist monk, who lived in the high mountains. There were five other monks in that area, but they did not associate with him, because they believed that he wasn't careful about whom he was teaching his great wisdom, and they argued that if an ill-intended man learns about this powerful knowledge, he could use it for personal gains and that may cause great pain for lot of innocent people. One day a young man who was a thief came to see this monk, because he knew this monk has all the answers and will freely share his knowledge with any one no matter what the asker's intention and motives was, so he asked him, how can I improve my stealing skills to make more money? The monk said if you don't have a weapon get a weapon it will cause fear inside of the people you rob so they will easily give you all they have without resistant. The thief who was a very poor man and had to take care of his family and his blind mother thanked him and left. He bought a knife, and soon his earnings from stealing doubled, but still he wasn't satisfied, so he went to see the monk again, and thanked him for his previous tip about the knife, but said I need to yet again improve my skills, The monk said find few other people to join you, and if you attack the caravans that are traveling between the cities, you can make lots of money, he thanked him again and went to his neighborhood, and since the king was so cruel and selfish there was no jobs or money to be made by young people, so it was very easy for him to gather lots of people, and soon he became very rich and now he had a large group of tugs, which were very famous and feared by everybody, even the king's army. At this point the other five monks went to see this monk, and asked him to stop giving advice to this man, because he is doing lots of evil and the peace and order of the whole area is endangered. But he did not accept, and said that I have made a promise to god to share all my knowledge with everybody regardless of the asker's social background, because there is a reason why god has put him on my path, so I should answer and help him with any thing he asks me. So the thief came to see him, and thanked him again. He was very happy because now, he was not only rich himself but also he had helped many other families to acquire foods, clothing and shelters that they never had, so he asked what can I do to even improve my skill more? He said you should increase your group's number to thousands and also train them for combat, in that way you can capture the cities and take every thing you desire, so he did and soon he captured the whole region. At that point the king was really upset and felt threatened by this man, and soon war broke out, and since the king was not a popular king, people turned against him and supported the thief leader, and kingdom fell in few days, and this young man became the king of the whole Indian empire.

And since he had lived in poverty and hardship all his life, he understood people and as a result, he cared for them and became the most popular and loved king of India's whole history up to that point. He continued to visit the monk and ask for new advices, but now different kind of advices, about building and improving the life setting of all citizens, since he started robbery not for personal gain, but to support and help his family and his fellow men. The five monks who were dumbfounded by this monk's attitude and his wise choice of helping the once thief man whose efforts, lead to the liberation of the whole country from the oppressive rule of the king, came to learn his secret of how did he know that this man will become the next king, when he was just a normal crook at the time. So they asked him how did you know this thief would become a benevolent king? He smiled and said I didn't. I just told him any thing I knew, because I follow god's rules which are impartial, meaning if god gave me his knowledge, it is not for my personal use, and I am responsible for giving this knowledge to anyone who asks me, because this knowledge does not belong to me, it belongs to everybody equally. And furthermore unlike you, I did not see a thief asking me question, I saw a man who has a part of god within him asking me for advice, and since one can never be aware of anyone's intentions or outcome of their fate, we have to help and teach to whomever god puts in our path, because some times what we judge by our limited mind as a terrible person, ends up to be the greatest thing that ever happened to us. So you have to simply act as a divine channel and without judgement and prejudice against the asker, tell them what god has allowed you to learn.

The wisdom of the story is that we should not be prejudice in helping others. If anyone comes to us for guidance and help, we should help them, because god has put them in our path. Most often we logically judge whether helping someone is right or wrong. Since our belief systems are biased by our limited personal learning experiences of the past, we often are biased and unable to make the right decision. On the other hand our soul sees the big picture which views us, not as a separate entity but as a harmonious and interactive part of the whole. And sometimes it is to the benefit of the total consciousness in a collective manner, for us to act against our immediate conscious judgement. When we are faced with these type of situations in life, we have a chance to reevaluate our belief systems, and to change them to more spiritual and compassionate ones. And when you eliminate these limiting beliefs which are self-centered and develop a view of generosity and sharing, you will be rewarded by receiving the same types of unexpected helps which people call miracles in your life. If you go out of your way to help someone, then the universe also will go out of its ordinary ways and helps you in miraculous ways. But in order to do this we have to be brave to break our belief system, which we are strongly attached to it. For example one day, about ten years ago I and my room mate were walking toward a restaurant in down town area, sitting in a street corner was an alcoholic man, he looked at us and asked for some change in order to eat some thing, my friend told me not to give him any thing because he was surely to use it on buying alcohol and all we have is twenty dollars, and our food at the fast food restaurant would probably cost fourteen dollars, so we should hang onto our money.

But I told him, let's break a pattern today and not to prejudge this man only because of his present condition. My friend agreed and we told him that we will give you some money, but since we do not have any change, if you are hungry, you can join us for lunch, he was surprised and agreed to come with us, even though he smelled strongly we decided to go on with our plan. We bought him some burgers and fries and we sat with him on the same table, after eating his food frantically and quickly, he told us about his life's sad story, and he thanked us for our generosity and promised that he will change for better, Anyway shortly after he left, my friend and I started talking about our experience, he told me well it was good but now we have only two dollars left till tomorrow and we laughed. I was also very preoccupied about my next month's trip to Sweden, where I was suppose to visit my mom whom I hadn't seen for three years, and I had no money saved up for the trip. I needed $550 for the ticket and about $350 for spending money and souvenirs. I needed total of $900 for the trip. That day I went to my work, where I was working as a supervisor in a customer service department of pizza company. I received my cheque, in the "other" section of my payment statement $905 was added. At first I got so happy, but then I thought they may have made a mistake and over paid me, and since they would deduct it from my next cheque, I thought it is better to let the management know, and correct my cheque.

When I went to the office, The manager said your cheque is right we gave you a raise of $1 an hour. I told him but this is $905 extra, I worked only 35 hours this week. He said we evaluated your performance for the past six months, and we found out that you have been under paid for that period, and we decided to give you the raise starting from six months ago. I was shocked and happy. I thanked god for his last minute help. Later when I looked back, I realized that since I decided to go out of my way and give genuinely when I myself was in need of that money, God also gave me what I needed in an unexpected and miraculous way. From that time on, I have been experimenting with these type of giving to others where the person would not usually expect to receive, and I found that god and universe also gave me any thing that I wished for, in a mysterious and magical way. God helps you, when you help one of his children, so we should have a universal and unbiased love toward all people and living beings.

Exercise; This week, keep this story in mind and decide to make a plan to help someone that may ask you for help. Go beyond your usual standards. That means do not give just what you have as "extras." Give him more than what you usually do, for example if someone tells you, oh I love your favorite new T-shirt, decide to give it to him. It may bother you in the beginning, because you are breaking a very strong pattern which is caused by your subconscious and emotional bond to your material belongings. When you act this way, you will show an active faith that you deserve to have any thing you wish all the time, because you believe that you are the beloved child of god, and he will help you get any time you need any thing in life, and since you are going out of your way and giving others what they want, god will also give you what you want. On the other hand, if you limit yourself and stick to your old possessive beliefs and patterns, and not giving any of your possessions including material things, time and energy to anyone, then god also will not give you his possessions and gifts of love, happiness and wealth neither.

Since the god's treasure house is full of infinite blessings, and is much greater than our possessions, it is wiser to follow god's universal rule, that states "Give freely, love all and serve all, and as a result you will receive freely, and you will be served and loved by all, including god." This exercise will empower you, and enrich your life in every dimension. Remember your giving should not be limited to money and material things, it can be giving of your time, energy or simply being there for someone when they are going through a hard time. But the important factor of this exercise is to give unconditionally without expecting any return from the person(s) that you are helping.

35. Who decides what is possible and what is impossible?

Once upon a time there was a young man who was a grade twelve student, he had a very serious and demanding math teacher, who was always checking every body's home works specially those of the lazy students who had previously gotten poor marks and results, and since this young man was not really good at math, The teacher not only checked his home works with extra attention, he also called him to the blackboard to solve the problems in front of the class to make sure he didn't cheat or copied it from another student. And if the teacher found out that anyone couldn't solve a math question, which he had answered in one's notebook, he would automatically consider it cheating, and he would not only deduct 5% of his final mark, he would also punish the student by reporting his name to the school principle and also to the student's parents, and he would also punish the student by embarrassing him and making him feel guilty in front of the whole class. Of course his intention was to make sure nobody else dare to cheat again, however his attitude had created a very tense environment in his math classes. So this young man was always trying to stay extra alert and careful about his homework, because he didn't want to go through the harsh punishments that he had actually experienced personally earlier that year. But one day, he was playing soccer all day and he didn't get enough sleep from the night before because he was memorizing all the math answers in order to avoid any punishment if he was asked to go to the black board. Any ways when he went to the math class that day, he was very tired and he could hardly keep his eyes open. The teacher did not ask him to go to the blackboard. However, toward the end of the class when the teacher usually gave the new math questions, he fell asleep. And when he was asleep the teacher started writing the questions on the board, he wrote five questions for next week and when he was done, a student raised his hand and asked a question from the teacher saying, "Is it possible to solve all math questions all the time?", The teacher said wonderful question, The answer is no, there are certain mathematical problems that have not been solved and are mathematically impossible to solve, and after a short pause he said as a matter of fact I have one that I can think of right now, that I recently read in a math journal that is impossible to solve, even when worlds top 10 mathematicians tried to solve it for a year, they could not solve it. Then he smiled and said then I guess it is absolutely impossible to solve that, and then he wrote the question on the board, and he wrote it right under the other five home work questions. Right at that time school's bell rang, and everybody got up quickly to leave the school, the young man jumped, got up and saw the teacher is looking at him and shaking his head in a disappointed way as he was leaving the class, he said, make sure to write and answer the math problems which are on the board, because I will ask you to solve all of them in front of the class, this is your penalty for sleeping during my class. So he quickly wrote all the six questions which were written on the blackboard in his notebook, and he didn't realize that he needs to just answer the first five, and the sixth question was impossible to solve, even by the most intelligent and expert mathematician. So he went home and worked all day to answer the questions, he answered the first five, but he got stuck about the sixth one which was the impossible one. But since he didn't know that it was impossible to solve it, he thought for sure there is an answer so he went to the library and researched for three days and night but still couldn't find the answer. The night before the due date before he goes to sleep, he asked god please help me find the answer for the sixth question to avoid embarrassment and punishment from my teacher.

He prayed whole heartedly for 20 minutes for the answer and fell sleep, in his dream state he saw himself at the black board in his class room, and he clearly and easily solved that so-called impossible sixth problem, and his dream was so vivid and clear that he remembered the complete answer as he got up at 6:00 a.m., so he happily wrote the answer into his notebook and very confidently and he went to school. His teacher without any hesitation or second thought called him to the black board, and told him to start from question one and to answer all the questions. He started by quickly and flawlessly answering all first five questions, as he finished the question number five, The teacher said bravo! I am impressed you have done your home work perfectly, but the young man said I am not finished yet, there is question number six that needs to be answered still. The teacher asked: What sixth question?, There was only five of them. He said no, I am talking about this one, and he wrote question number 6 on the board.

The teacher laughed and said this is the impossible question, I hope you didn't waste all of your time and weekend on this unsolvable question. The young man said I did spend all my time on the weekend, but I didn't waste my time because I did solve it, it is not impossible. The teacher smiled sarcastically and said go ahead genius. Solve the most impossible math question that the best contempo-

rary mathematicians in the world have not been able to solve!, So he wrote the
solution very quickly and confidently, and to the teacher's amazement it was the
correct answer. Then the student turned to the teacher and said I guess it is possible, isn't it? He later became one of the greatest math experts, winning all kinds
of awards in pioneering and inventing new math methods. And when they asked
him how did you solve that problem? He said, since I wasn't told and I didn't
believe that this question is impossible, and since my mind felt the urgency and
importance of the solution to this problem, it gave me the answer when I wholeheartedly ask for it from god. You couldn't solve it, because you already had a
negative mental expectancy of not being able to solve it, because nobody had
been able to solve it before. And what you believe is true and nothing else. So we
are the one who chooses what is possible and what is impossible, and if no one
tell us that something is impossible, and we whole heartedly believe that it is possible, our positive mental expectancy will make it possible for us.

The wisdom of the story is that our belief system decides what is possible and
what is impossible in our life. We have a belief about our levels of abilities in any
of life's many circumstances and tasks. And these belief systems are completely
different, or different to some degree in every individual. Our beliefs have been
learned and recorded by our experiences from the moment that our mind has
started learning through the usage of its five senses. The sources of our beliefs
may be direct, meaning it is some thing that we heard, felt or experienced ourselves. This includes our encounters, communications and experiences with our
parents, teachers, friends and any other sources. And the indirect source of our
belief is originated when we believed that some thing is true, even though we had
not experienced it, first hand, but we had been convinced at that time that probably the information, that we are receiving, is true and it can be applied to your
own situations. These sources include but are not limited to, what we read, hear
in the news, gossips and so on. It does not matter whether our belief system is a
by-product of direct or indirect experience, because once believed to be true, both
of them will direct and control our behaviors in complete accordance with those
beliefs. In a way our beliefs function like a lense that allows us only to view and
see the things that we believe in. And if we have limited and wrong set of beliefs
about our true potential and abilities, then our mind allows us to notice only negative and limited opportunities and choices in life. As a result of being faced with
only negative and limited options, we are forced to make a choice which is least
negative one, and then our behaviors have to match these beliefs, and the final
result is a limited and negative outcome. Therefore we can see that the only way

to be free from these types of limitations, is to expand beyond our limiting and disabling beliefs system, and replace them with the positive and empowering belief system. For example, if you have been programmed to have a negative belief that it is impossible for you to own a nice home, or to buy a brand-new luxury car, or it is not foreseeable for you to have a perfect athletic body, or any other blessing in life. This belief alone will block the flow of information and solutions from your subconscious mind into your life, because our subconscious mind works based on its existing beliefs and programming, and when we talk about how we feel, and express our negative mental expectancy about life in general, it reinforces the existing belief system and makes it even stronger. Our subconscious mind is our servant and protector, and always wants to make sure that whatever we believe happens, so we won't feel bad. However the problem is if what we believe, is negative and disastrous, our subconscious mind does not have the judgement and decision making ability, and it will automatically produce the negative results that you are talking about or thinking about. Our subconscious mind is best compared with a fertile soil, whatever you plant the seed of, will make it grow and manifest. Whether it is positive and empowering, or negative and destructive in nature. Therefore we must choose to focus only on the positive things, meaning only focus on what we really want, instead of what we want to avoid. And we should also have a positive mental expectancy about all the new situations in life. In fact all situations are new, because nothing repetitive ever happens in the nature. We must live with our soul's belief system which is boundless, limitless, omnipotent, omniscience and creative.

Our soul has its essence from the holy spirit and god. Thereby has access to all the blessing and powers in the existence. However only a universal, unbiased, and boundless mind can attune, to this universal, unbiasedly pure and divine energies. Therefore we should attune to our true nature, which is a soul, and view ourselves as a part of god himself, and view ourselves as beloved children of god. With this belief system, we will always be protected by god, and we will receive the necessary guidance and help whenever we need it. Worry we must not, because god is in our heart and is always with us, and will protect and help us all the time. Therefore we must believe that any thing is possible, only if we believe it is possible deep down in our heart. The opposite is equally true, if we believe some thing is impossible, no matter how hard we try it will be impossible for us to solve it. Therefore instead of looking outwardly, when you are stuck in a situation and can't find a solution, one must look inwardly, and by evaluating and expanding his belief system to a higher level, he will be able to overcome his challenge easily.

Exercise: This week keep this story in mind and decide to evaluate your life and make a list of your goals, your dreams and your overall condition at The present moment, in your work book. In front of each goal or dream right down how far you are from your desired goal at the moment. Then find and write down the reasons you believe are the cause or the obstacles that have not allowed you to reach your goal. After finding the underlying cause, write as many alternative solutions you can think of that will help you pass those obstacles, and achieve your goal. Remember these solutions should not necessarily seem logical or possible to you at the present moment. Simply write them down, regardless of to your present circumstances. This will help your subconscious mind to access to new resources and information that will mysteriously lead you toward your goals. One easy and best way to get your subconscious mind to believe in what you want to achieve, is by imaging what you want from the end, meaning seeing it as if it as happened already. By repeatedly focusing on your new goals, visualizing and feeling it in your thoughts and reinforcing it by constant self-suggestions. Your subconscious mind will believe this new image to be as true, and as a result of the mental law of attunement and manifestation, which states any condition or circumstance that we focus and attune to mentally, has to manifest externally in the physical world, if and when our focus and attunement is the dominant one. Meaning what we focus mentally on the most at any time, will drive ourselves and our lives toward the exact similar conditions. Therefore we should create the image of the outcome of our desired goal, find a quiet place, close our eyes, take five deep breath, attend to our breathing for 2-3 minutes, which will allow our mind and body to relax. In this relaxed state our subconscious mind is more receptive and suggestible to our suggestions. Visualize your goal in your mental screen which is located between your eye brows and is called the third eye.

See it as if it has happened, the exact way you desire, role play in a very descriptive manner. Add feeling, language, colors, odors, and even add taste if applicable. For example if you wish to buy a house, you should imagine yourself in the house, your loved ones are present and they have brought you house warming presents wrapped in colorful papers, enjoy and store the pleasant feelings of satisfaction, pride and happiness that you feel because you have succeeded, and imagine your mother has cooked you a home made cake, which is your favorite, smell it and taste it, enjoy and store the feeling of love and warmth, and thank them for coming. Act and role play, absolutely as if it has happened already. Then, when you are ready to leave, imagine telling them that you have an important business meeting and you should leave now, tell them that they can stay and enjoy, because you will be back soon. At the count of three open your eyes, feeling wonderful, happy and empowered.

What your subconscious mind believes, we tend to realize in our lives. This is a very simple principle, that all of us have used to be where we are right now. What we thought and focused about, in the past has brought us here, and by the same token what we think about and focus about right now will take us to a place which is exactly corresponding and matching to the quality and nature of our mental focus, words and thoughts. Therefore decide from now on to focus only on solutions and outcomes, and your goals, this will create a positive mental expectancy that will get you where you want to go in life, and leave the possible obstacles for god to take care of them. When we don't focus and don't believe in obstacles, we will not find them or be affected by them in our lives. Be like children, they simply and freely ask for what they want, without considering the circumstances, and amazingly they usually get what they want, however illogical it may seem to an adult.

Remember we are the beloved children of god, and he is the richest and kindest father in the universe, and he will give us any thing we wish for, as long as it does not harm others including ourselves.

36. Who was the true emperor, Who was the true beggar?

Once upon a time Alexander the great and his army which had invaded the western part of India were traveling toward east to conquer the whole India and later prepare to attack China. Somewhere in the road they were passing from a beautiful valley which had become very lively and colorful because of the Ganges river, and it was covered by beautiful and colorful flowers and vegetation. As he was crossing a village he asked the villagers where is the most beautiful site that he could rest in this area, before moving on? And one of the villagers showed him a water fall that could be seen from the village and he said it is the most peaceful and quiet place in the whole of India, and you can also meet one of the greatest masters there who is usually there praying or resting. Alexander got excited, because it was a long time since he didn't have a quality intellectual and spiritual conversations, and he was eager to meet this master and learn some secrets and wisdom that he maybe, able to use to facilitate his victory against The Indians and Chinese empires. So he ordered his army to take him there, where they would rest for few hours before continuing. He was hoping to meet a great, elegant, old master, but when he got there he saw a man in his early forties with long black hair lying down and taking a tan beside the waterfall, and he rarely had anything on, just a torn piece of cloth covering his private parts. He thought it will be really embarrassing to ask for an advice from such a person who looked more like a beggar than a master, instead he decided to make the master embarrassed in front of his army, so they would respect him more since he could even take control of, and belittle the greatest of all masters. So he approached the man and said I am Alexander, he replied with a warm smile and said do you want to join me for a sun tan and a warm conversation? Alexander said you don't realize, I am the famous almighty Alexander the great who have already conquered half of the world. The master smiled and said: So do you want to get a tan or not? Alexander looked around, he loved the beautiful scene and atmosphere of the water fall, and he also kind of liked to take some time to relax, take a tan and talk to this young master, however his strong ego and pride didn't allow him to accept getting naked and taking a tan with a man who looked like a beggar. So after a pause Alexander responded with total arrogance, that I really like to take a tan and relax here, but I am not a beggar like you, I am the greatest emperor of all time, now I have to go conquer the other half of the world. But when I do that, then I can come back here and enjoy the sun and scenery of this beautiful place. But since I really liked you, I don't want to see you in such a state of poverty, without any clothing, home or foods, so I will give you any thing you need.

But the master smiled and said my body is enough for my spiritual journey in this world, I put this piece of cloth only because I don't want to offend other human beings when they come and visit me, otherwise I wouldn't even need that, I am content and fulfilled by this simple opportunity that god has given me to enjoy the fall and sun and I don't need any material thing to feel happy. Alexander whose intention was to try to buy the master, and to prove to his army that he is not a real master, failed in his attempt, then he tried to save his face from embarrassment and told the master: Oh, I liked you even more now, a beggar with pride, so I will give you my own precious red silk rope, which is not only materially valuable, it also carries a great honor for anyone to have it, he then took his rope off and attempted to hand it to him, but the master refused by saying thanks but I don't need it, and I will not use it. Alexander which was getting really frustrated with this man whom he viewed as a simple beggar, said in an angry tone, then give it to the neediest person you know so he can use it. The master took the rope and said okay I have to give this back to yourself, because you are the neediest person I have ever seen.

Alexander said but I have half of the world, what are you talking about? He smiled again and said you have half of the world at your possession but you still feel poor and dissatisfied and you have to have the whole world to feel adequate since your journey and desires are the hardest to achieve, thus you are indeed the neediest. Alexander took the rope and said no problem, it is apparent to everybody who is the rich and emperor and who is the needy, and the beggar one, he laughed loudly and his whole army laughed with him in agreement with what he said.

Alexander who now felt like a winner in his challenge to embarrass the master told the master in a calm way that anyway I am still willing to give you whatever you need before we leave. At that moment the master was lying down and Alexander was blocking the sun, so he smiled and told him if you really want to do some thing for me, there is only one thing you can do for me!, Alexander smiled victoriously and said whatever name it, he said, please move away and stop blocking the sun so I can continue enjoying the sunshine as I was doing before you got here. Alexander just shook his head and jumped on his horse, and said I guess some people are meant to become true emperors like me, and some people are meant to be and remain beggar and loser like this man, and he ordered his army to leave that place.

Incidentally both Alexander and the master died on the same day, and on the road to the court of god where they had to stand and answer for their deeds, they had to cross a river and they both reached that river at the same time. An angel was also present to accompany and direct them to the divine court. Alexander recognized the master, but he was shocked to see that he is dressed like a king, and when he looked at himself he just had a little cloth short on him. He started complaining to the angel that there has been a mistake, I am the true emperor, you have given my clothing to him by mistake, he is the true beggar and you mistakenly given his short for me to wear.

The angel said in an imperative tone, we never make mistakes here, that is the right way. Alexander said but, I was the true emperor in my real life and he was a poor beggar in his real life, how can that be?

The angel said, you are, and you were the true beggar and poor person both in this world and also in your physical life on earth, because in your past life you were given the opportunity to expand, you had half of the world, but inside of you, you still begged, and were hungry for more to feel enough, you needed to conquer everything, to feel enough and equal as this man, he pointed to the master, and in this world you are still begging for more. On the other hand this man was content and rich already because inside his heart he didn't need anything, because he felt the love and protection of god within his whole being, he was a king then because he was living like a king which doesn't need anything to be happy because he already has every thing. And in this world too, he is content because he has faith in his heart that god is kind and fair, and will give him exactly what he deserves, so he is neither worried nor begging. True riches and kingdom are within not without.

The wisdom of the story is that the true wealth, is not only what we own, but is how we feel and how much we enjoy with what god has given us. Most often people fall into the trap of material greed. They believe more they have, more they can enjoy in life. They start with this presupposition and belief in early stages of life where they did not have any thing. As they grow up and become financially successful, they get married and have children, and at subconscious level their mind equates love and recognition with material wealth. This archetypal belief will make them worrisome all the time, because now they want more enjoyment and recognition at subconscious level, since our subconscious mind always seeks to maximize pleasure. Therefore the individual feels that he should work even more and harder, and buy more material things to be loved and recognized more by his loved one and society. The problem with this belief is that it causes our mind to neglect our other aspects. For instance many people have damaged or even lost their physical health and emotional well being because of their greed and thirst for financial success and power. Many professionals and lay people have experienced this phenomenon, working late all the time, not exercising, not paying attention to hygiene, neglecting of family and children which has lead to a divorce and/or physical and emotional break downs. One should realize and remember that we are actually a soul, and our soul has other priorities than those of our greedy and competitive social mind. Our soul wants to experience peace, love, wisdom, growth, creativity, happiness and closeness to god. Our soul loves to enjoy and embrace every single moment of life, and is not concerned about what material possession, or what social status or power we hold, because it is omniscience and knows that we cannot even take a dime with us to the next life. The proper spiritual belief is to enjoy and use whatever god has given you today, but do not come to believe that you are the owner of these blessings. Every thing belongs to god, they have just been lent for us to enjoy and learn from these blessings while we are here.

At the end, all we can take with us to the next life, is the level of peace, harmony, love, self realization and wisdom that we have learned and experienced in our life, because you can only take spiritual things to a spiritual plane of existence, no material entity or object is allowed or is able to exist in higher planes of existence. Similarly in our present life, The level of our enjoyment depends on our inner level of peace, calmness and spiritual balance. In summary more you focus and live by spiritual values of love, peace, happiness, harmony, and self development, happier and more vibrant you become, and happier and healthier you are more you can enjoy life.

Exercise: This week, keep this story in mind, and decide to examine your life, specially the way you are handling your finances and your job. See how it is affecting your emotional and family life at home. If you found that you have been over working, look for ways to alleviate these situations and balance your life. Also check to see what effects do your over working has on your physical health. Make a list of the possible effects and harms that you feel applies to your case. In front of each of these harmful results, write a solution and incorporate and make some time to balance those imbalanced aspects of your lives, whether it is your physical, emotional or spiritual aspect. Also in another page of your workbook, make a list of possibilities that can help you make adjustment to your working hours, so you can designate some of those hours to another type of activities, which will fulfill your other needs. You can cut some hours, or reduce some of your unnecessary spending, or a change of a job that will give you more income but fewer hours. You need to write down all the possibilities freely and without judgement first, and then, choose the best possible option.

Also you need to be attentive and catch yourself, whenever you find yourself being greedy by over working yourself, or competing with others in an unhealthy and destructive manner. Catch yourself when you are sacrificing your physical, emotional and spiritual life, and when you did catch yourself, immediately change the pattern. For example, if you have planned to take your children to church and later to an amusement park on a Sunday, and they call you from work and ask you if you want to come in and make an extra $200, if you are tempted to go to work instead of your previous plans, stop right there! Tell your-self, no I am the one in control of my life, not the financial circumstances, I choose to live a balance life, and take care of my family and spend some quality time with them, because it makes both me and my family emotionally healthier and more balanced, and I will also go to church and pray, this will make me and my children's spiritual life healthier and more balanced. Decide to live a balanced life, no matter what, because if you neglect different aspects of yourself, you will not be able to be happy and enjoy life today, and neglecting your other needs for financial goals will defeat its own purpose anyway, because later on you have pay dearly to balance those physical, emotional and spiritual aspects. Because by neglecting yourself physically, your health will deteriorate and you have pay lot of money and time to balance and fix the problem if it is possible, in most cases irre-versible damage is done to our tissues and organs because of, our unhealthy diets and lack of proper rest and exercise. Similarly emotional negligence toward our family, may lead to conflicts and divorce which can also be very costly both finan-cially and emotionally, and the list goes on and on.

So decide to live a balance life, and live by healthy and spiritual values. Your priorities should revolve around your soul, not your finances. Our soul loves to love and be loved, it loves to teach and learn, loves to cause happiness and to be happy, and loves charity. For a soul, this moment is the most precious gift of god, and wants to enjoy it to its fullest, because it knows that tomorrow never comes, all there is, is now. Decide not to lose your best moments of life, worrying about possessing more material things, but enjoy and live the moment. Develop a "Don't worry, be happy" attitude. Because you as a child of god deserve to be happy and enjoy life to its fullest.

37. Who makes the decision how much of what you make is yours?

Once upon a time in Syria lived a young man who was a very serious and hard-working man, and since his father passed away he was forced to work full time at his late father's carpentry shop, where he was making beautiful and stylish furniture. Since he was more educated and creative than his father, he made serious changes about the way he was building and selling the furniture, he made many different modern looking furniture and he also used his knowledge about commerce to market his products to other bigger cities. He soon started to triple their income in compare with what they were making during his father's time. Since he was a very serious person and was spending all of his time at the store, he was giving all of his money which was about 1500 dinars every week to his mother to keep it in a safe place for him. His mother was really proud of his only son, who not only managed to run the business but also to buy a new house and a car. She had become his accountant and knew exactly how much he was making. But after a while the young man got tired of his loneliness and lack of social life, so he decided one day to visit the restaurant that was serving alcoholic drinks, to have some beers. As he was sitting at the bar, he met a very attractive lady there, whom he later found out to be a prostitute, after getting really drunk he took the working lady to her place. At the end of that day he realized that he had spent 250 dinars on drinks, and 250 dinars on that lady, but he did not regret it at all, and as a matter of fact decided to the same twice a week. That meant he would spend 500 dinars on drinks, 500 on that lady and take home only 500 dinars a week. But he figured he doesn't need to save all those monies, and he had a right to enjoy his life. However he was embarrassed to tell her mom about his activities after work, because he was sure that she would not like or agree with what he was doing, so he decided not to tell her the truth, but to tell her that the business is slow and the store is not making money as it use to, and it has returned to its normal level of income as my father's time. So end of the first week, the mom was surprised to receive only 500 dinars from his son, so she asked him did you by any thing this week? He said no, the business was bad this week, I could make only one third of what I usually make, but don't worry the sales should get back to its usual level next week. But week after week he kept bringing home only 500 dinars, and kept playing the role that business is not picking up, and he kept visiting the bar and that working lady. The mother finally got suspicious and decided to follow his son after work, she found out that he was spending 1000 dinars which were two third of his income on these unhealthy and immoral activities. She decided not to tell him any thing about this, and pretended that she didn't know any thing about his life after work. Instead she figured it is a wise idea to find a nice and loyal girl for him to get married, in that way he would not waste two third of his income on drinking and working ladies to fill his loneliness.

So she convinced him and picked one of the most beautiful and faithful women in town for him to get married. He got married and actually fell in love with his wife so much that he would directly go home after work, he didn't even think about that bar and working woman anymore. But even though he was not spending any money on drinks or that working lady he was still making only 500 dinars a week and his income dropped to 500 dinars exactly when he got married and stopped going to the bar and to visit that working lady. So every week he kept giving his mother the same 500 dinars. The mother was surprised, she couldn't believe that his son can be such a horrible and immoral person, that even though he was married, he would still cheat on his wife and drink twice a week. But she decided not to say any thing, but to follow him again the next week. But to her out most surprise she found out that this time he was telling the truth and was making only 500 dinars a week. She knew a wise master who lived in a nearby village, she decided to go and see him, and ask for his explanation and also to ask him to pray for more income for her son. She met the master and explained the situation and her dilemma. The master smiled and said, "what we call income, is actually our divine share", and in your son's case his divine share has not changed a bit. It was always this much. But the mother reminded him, that her son was making three times before his marriage, but spending it wrongfully on a working lady and alcohol. The master smiled, and said first of all, only god knows and can be the judge of whether what your son did was wrong or right!, Secondly even though 1500 dinars came to your son's pocket, however his divine share of that money, was only 500 dinars, the rest belonged to the working lady and the wine seller, 500 dinars for each. Therefore when your son stopped spending that money, and giving their divine share, there was no need for him to make that extra 1000 dinars anymore. Somebody else will make that amount, to spend it on that lady and wine seller, and to provide them with their designated divine share. The master told her that god's rules and wisdom are mysterious and most of the times beyond the comprehension of human beings, and she should know that no one can temper with god's decision about how much his or her divine share is. But the general rule is, more you give to others, more, your income will be. Because you are asking for income to share it selflessly with others, thus god allows the universe to provide you with what you ask. But if you continually ask things for your own selfish desires, then it will not be given to you. We must all learn to share our gifts and blessings with others, if we want to enjoy a happy, healthy and abundant life. Remember god is generous, thus he loves generous people. She thanked the master and realized how her selfishness and greed have been causing her lot of mental and emotional turmoil, and from that time on she decided to be content with whatever god was providing to her and her son.

The wisdom of the story is that god and universal consciousness decides how much is given to each individual. Of course god has given us the total freedom by choosing our way of life and our profession. And a person who is more focused and specializes in one art or science will succeed financially and socially at a faster rate. However there are also karmic effects from our past lives and experiences that affect our present life. Law of karma, is the law of cause of effect which states that every thought, emotions and actions, will have its exact reaction and effect. For example if one kills someone, even if he gets away from it in this life, he has to be reincarnated, and be killed in a similar fashion in order to clear his karmic debt. That is the idea, behind the death penalty. Even though it seems inhuman, but religiously and spiritually, it helps the murderer, because if he gets killed in this life, he would clear his karma and should not be reincarnated and go through long years of hardship, until he meets the inevitable. Not all karmic conditions are as extreme. But it is so precise that even if owe money to someone or harm him emotionally, and you fail to make up for it in this life, you will have to come back along with those people, to clear your karmic imbalance. Remember the essence of life in the planes which are lower than the spiritual planes, which are referred to as lower worlds, are moderation and balance. Meaning you should receive as much as you give. If you give more unconditional love and service, you will store positive karma, which will help to clear your previous or future negative karmas. Furthermore, more you give more you receive. So we should decide to be generous, and keep in mind that the true owner of every thing is god, and what we call "ours or mine" is given to us as a temporary gift to use, and we should pass on and share the gifts that he has given us. In this way the flow of energy and love is increased and as a result the number of and quality of our gifts is also increased in life. Share your wealth, happiness, wisdom and love and you will grow tremendously beyond your wildest imagination. Furthermore you will be blessed even after this life and save yourself from other karmic reincarnations.

Exercise: This week, keep this story in mind and decide to be more generous and giving in life. Remember giving does not have to be limited to money. You can give your old stuff that you are not using to goodwill stores and other charities. You can give your time and energy to help someone in their project. Do every thing in the name of god, and believe that by giving to others, you are actually increasing the flow of wealth, health. Wisdom and love into your own life as well. Because we are all connected together with an invisible web of divine energy and love, and more positive exchange of energies among its energy fields, the more powerful the whole energy field becomes, and as a result each member of this totality is flourished as well. It is like, if you act and think you are a separate entity from the whole universe, others and god, then you are just a drop in the desert, but if you believe you are one and an active part of the whole, then you are a drop in the ocean, and can enjoy all the privileges and powers of the ocean. Keep saying this mantra, or self-suggestion to yourself, whenever you have free time," I am a soul, I love all, I serve all, I am part of the whole, we are all equal and interconnected by love." This will help you to destroy your old limiting beliefs, and replace it with the correct and positive beliefs.

38. Which is more important, the source of help or getting the help itself?

Once upon a time in China, there was a monk living in a small village which was in the middle of a thick jungle. It was a period when the Japanese army had invaded China from the east and was rapidly and ruthlessly moving toward west and destroying and killing all the people in their path. This village was hidden in the middle of the jungle and had remained un attacked from the beginning of war, which had started about a year ago. But one day as the Japanese army was looking for food in the jungle, accidentally found this isolated village, so they went back to their moving army's head quarter which was resting at the edge of that jungle, and reported of a village that have not been destroyed yet. The Japanese general decided to attack the village immediately, because he figured that they may have found out about the presence of the Japanese army and they may escape or even worse they may plot an attack against his army, and furthermore he figured that, he could find enough food to feed his starving 5000 man army. So even though he knew that it was the army's policy not to attack at night times because of many dangers involved, but he decided to attack immediately, so he ordered his troops to move toward that village, and in about one hour they arrived and, after facing strong and unprecedented resistance, they captured the village around nine o'clock at night, the general ordered his troops to kill everybody and get the food. But one of his advisors told him that it is wise to keep one wise person alive, so he could guide them out of that jungle, so they decided to keep the old monk alive and kill the rest, they also prematurely burnt the whole village. After they were finished and the fire from the houses was turned off, the dark night set in, soon all the soldiers started to get frightened because they knew lots of dangerous and wild animals were living in that jungle, that would attack them in the dark, so they decided to leave and ordered the monk to lead them. But the old monk said: I can't lead you in this complete darkness, but I can pray for lightning and we can use its light to get out of here, the general who was really

134

angry and pessimistic about this monk and his ability, gave him only half an hour to fulfill his promise. So he started praying and meditating in a corner, shortly after there was a major sound of thunder, when they looked up, they saw thick clouds gathering and soon they saw a very powerful lightning in the sky, which brightened the whole jungle for few short second. Everybody became happy and amazed and stopped to watch the beautiful lightening, and they were talking and arguing among themselves that, did the old monk really cause the lightening? or, was it a coincident?

So instead of finding a way out of the jungle, they stared at the lightening which lasted only for 30 minutes, that is how long the lightening usually continues for. On the other hand the old monk and few of the Chinese women who were not killed because they were beautiful, used the light that the lightning provided and found their way out of jungle, but the Japanese army who was so prejudice and could not believe that an inferior Chinese man can cause lightning, but they who considered themselves as a master race at those days couldn't do the same. So they spent their time and for them, the source of that light was more important than the way and as a result they could not take advantage of the benefit that this light provided. And as a result of ignorance and arrogance in taking the proper action by using this provided light, they missed their chance and they fell pray to hungry wild animals, but others that decided to follow the old monk and use the opportunity that this lightning provided escaped death.

The wisdom of the story is that it does not matter where we are getting our help from, and we need not to be prejudice and block ourselves from receiving help from others. We all have a mind set that certain things and people are worthy enough to be listened to and looked up to, by the same token we have a mind set that certain people are not qualified to give us any advice or help. That means we have a set of beliefs and value system that filters the information that we are receiving. For example it is very difficult for a doctor who is financially and socially at a higher level, to accept an advice about his health from a lay person. Even though the lay person may be right about his comments. For example he may tell the doctor who may not be watching his diet, or not regularly exercising, that, he should watch his diets to avoid health hazards and heart attack, and he should consider regular exercise to keep his heart healthy. However unfortunately in most cases, the source of information is more important to people than the benefits of the information itself. So the doctor, resists listening and taking the advice seriously, and misses on a great motivational opportunity which could lead him to a better, healthier and eventually a longer life. But our limiting beliefs

blinds and deafen us from receiving all sorts of positive and empowering suggestions and helps that are readily available to us. One should decide to change his
point of view, and to have an open eye, ear, mind and heart to be receptive and
accepting to any good advice, suggestion or help from various sources regardless
of the persons' religion, nationality, race, social status, sexual orientation and life
style. Because we need to remember, we are all souls and we are all part of god,
therefore we are all potential sources of infinite blessings and resources. We need
to choose to accept the gift of others freely. As Jesus has said, "Ask and you shall
be given." But we may add to that statement that you need to open your heart
and mind to receive what they give you. Otherwise it is like the mail man brings
you $100,000 check to your door. But you never open the door for him, he will
wait and ring the bell for few times, but then will leave with your check. So gifts
of god are infinite and many, all we need to do is ask for them, and then accept
them, when they are given to us.

And we should develop a mental set, which helps us to focus on the possible
benefits that are available in any given advice, instead of judging the source first,
and if he is not fit to give us advice based on our existing limiting belief system
and then attacking him instead of thanking him.

We should always thank the source of our help or the people who are offering
it freely to us, even if we choose not to use it. Because by thanking them, you
show your appreciation, and that will keep the healthy channel of energy, support
and love among you, and it can easily be used mutually in the future.

Exercise: This week, keep this story in mind, and decide to expand your horizons and belief system. Start to respect and be attentive to anyone who is genuinely and freely is trying to give his advice or help. Take the time to listen to each
person that you meet this week. If we just develop the art of listening, our whole
life will be transformed for the better. True listening means, when the other person is talking, we should only focus and listen to what they are saying, but in
most cases even though we may be quiet when someone else is talking to us lets
say about his dog, as soon as we know the subject, we are reviewing one of our
own experiences and memories about dogs and we are involved in our own inter-
nal world of thoughts and memories, and we are not really there, listening to
them. When we think about some thing other than the present conversation,
parts of our soul's energy moves away from our energy field or aura toward those
thoughts and memories, and that reduces our vital power and our ability to be
focused. To be focused, means to be in present. Since real things and real
improvement in any areas happen now, then if we are not present, nothing is

happening in real terms. Meaning there is no exchange of energy or love between the people. That is why we feel drained and tired, when we have long conversations with people who are not genuinely receptive, or people who always talked about the things that they can't get in their life. The reason is, they drain our vital energy, similarly we may drain them. And by the same token, when we have a simple conversation with family or loved ones, since they love you and take the time to listen to your concerns, you feel relieved and vibrant after talking to them. Because our soul which is part of god, is omnipresent and omniscience and knows the intentions and quality of the person who is communicating with us. If it is not from heart, and is just for show off or convenience or guilt then your soul will not receive or send any of its energy, and if there is no flow of energy and love, we start feeling tired, bored and even may lead to physical symptoms if it is continued. Holistic practitioners of the eastern Asia believe that all the diseases are created because of our lack of ability to give or receive love and universal energy, which are caused by our wrong and limiting frames of mind. Because the universal flows of energy and love, flows into our energy field via our mental frames, which are created by our belief system.

More limited our belief systems, meaning more prejudice, self-centered we are, less energy is allowed.

Since the nature of the god's love is universal and impartial, our belief system and mental filters should be universal and impartial if we are to receive more of those divine energies and love. So believe that you are a soul, you love all and serve all to best of your ability, and everybody else is as good as you, and deserves to be listening to. Remember god's ways are mysterious, you will never know where the help is coming from.

So give freely and receive freely, and watch your life grow in every dimension.

39. Does it matter, in what field you become a master?

Once upon a time in Japan, lived a tea master in a Japanese palace, where he was in charge of making the best tea for the king and his royal family. Serving tea and drinking tea was a very special and sophisticated activity back in those days, the master had to preform a special dance which involved very smooth and gentle movements of legs and arms while he was pouring the dry tea from its container to the pot, and while the tea was being boiled in the pot he would chant special prayers and mantras to bless the tea, so it would bring health, wealth and happiness to the king and royal family. This tea master was so elegant and expert in his tea servings that he had become so famous and popular by all the family, specially the king himself. The king loved and respected him so much that he decided to make him the secretary of treasury, which was the most respected and powerful post in his dynasty. One of his duties was to visit all provinces and gather the collected taxes from each governor and check their records to make sure every thing is right and there is no corruption or stealing, and to bring it back to the king's main palace where they stored the collected taxes which were golden coins.

This period coincided with the rise of the samurai fighters, which were the brave and ruthless fighters who rebelled and challenged against the king's unfair and oppressive tax collectors who almost collected ninety percent of whatever any farmer made. The samurai fighters would kill any tax collector or king official that they came across.

One day when they were passing by a small village, which was known for its perfect tea. He decided to stop there for few days to collect and buy some tea, which was the finest tea in the whole of japan, but his advisors told him that they cannot stop, because the governor of the next province is expecting their arrival in few hours, so he ordered them to go and gave them a letter with his special seal on it that gave them the authority to collect tax, and he decided to stay. The advisors warned him that this village is a home to many samurai fighters, which if they found a royal official will kill him without any hesitations. He smiled and said don't worry I am gonna wear a villager customs on top of my royal uniform so no one can recognize me, and I will do my purchases and I will then wait for you here after two days when you are back from the neighboring province.

They reluctantly agreed and left him about a mile to the village. He walked to the village and found a tea shop which had all different kinds of tea, and being a tea master and in love with tea, he spent about three hours in the shop and bought lots of teas. When he was done, he asked the store owner, if he can find him place to stay for two days, the owner said there are no renting place in this village because strangers are not welcome in this village, but he can rent, him a room in his own house since he purchased a lot of products from him, and he agreed. The owner said we will go home in two hours when his business hours were finished, the tea master agreed and said I will go look around other shops and I will be back in two hours. He walked around the village's small but busy market, as he was walking around he saw a beautiful royal vest hanging from a clothing shop, he thought it was probably taken or stolen from a royal victim, He decided to buy it, he entered the shop and agreed on its price. The shop keeper told him would you like to try it on and see how it fits on you? Because I will not refund your money if you bring it back later. He agreed and took out his villager's clothing to try the vest on, and suddenly the shopkeeper saw his royal uniform underneath, and started yelling and screaming, and soon after, a very strong and tall samurai walked in with his sword. The tea master was shocked and taken by surprise, he started to explain to the samurai who was very angry that he was just a tea master, and he is in their village to spend a lot of money, not to take or collect any tax, But the samurai told him that I shall kill you right now, however our tradition states that I should challenge you by the next dawn, because I should not kill you because of my personal rage, but I should want to kill you for our collective purpose to free Japanese people from oppression. And he warned him not to try to escape, because his fellow samurai fighters would be chopping him to pieces, and it would be better to at least die with honor. He came back to the store with a long face and frightened, The store owner asked him why are you so pale. What is the matter? The tea master told him what happened. The store owner told him that, this samurai is the toughest samurai in Japan and there is no way to win against him, however I have a sword at home and I know some tricks that I can teach you. The tea master reluctantly agreed. When they got home, the man brought the sword that he was hiding in his closet, and showed the tea master few moves and then asked him to try it. But the tea master that was a very peaceful and spiritual man had never touched a sword in his life, could not learn or replicate any of the moves. His movements were preposterous, so the man said forget it, you gonna die. The tea master thanked him anyway, and being a spiritual man told the man that he should repay him for all the things he did for him. The man asked him to prepare a tea for him, because he had never watched a real tea master prepare and make a tea. The tea master agreed. And he automatically started his beautiful smooth dance which was consisted of rapid but harmonious movements of his arms and legs and whole body, he was so agile that the man could not believe his eyes, and all of the sudden the man said "just do that," The tea master stopped and said, Do what?

The man said tomorrow just hold the sword in your hand, close your eyes and pretend that you are preparing your tea, because in that way you move and look incredibly, and I guess you would survive his attacks for a while and at least would show some grace and die with honor. The next day, they met in the hillside where lot of people had gathered already, to watch the tea master's death. They made a large circle by sitting down in a circular fashion, and the tea master and the samurai, were the only one inside the circle. The samurai started his warm up movements, by moving his sharp and long sword in a very quick and artistic way.

The tea master simply closed his eyes, and with the sword in his hand, started to preform his tea preparation ceremony that he was the greatest master of. He moved in such a beautiful, artistic and flowing manners that everybody was amazed. The tea master was so immersed in his ceremony that he had forgot all about the battle. One the other side of the circle, the samurai was also dumfounded by his opponent's beautiful and harmonious movements. Then some thing very unusual happened, the samurai who could easily kill his opponent in less than one minute, put his sword back to its cover, and said: There is some thing in you which is very similar to me, and that is your self-mastery. A master can never kill another master, because it is like killing himself, or killing one of the god's greatest masterpieces. He bowed to the tea master and congratulated him for his achievement, and told him that he had just demonstrated the flow and action of the god through a human being, and this is exactly how I feel when I am using my sword during the fights, I am no longer present, it is the god within me that is moving.

He continued by saying that he was wrong to believe that only the samurai fighters could be unified with god, however now he knows that no matter in what you become a true master in, you become one with god. Therefore from now on I will respect and love all masters, because they are the closest manifestation of god in this world.

The wisdom of the story is that it does not matter in what area in life, we become an expert and a master. Our society unfortunately programs the majority to focus on mastering and becoming the best in only few fields. Mainly the parent's focus is to force their children to become a doctor, dentist or a lawyer. Their base and logic of this strategy is solely based on the financial rewards that these categories of jobs provide. However only those few percentage who really love these subjects are persistent enough to get into these difficult and competitive fields. And what happens is, many young students which were forced to give up their own dream that may have been becoming an artist, musician or a carpenter, to live the dream of their parents, get frustrated and confused when they fail to make it to the medical or law school. And then, they have to start all over again and start focusing and studying on some thing else that they may like. Usually these students feel bad because they think that they have disappointed their parents, and these negative feelings of failure, guilt and disappointment do not allow them to focus and find out what they really want. And we can find many of these students that wonder around in universities for 5-6 years without choosing a career yet. The initial parental pressure, and later their failure to fulfil their parents dreams, causes them to lack confidence in making the right choice. Because they are consciously and subconsciously are afraid that they may fail and not make it in that field, so before finishing they switch to another subject. But the reality of the matter is, if we focus our attention on any profession, even if society discredits it, we will make it and will be successful. All it takes is focus, planning and persistence. There are millions of examples of people who make millions of dollars, and are completely satisfied and fulfilled in life who have mastered in different fields of business. For example an artist, which has invested his time and energy in years of drawings and practice, can make a fortune and succeed in life even faster than the most educated people. I do not want to under value education, on the contrary I believe education and training is a must for every individual. But the point is, every individual should find out what he really wants to do in his life. Before starting any subject, he should discover his inner tendencies. Because the strongest and most consistent force in the universe is love. If a person does not love the thing he is doing, he will not be able to focus on it and he will try to run away from it as soon as possible, therefore he will not be successful in it. Because it is a mental law, that whatever we focus on dominantly in our thoughts, we will realize the same thing in our life. And in order to be able to keep some thing in your attention all the time, it has to be something you love to do. So we need to pick a profession and subject of study that we love. The power of love will give us the stamina to carry on the long hours of works, which is necessary to achieve mastery in that field.

In today's competitive society, everyone who wishes to succeed financially needs to specialize. And if you become one of the top 500 people in any field, such as plastic, fruit, computer, art or any other field, you will be in the top of the ladder of success. Furthermore becoming an expert will also fulfil your other emotional, mental and spiritual needs. Because by becoming an expert, you can help making the life of many people easier, by offering them your innovative products, services or information. So you will feel useful and proud of yourself. And since you naturally add to the quality and well being of the society as a whole, spiritually you grow as well.

Exercise: This week, keep this story in mind, and make a plan to improve and upgrade yourself academically or professionally. Depending on your field of activity you can find courses, workshops or even books that can expand your horizons and broaden your opportunities. Decide to make growth and learning to become part of your everyday life. And if you are young and have not chosen your profession or subject of study, take some time and clearly think about what you really love, and what is the subject that you can be involved and live with, for rest of your life. Remember choosing a profession is like choosing a partner, you cannot stay with a partner that you hate for rest of your life, you may hang onto it for a while for immediate needs, or for pleasing others but in the long-run heart wins over the mind, and we cannot stay in something or with someone that we do not love. So the basic rule number one is that you must love whatever you are doing in life, and then you will love doing it. And as a result the process will become effortless and even joyful, because it will be like having the person you love beside you all the time. And if you are a parent please do not force your children to some subject of study or profession only because you believe is right for them. Of course as parents it is natural to have concerns about the future of our children, but the better approach is to present them with the choices and opportunities, but give them the privilege of choosing for themselves.

Because it is their life, and they have to live with, that profession for rest of their life not us. And after they made their choice, even if it is not your preference, you should encourage and support them any way you can. Because remember love always wins over logic. So let them live their life doing what they love. Because when you constantly have love in your life and in what you are doing, you are actually inviting and being embraced by god every day. Because god is pure love. And when you have god in your life, your prosperity, security and happiness are hundred percent guaranteed. So let your loved ones be happy, by having love in what their doing, and their happiness and fulfilment will make them more successful and that in turn will serve your intention which is wanting the best for them in life.

40. How important are we in the eyes of god?

Once upon a time in Persia a young man heard of a master living in the neighboring mountains beside his town, he heard that this master is accepting disciples for enlightenment, He decided to give it a try, even though deep down he didn't feel that he was worthy of becoming enlightened, because he figured that he is just a normal person without any religious or spiritual background, plus he had committed many immoral acts in his past. So one day he gathered his personal belongings and enough food and waters, to make the trip which was about two days of walking and climbing of rough mountains. After about two days he reached to the cave that this master was living in. He cautiously entered the cave, and saw that the master is meditating with his eyes closed, so he waited quietly for the master to finish with his meditation and prayers. After about one hour the master opened his eyes and greeted him with a friendly smile, The young man introduced himself and also told the master that I am here to become your disciple with a hope that one day I will reach to the same state of bliss and enlightenment that you are enjoying right now. But he continued by saying, my only concern is that I am just a normal person with no religious training, I don't know if I am important and worthy enough in the eyes of god to be allowed those divine levels!, The master smiled again, and spoke for the first time since the young man had arrived, and said it is easy, lets find out how important you are in the eyes of god, I will ask you some questions and you answer and at the end we should find out how important and worthy you really are, and whether you are fit to become enlightened and reach divine's consciousness. The young man nodded his head as a sign of agreement and consent, so the master started asking him the questions.

Master :Is your country bigger or the earth?

Young man: my country

Master :wrong!, your country is merely a small part of the earth, so the earth is much bigger.

Master :is the land area of earth bigger or the oceans?

Young man: The land is bigger.
Master: wrong again, two third of the earth is covered by water, so the oceans are bigger than land.
Master: Is the ocean bigger or the sky?
Young man: The ocean is the bigger one
Master: Wrong again, the sky is so big that every thing, including the ocean is contained within the sky
Master: is god bigger or the sky?
Young man: I am sure about this one, Of course god because he has created everything including the sky.
Master smiled and said: Now, I can tell you how important you and all human beings are for god. God loves us so much and attaches so much importance to us that he decided to live and reside in our heart, and by doing so he has given us access to all of his divine and powerful attributes and consciousness. To answer your question, we are god's most important and precious beings, because god 's imagination and wishes are transmitted to us in the form of thoughts, wishes and desires and then we manifest those wishes in the physical world, so you are ready for enlightenment as any other human being is, because the state of enlightenment is already available within your heart and soul, you just have to uncover it, spirituality is not a field of which one need to learn some thing new to be enlightened, it is a field of recognition where you recognize and realize more about, who you really are, by walking in the path of spirituality. And as long as one desires to reach god, it means that he has received the proper message and signal from god and this alone makes him eligible and successful in the road of enlightenment and spiritual freedom.

The wisdom of the story is that we usually underestimate ourselves and our potentials. We are the most advanced, and most capable of reaching highest goals and potential in this universe. God loves us so much that he has given us all of his blessings, powers and love. We are the only beings that can use language, visualization and our mental faculty in a volunteer fashion. Human beings are the only beings that are not merely responding to their physical instincts and impulses, we are loved and trusted so much by god, that he has given us the freedom to choose, which means we can form our destinies by using our mental focus. God has given us this gift so we as souls can experience and experiment in this physical world. Because if it was not so, we would become like a preprogramed robot. God has created universes, and all kind of other features and blessings in them, for us to use, enjoy and live in order to experience and learn our necessary lessons.

There are some universal laws which are precise, affirmative and impartial. The universes in the lower physical and mental planes, that we live in, are subject to laws of cause and effect meaning whatever we think, say and do, will attract the similar things and circumstances to us in exact proportions and quality. Our mental reality is also subject to, and operates by the law of attunement, meaning whatever we attune to internally by using our imagination and thinking process, we tend to meet in our real physical life. Even though god's rules are complete and perfect, and even though he has intentionally and for our own good has allowed us to independently experience and manifest in this life, however he will still help us by giving us guidance whenever we are lost, or whenever we are going the wrong destructive way. But we need to ask for god's help and guidance, and we need to listen to his advice. But still god always leaves the final choice to the individual, he shows the road, he provides the vehicle and other necessary supplies for us to walk on the path, but the actual walking is our job. It is like someone gives you a car and its keys, but if you want to go somewhere, the car won't go by itself, you need to drive it. And god loves us so much that he has made it really easy for us to contact him, he is always in reach and by our side, because he is in our heart. Whenever we really need him, he will respond.

All we need to do is to ask. As Jesus said, "Ask and you shall be given." But unfortunately we are usually too busy to talk to god, and he is usually our last resort. We only call him when every thing is going bad, like we are very sick, or a loved one is dying. Why not develop the habit of talking to god more often, and ask for his help and guidance on a regular basis? Because he is the creator, provider and giver of health, wealth, love, understanding and happiness. If we don't use this infinite treasure within us, is like having one billion dollars in your account but never spending it. So we must choose to talk to god more often, that way we will embrace more of his blessings, love and protection.

Exercise: This week, keep this story in mind, and do the following exercise that will help you to expand your horizons about your self image and intrinsic values. Find a quiet place where you would not be disturbed for 15-20 minutes. Close your eyes, take five deep breath and relax your muscles. Attend to your breathing for 2-3 minutes that will allow your mind to calm down and relax like your body. Then with your eyes closed imagine yourself being a soul, and being surrounded by an energy field which is called the aura. A healthy person's aura is perfect egg shape, and the diameter of his aura is about 8 meters. But you can use the exact size that you see on your mental screen when you close your eyes. Feel your aura's energy and vibrations for a couple of minutes. This is your true self, and it is your soul within your mental body. Now that you feel comfortable with that image of yourself, you will expand your aura, you start to imagine that your aura is expanding and getting bigger and bigger, it becomes as big as the room. As your aura becomes expanded, your awareness of your surrounding also expands from the immediate previous surrounding to a bigger area which now contains all of the room. Next decide to expand it even more, imagine it is getting as big as your building, and be attentive of your awareness of the new surroundings. Expand your aura even more, make it as big as your neighborhood, your city, your country, your continent and then expand your awareness and aura to become as big as the planet. Now become aware of your surroundings which are now the outer space and galaxies, and within your aura you contain the whole of the globe, with all his people, oceans and landscape. Next decide to expand even more, to make your aura contain all galaxies and unexplored places. You will experience a great sense of harmony, peace, power and love, because you have become one and unified with every thing in the universe. Hold on to these wonderful and empowering feelings and tell yourself that whenever you wish, you can experience these feeling by simply closing your eyes and expanding your aura. After you do that, you will start to, gradually shrinking the size in the same but reversed order, meaning, shrink it from galaxies to the size of globe, continent, country, city, neighborhood, building, your room and finally to its original size. Please do not rush the process so your soul can adjust its vibrations as it shrinks your energy field. When you are ready, count from one to three, and at the count of three, open your eyes, feeling powerful and energized.

This is the reality of the soul, which is a part of the whole, contained in the whole and also the blue print of the whole is contained within it.

That is what the ancient masters of the east called small world, and big world. The small world or reality is in our soul, which is actually a small piece of god itself, and the bigger world or reality is the world outside of the soul's energy field, which correspond exactly to the individual sense of reality. Meaning we see only what we believe. Therefore we will worth, succeed and enjoy in life as much as we believe we deserve. Now having this story in mind, and this exercise to use you can tell yourself during the exercise that you are part of god, thus you deserve to have any thing you want in life, without harming anyone else.

41. Should I give him what he needs or teach him how to get it himself?

Once upon a time in China, lived a generous fisherman, who used to be an expert in setting the traps and nets in the right place in the river, as a result he was catching almost five times more fishes than other fishermen. Being a very spiritual man, he loved to share his catches and give away half of his catch to the poor people, living in his village. Soon he became very famous and popular because of his kindness and generosity. In the beginning he started by giving fish to ten of the poorest families in his village, but as others heard about his giving, they all lined up beside the river to get a free fish. Now the fisherman had about fifty families who were asking for fish, and since did not have enough fish for all of them, he was forced to give most of his own fishes to these people.

Furthermore he also found out that all these people have given up trying to find away to earn their own living, they had become lazy and completely dependent on him, that was making him very upset, because his inner intention was to help those people to survive, but he also felt that he is making them weak and helpless by giving them free fish. He was also upset because now, he didn't have enough fish to sustain his business and home because he had to give away most of his catch. So he decided to go and see Lao Tzu, the great Taoist master and ask for his advice. He went to Lao Tzu's monastery and explained to him his dilemma, and asked him, should I give free fish to whoever needs it, or should I not? Lao Tzu smiled and said neither one. He said not giving any thing and turning your back on them, will not be spiritually correct, because if god puts someone in our path we have a responsibility to help them the best way we can. However, giving them a free fish or any other thing freely is not the best possible way to help them. The fisher man who was confused by Lao Tzu's comments, said then what should I do? He said instead of giving them a fish, teach them how to fish for themselves. Because by giving them the fish only, they will become completely dependent on you, and one day if you move or die they will be back to their helpless and disabled state. On the other hand if you teach one how to fish for himself, first of all he won't need you, that will relieve both him and you, and secondly he will have fish for rest of his life, and most importantly instead of feeling weak, helpless and dependent, he will feel strong, secure and empowered. So always instead of just giving someone on a regular basis, what they need, show them how to get it for themselves.

The wisdom of the story is that, it is wiser and more productive to help someone to become independent and self-sufficient. Because if you encourage someone or teach him some skills that will enable him to support his living costs, you have empowered him permanently, and he no longer needs you or any other external support. Of course there are conditions that we must simply give someone what they may need urgently, for example if an orphan is in the hospital bed and needs money for operation, however in most cases it is better to take the time to teach someone, or help him to get to the appropriate sources where he will learn a skill to support his life. Similarly we must focus our own life on creativity and constant and ongoing improvement of our skills and expertise. It is not wise and appropriate to only beg and pray god for better life style and more money, without putting the necessary efforts and training. One must remember that god's rules are precise, just, fair and exact. Meaning there is set divine rules, if we want to get somewhere better in life, we need to think, focus, talk and act better. Similar to this story, god loves those who put efforts toward their goals and self-improvements, as the Moslem saint Ali has stated "god's help reaches us at the exact rate of our efforts." And another of his sayings states "movement and efforts from your part, and blessing from god's part." Meaning god will always support anyone who focuses and acts toward the achievement of any physical goals. God has set a universal system which works with mental waves which connect our thoughts to their similar physical resources. It is called the law of attunement, which states, whatever we attune to mentally, we will meet and experience in the outside world. But the speed and quality of our reaching depends on our efforts, training and persistence.

Exercise: This week keep this story in mind and decide to review your life settings and life style. In this particular exercise we will focus on your financial and professional aspects of our lives. You need to clearly find out and write down in your work book where you stand at the present moment. We will call this the original point.

You will need to write your exact level of income, number of hours required to make that income, physical quality of your job, emotional quality of your job, social quality of your job, intellectual quality of your job and finally the spiritual quality of your job. After finishing your answers, rate your present condition for all the questions and categories from zero to 10, 0 being the least satisfactory and five being normal or the average acceptable range, and 10, being the most satisfactory situations. Then, After you finish the rating of your financial and professional's different aspects. The weakness and shortcomings in those aspects will be evident to you.

Then you need to think of and write down the possibilities and opportunities that you have available to you, and also to write down the extra resources that you need to get, to improve your financial and professional life.

Your list may include but not be limited to, upgrading yourself by taking extra courses and certifications in your related field of expertise, considering opening your own business, getting help and support from loved ones, obtaining loans and grants from different financial institutions to expand your business, and so on. After doing so you will realize that the possibilities are endless. Then you need to make a precise and practical plan, which requires your daily or weakly actions toward your goal. Your goals need to serve and improve all different aspects of you in a harmonious manner, which are your physical, emotional, social, intellectual and spiritual selves.

After writing down the exact and final format of the goal. You need to find a quiet place, take five deep breaths, attend to your breathing for 2-3 minutes, allow your mind to settle down, and then visualize yourself, physically, emotionally, socially, intellectually, financially and spiritually satisfied and happy with your new self image, which is enjoying the blessing of having achieved his goals of self-improvement. In your mind's screen imagine and act as if you have already obtained that goal. Because for our subconscious mind can comprehend only the present time, so if it sees your goal as a happened situation it will use all his resources to drive you toward that goal and help you obtain it. Again we need to remember whatever we believe internally we tend to realize and experience in our real life. So choose to decide to improve your life, focus on your new desired goal, make a plan of action, and take consistent action until you get there. Also remember what Jesus said "ask and you shall be given." God is the fairest employer and father, he will give us exactly and precisely as much as we ask for. So choose to ask for more and go for it, and god will support you and be by your side all the way.

42. How should I react when somebody is bothering me?

Once upon a time in China, a young man lived, who was a disciple and follower of the great Taoist master Chuang Tzu, he had been successful in overcoming all of his behavioral shortcomings and problems, and he was almost in full control of his emotions, thoughts and actions. However he was still occasionally felt outraged or frustrated with other people when he was trying to teach them the Taoism and the better ways of life. He was being challenged, laughed at and even mocked for his views, and he was just becoming fed up by those people's attitude and ignorance to a point that he even considered giving up preaching all together. But since he had invested most of his life in the way of Taoism and god, and for the strong respect, love and trust that he had for his master, he decided to give it another try, but before doing so he wanted to talk to his master and find out the reason for his frustration and anger, and also to ask for a remedy to fix and control his rage and anger toward the ignorance and lack of understanding of most people regarding to his teachings. So he went to a riverside where Chuang Tzu was living in his little temple, he went inside and saw the master, who was doing some gardening in the front yard. He greeted the young man with a smile, and as if he was reading his mind, said some thing seems to be bothering you! How can I help you? The young man explained his problem, while the master was listening to him attentively. Then master told him, let's take a walk on the riverside and we will talk about your problem. They walked for five minutes but the master didn't say a word, he was chanting and looking around, all of a sudden he stopped where, a Shepard was grazing his herds of cows. He pointed to a particular cow that was drinking water from the river, he asked the young man to listen carefully and pay attention to what is happening. Chuang Tzu who, was able to understand the language of all animals and beings, showed him that a mosquito is sitting on the cow's horn, the mosquito sat there for few seconds, and being a polite and considerate mosquito, when he was about to fly away he talked to the cow and told him; I am sorry, I bothered you and sat on your horn for few minutes!, The cow looked at the mosquito in an indifferent way, and said I didn't even

151

notice when you landed on my horn, and I probably wouldn't even know when you would have left, if you hadn't told me. Then the mosquito flew away. Chuang Tzu turned toward the young man and said, here is the answer to your question which was How should I react to someone that is bothering me? As you just witnessed a stronger being does not react to little things, because it is sure that, nothing that small, can hurt him.

Similarly a man that lives and is guided by god is not afraid and does not feel threatened from anyone, because his connection with god, gives him such an inner strength that he doesn't even notice what other people are saying or doing to him. A man of god never reacts, because his is one with god and the holy spirit, which makes him greater and stronger than any other being, a man of god just acts based on his own inner divine morals and beliefs and is not affected by the actions of others.

Only the one that doubts and feels threatened reacts and fights back, the man of god acts like that cow, which means he acts with indifference and calmness meaning he doesn't lose his temper nor feel threatened by anyone. Because his higher understanding makes him a stronger being like that cow, which no man with little understanding which makes them like that mosquito, can cause any harm to him. However if you react, you have lost the battle, because you have brought yourself down to their level, and they have succeeded to move you away from your path. And if you get away from the path of god, you will lose your powers and higher understanding, and as a result you will be at the same level of those people with lesser understanding.

The wisdom of the story is that when we encounter someone who is being rude and offensive toward us, we should not react, instead we need to stay calm since we are now enjoying a higher level of spiritual awareness, and we should not be bothered, and should not punish ourselves with somebody else's shortcomings. It is always the responsibility of the one who knows more, to take charge of the situation and try to resolve it in a peaceful and positive way. Because showing a negative and hostile reaction, will only make the situation more hostile and the conflict will be escalated. The spiritual man knows that moderation, peace and balance are the best ways to resolve his challenges, therefore he is never defeated by badness and negativity, instead he will defeat evil and negativity with his good and divine acts. Even if the situation does not permit him to respond in a positive fashion, he decides to remain quiet, not to respond and not to be bothered with what the other person is saying. And by practicing this type of positive and "in charge" attitude, very soon he will not even feel offended by other people's negative comments, because he is very certain about himself and his identity, which is a spiritual man, therefore he enjoys all the attributes and positive traits of god, and he feels too powerful and secure, so he does not even feel the necessity to even think about what others are telling about him.

Exercise: This week, keep this story in mind and decide not to react to whomever that may try to intentionally or unintentionally put you down or belittle you verbally. When that happens, take three deep breath and tell yourself that you are a part of god, and you are protected and loved by him, like all other souls including the attacker. Tell yourself that I trust god and fully believe in his justice system, I know if any thing negative is intended toward me which is unjust, god will protect me and reverse the situation, by sending the same negative force toward its sender. Furthermore you can also send love and good will for the attacker, and offer your help, in most cases this will reverse his mood and behaviors. If he didn't, then simply do not respond and leave. In the beginning this may be emotionally overwhelming, and after we leave that negative incidence without reacting, we may feel bad about ourselves, we may think of ourselves as cowards, and we might be overwhelmed by rushing negative thoughts about our negative encounter.

In these cases try this exercise which will help you to get rid of the negative emotional effects that are associated with your experience.

Find a quiet place where you won't be disturbed for 15-20 minutes, lie down or sit in an upright position, close your eyes, take five deep breaths, attend to your breathing for 2-3 minutes, this will help your body and mind to relax, then imagine and relive that negative encounter, feel the outrage and frustration within yourself, let it be expressed in its total form, then imagine there is your guardian angel standing beside a table holding a glass of divine water in his hand. Imagine him telling you that, this divine water is actually not water, but is pure godly love, and is the cure to your negative emotions of anger and frustration. Then visualize him, handing you the cup of divine water and points you to drink it, and as you drink, imagine and feel the blissful and calming sensation that it gives you, it almost immediately enlightens you and makes you more peaceful. As the angel is about to leave he also tells you that when you go to washroom today, you will get rid of any residual of these negative feelings that may still be remaining in your body. He also directs you that whenever you feel the same way, you can come back here and drink from this holy water. Then thank him for his help and guidance, and also thank god for making all this possible, whenever you are ready, start counting from one to three, and at the count of three, open your eyes, feeling happy, healthy and energized. In order to make the exercise more effective, you can actually get a glass of water, put it on the table, and tell yourself that this glass of water contains the solution and cure to my anger and frustration and drink it, and as you drink it visualize it cleansing your system, and filling it with divine love, and also when you go to the washroom, tell yourself, that the negative emotions are leaving my system now. Since our subconscious mind works in a symbolic way, it will also match our efforts in a similar way, and will get rid of the negative emotional effects of that experience.

43. Make room for miracles to happen in your life

Once upon a time in America, lived a man who used to go dock hunting with his dog. This dog was a very smart and a fast and a perfect swimmer. Usually he and his dog would get on his boat, and get near the area that docks rest, and hide behind the bushes, until it was the proper time for him to shoot the docks, and the dog's responsibility was then to swim and bring the dead docks back to the boat. But an unusual thing happened one day, when he shot five docks, when he ordered the dog to go and get the docks, the dog ran on the water, without sinking or getting wet and picked up one of the docks and brought it back to the boat. The man thought maybe he had a "deja vu" or maybe, he was dreaming all this, so he slapped himself a couple of times, and put some water on his face, and ordered the dog again to go and get another one of the dead docks, to his outmost amazement the dock did the same thing, ran quickly on the water, without sinking. The dog brought all five docks to the boat, by simply running on water. He was so dumfounded and confused, he thought he is gonna go mad. He decided to go back home, even though it was too early in the day, because he was too distracted and even scared to stay there in the wild. He was not sure, if he should talk about this incident with anyone, because he was sure that no body would believe him, and they gonna make fun of him or worse think he is losing his mind. But his curiosity and astonishment overwhelmed him to talk about this incident, but he chose not to say any thing to his immediate family, because if he couldn't prove his claim that this dog can and did walk on the water, they will remember, and make fun of him for the rest of his life, so he called one of his friends who was the most cynical and pessimist person one can find, he was a kind of person that can discredit and criticize any thing, and can make a best event look like a horrible event, by finding some flaws and short comings in it.

The hunter chose him specifically, because he figured if this guy believes me and confirms my experience of witnessing the dog running on the water, then anyone on earth will be convinced about it. So he made an arrangement with him and asked him to come and try hunting with him next weekend. After resisting for a long time he agreed to go. The hunter decided not to say any thing about the dog's extraordinary ability, because he did not want his friend to have presupposition in his mind, he decided to just let it happen and then ask for his opinion after. So they arrived, and got on the boat and he shot few docks, and then ordered his dog to go and get them, and again similar to the last time the dog ran on the water surface and brought the docks. The hunter looked at his friend's face, waiting for his comment, or to witness his astonishment, but his friend seemed to be thinking very deeply with his right hand on his chin. After a long pause, he said let him try it again, and the dog successfully walked and ran on the water and brought all the docks back to the boat. His cynical friend didn't say a word, while they were driving back, and the hunter did not want to interrupt his friend's thought process, so they drove silently and without saying any single word, until they reached to his friends home, he pulled in the drive way, and said so what you think? His cynical friend put his right hand on his chin and in a very philosophical way said, well it is clear, your dog does not know how to swim and got out of the car.

The wisdom of the story is that so many times, great things and miracles are happening in our everyday lives, but since our mind does not believe in miracles, and is focused only on the negative and miserable outcomes that, even when some miraculous opportunities happen in our lives, we fail to notice and take advantage of them. We need to expand our horizons and widen our belief system, we should be expecting good things and miracles to happen in our lives. Because if we don't think and focus on some thing or the possibility of its happening, it won't happen in our lives. Because as we found out earlier the seed of anything or circumstances must be first planted within our subconscious mind, and be watered by our mental focus, and then and only then it can be manifested in the outside world. So we should believe that god loves us, and have provided for us lots more blessing than we have ever imagined before. We deserve to have lots of new blessing in our lives, because we are the beloved children of god.

Exercise: This week, keep this exercise in mind, and find a quiet place where you would not be disturbed for 15-20 minutes, close your eyes, take five deep breath and attend to your breathing for 2-3 minutes, that will help your mind to settle down and be free of thoughts. Then visualize yourself in your soul form that is in reality your true self, and also imagine that you are surrounded by an egg-shaped energy field. Imagine golden and white lights are emancipating from you. Then visualize a huge energy field in front of you, it is so big that it blocks your entire view, all you can see is this huge vibrant suiting energy field. Then imagine that, some pink, gold and white beams of energy, light and sounds are coming from that energy field toward you. It is god who agrees to grant any wish you may have in your life. Then simply say what you want from him, be as specific as you can. Then imagine that, god grants you a golden bubble, and asks you to put your wish in that golden bubble. He asks you to add and include the picture of what you want in that bubble, he asks you also to add your desired feelings into that visual image. Then he directs you to add sound and language to that holographic image in the golden bubble so it would include the words and sounds that you wish to experience. Then imagine that he is asking you to include the people that you love and want to have beside you when you get what you wish for. Next he will ask you to add any other little details like the location where you want your wish to happen, and the time and date of your wish. Then imagine he asks you to seal that golden bubble, which was opened in order for you to construct and put your wish inside of it.

Then imagine god grabs that golden bubble and fills that bubble with his love, blessing and energies, and see the bubble getting vibrant, and lively. You can see your goal happening by the command and love of god. Visualize that image vividly and remember the feeling of joy and victory which is taking over all over your body. You may feel an upsurge of divine energy, which comes directly from god. It is god's love, embrace it, and store it in your heart. It is yours to keep for the rest of your life.

Then imagine god is directing you to look at the bubble that he is releasing in the world of thought which is the fourth dimension, where there is no limitation of time or space. And he points to you and tells you that your wish has been granted, and you will receive it in your physical life when it is the proper time. Then you watch the golden bubble comes closer and closer to you, and enters your energy field. It is an inseparable part of you now, and you can believe and trust that it will happen in your physical life shortly. Finally thank god for all of his blessings and miracles and open your eyes.

You should do this exercises twice a day. And if you don't have too much time, you can do this exercise in five minutes when you have mastered its mental details. But for the beginnings take at least 15 minutes to preform this meditative exercise.

This exercise will create a clear inner image of your goal, which in turn will make its manifestation easier, quicker and more efficiently. Furthermore it is great way of prayer and communication with god. Buy doing this exercise you will raise your consciousness, and you will be protected from any negative force, because you have your focus on the love and support of god on a regular basis.

Remember we become what we mentally focus on, so focus on god and acquire godly wisdom, love and understanding. Choose to believe in the possibility of miracles, and infinite abundance of blessings in your life. This positive mental expectancy will attract and bring you whatever you want in life. But you must do this exercise routinely and with effortless concentration. Do not try to rush or push the process. Do not worry about when you will get it, simply focus on it during the exercise and act as if it had already happened, and then release its outcome to god's decision, and have full trust that it will be granted to you.

44. The power of persistence

Once upon a time in Arabia, lived a prophet and king called Ayubb, he was famous because of his patience in enduring all kind of defeats in the previous battles, and still being able to work hard to rebuild his army and become victorious at the end. His city had been falling to enemy hands many times, but he managed to organize and train new soldiers and recapture and liberate the town many times. He was a very popular king and also a respected and trusted spiritual prophet, and after many hard battles, now he and his city were enjoying a period of calm and peace for almost 10 years. But the peace was interrupted when the Babylon king decided to invade Arabia over a dispute over the control of a main river which was vital for both of these two strong empires. Ayubb tried hard to stop the commencement of war, and tried to resolve the problem with negotiation and other peaceful means, but he couldn't convince the king of Babylon who wanted the sole control over that vital and strategic river, and he also used it as an excuse to attack and invade Arabia, because he was certain about the result of the battle, because of his army's superiority, he was sure that they can capture Arabia in less than two weeks. Ayubb which had not paid too much attention to his army for the past few years, since they were not threatened by any foreign forces for a long time, was not prepared to fight with the enemy's huge and advanced army, however he decided to fight to the end, because he knew if Babylon king took over his empire they would kill many people and destroy all cultural and historical places. So in a very short period he managed to prepare 50,000 soldiers to defend the capital. Battle started few days after the Babylonian king's declaration of war, their army was progressing toward the city very rapidly and with little resistance from arabic forces. In two days, they reached to the gates of the Arabian capital, and Ayyub and his army faced the bloodiest battle in their whole history, almost all of them were slaughtered by the enemy's superior army, who burnt down the whole city as Ayubb had predicted. He was also injured seriously by a spear that landed on his shoulder, and he was stuck in the middle of fire when they set his palace on fire, he also got burnt seriously in the fire. But one of his guards managed to save him and provide a horse for him and let him escape the burning town, from a hidden and secret tunnel that they had made for emergency situations like this, but the guard could not accompany him, because he had to go back in town to find and save his family. So Ayubb managed to escape his town, and as he was getting away, he would stop every five minutes and look back at his hometown which was burning, and he was thinking that this time it is finished, there is no way to liberate and recapture the town this time, his divine empire and his people's cultural identity and freedom was destroyed forever, he galloped fast all day long, until he reached a hidden destroyed building which was perfectly guarded and hidden by thick trees. That was, where he was going to meet his friends and guards that promised to come in few days to take care of his wounds and burnt body and to also bring him some food and water, because he only had enough water and food for two days. As he reached the front of that half wrecked building, he was so tired and exhausted that he just dropped himself to the ground and passed out. When he woke up at the middle of the night he found out that the horse had taken off back to his town, he crawled inside the building and ate a little bit of bread and drank a little water and fell sleep again. The following day when he got up, he found out that he had lost lots of blood, and his wounds and his burnt skin were showing the early signs of infection, and he had only a little piece of bread a little water left, because the horse took the food and water with it. Then he started talking to himself, he said this time it is over god, I am going to die right here, because probably all of my guards and soldiers were killed, no body is coming to get me. Two more days passed and he was so weakened that he could barely keep his eyes open, and worms and mosquitos were all over his body, he felt that he is going to die very soon, so he was about to say his final prayers, that he noticed an ant that was carrying a large piece of food climbing a very tall pillar, the ant fell when he was about a quarter way up the pillar, but he noticed that the ant didn't even wait for a second, and he started his climb again, this time it made it halfway up the pillar and fell again. He became so amazed by this little ant's persistence, and he decided to try to stay alive and find out to see whether this ant would make it to the top or not. The ant kept climbing and falling, and to Ayubb's amazement who was counting this ant's number of trials, it made it to the top after 161 trials.

At that moment his inner voice spoke to him, and said you have to learn from this little animal, this little ant just showed you the power of faith and persistence, that when you strongly believe in yourself and your abilities, it will give you the stamina to act in a persistent way to get to your desired goal. And the lesson is never give up, until you succeed, regardless of how big your goal, and how far you are from that goal, because if you have faith in yourself, the stamina for your goal's achievement will be given to you. Ayyub felt a sudden upsurge of energy and hope throughout his whole being, he told himself that I am gonna survive and liberate my town, no matter how unlikely and impossible it may seem right now. Since he was so hungry and thirsty he needed immediate energy to be able to move, so he decided to eat the worms which provided him with both food and water, and it also stopped them from eating his flesh, and soon he gathered some stamina to walk to a nearby river, where he washed and cleaned his wounds to stop the infections. Then he met some people at the river who recognized him, and helped him to get healed completely in about two weeks. After that he started recruiting and training a large army, which after many bloody battles which lasted about five years, he could finally recapture his capital city and liberate his people from the oppressive rule of the invaders.And he was able to do all that because of the turning point experience he had at his dying moments, and he learned all that from an ant which showed him that by being persistence and taking action in a focused way he can overcome any obstacle.

The wisdom of the story is that we should never give up on our goals and projects in life. Usually whenever we start a new job, project or goal we face many obstacles and challenges. The reason is because our subconscious mind has not yet been able to visualize and adapt its inner image and mental strategies to help us achieve our goals. Because for any thing to happen in our life, it must first be seen and imagined as feasible. And in order to be so we need to create the desired image of the final outcome in our mind. Our subconscious mind cannot differentiate between a real physical outcome, or imagined final outcome. So if we continually visualize and focus on our goal as if it has happened already, our mind will record our desired goal, and will program us automatically to move toward those goals and corresponding circumstances. And once you focus mentally on a circumstance, your mind will create a holographic image and energy field of that thought form which has a very specific vibrational frequency and it will be sent out to the outer universe, and as result of law of attraction, which means similar energy fields, are attracted to similar energy fields, we will be drawn and driven toward the similar circumstances which correspond with our desired goals. Similarly Persistence causes us to become really focused on our goals, and being continually focused on something, will create the inner mental holographic image and reality of that goal, and then the law of attraction, will provide the necessary conditions and circumstances for the physical manifestation of your goal. Therefore one should continue his progress and work toward his goals, even though it may seem impossible or difficult on the surface.

Exercise: This week, keep this story in mind, and decide to be more focused and persistent about your goals. Make a list of your goals and priorities. And prioritize your goals in order of importance. Then make a scheduled plan to follow up and to reach your goals. The most important thing is to have a positive mental attitude that means to have and develop a mental positive expectancy that your goals have already happened in your mind, and then it only needs certain easy to follow procedures and actions to manifest those goals in the physical world. Reduce your plan down to simpler steps. Then take prompt action. Then check the results, if it did not help you the way you expected, be flexible to change your approach. Change and adjust your approaches until you reach your goal.

The most important thing is being mentally focused on the goal all the time, and act as if you already have that goal and then with that positive attitude and positive mental expectancy take action. And be persistent until you get what you want.

Using this simple formula will make it impossible for you to fail.

Remember the only difference between a successful and unsuccessful person is that the successful focus on his goal only, but the unsuccessful focus on the obstacles that are between him and his goal. And since whatever we mentally attune to and focus on, we tend to realize and experience in life, thus the successful will realize and reach his goals, and the unsuccessful will realize and meet many obstacles and challenges and will never reach his goals. So choose to focus on your goals only, and have a positive mental expectancy by imagining the final image of your goal as already accomplished and acting as if you already have reached the desired goal. And take persistent action until you get to your goal. And never give up.

Remember a winner never gives up, and a person who gives up never wins.

45. What qualifies or disqualifies someone to be a master?

Once upon a time in Persia, lived, two great Persian poets, one was Rumi, who had become inspired by his master Shams of Tabriz, who introduced the beauty and bless of spiritual and heavenly worlds. He thought Rumi to make a special meditative dance, which involved spinning in a harmonious way around himself and gradually increasing the speed, and simultaneously chanting the secret name of god "hoo." This and other meditative techniques that Shams thought Rumi, led him to write many master pieces in poetry and writings, which are still available. Rumi's whole life was dedicated to Shams, whom he met in a marketplace by accident. He spent many years training under Shams guidance. But one day when he went to Sham's resident which was near the town main marketplace or Bazaar, he could not find him, and when he investigated, one of the neighbors told Rumi that Shams has moved away probably to Baghdad to learn and teach in there. Baghdad was the academic center of the Islamic world at the time. After waiting for 10 days, Rumi could not resist and continue living without Shams, so he decided to go to Baghdad to find his master. But when he got there and after searching all universities and schools and temporary guest residences and mosques he could not find him. He decided to stay in Baghdad for a bit longer, in a hope to find Shams. But he did not want to waste his time. And being a dedicated student of spiritual studies, he saw it as a great opportunity to study in these various subjects in Baghdad religious and spiritual schools. He spent about four years in school, without any luck in finding Shams, but every single night he was meditating and feeling the presence of his master, He felt the burning fire of Shams' presence, it was as if he was seeing and feeling the presence of god in Shams pure soul. But Shams was instructing him in his dream and meditative state to stay in Baghdad for now, and had told him:" I will meet you again when the right time comes, for now continue your studies and start teaching." So he decided to teach in Baghdad various schools. He soon became very famous in Baghdad and throughout the Islamic world. Many would travel thousands of kilometers to see and learn from him. He combined his newly learned knowledge

with the spiritual techniques and exercises that Shams had taught him, and in this
way he had developed a practical style of teaching which was showing people how
to use and apply spiritual principles to solve and overcome their daily challenges
and problems.

After spending total of eight years in Baghdad, One night Shams came to his
dream and instructed him to move north and also told him, that he will meet
him there. Without hesitation, he packed his belongings and moved toward
north, until he reached to a place that was called koniya which is now located in
Turkey. Over there, his inner voice which was Sham's way of communicating
with him told him to stay and make a living and to get married. He soon found a
position as a teacher in Koniya spiritual school, and soon after he opened his own
mosque, where he dedicated most of his time training and teaching his devotees
the meditative dance that Shams has taught him earlier. And he met a beautiful
lady and got married. Many years passed by, when he was in his 50's one day the
door was knocked, to his outmost surprise and happiness, it was Shams. He
invited him in, and asked him to stay with him forever. Rumi offered him any
thing he wished. Shams agreed, and he started taking Rumi to various inner spiritual journeys in meditative states, Where Rumi felt so close and in touch with
god, and so detached from his physical life, that he totally stopped his teachings
and training. Some of his disciples and devotees that were dependent on the
school and they were making a living by working in that school, became upset
with this situation and decided to make a plan to get rid of Shams, or at least
make Rumi hate Shams. Shams, who was a very pious but care free man, was not
conventional at all, he would do whatever he wished, as long as it was godly in
nature it was fine. First they developed a rumor that Shams is after Rumi's young
Daughter who was 18 at the time. When Rumi found out, he calmly said it
would be my honor, and my daughter's blessing to have Shams as her husband.
And both Shams and the daughter agreed and they got married. The plotters felt
really defeated, because now the situation was even worse, and Rumi and Shams
had become inseparable, and now they were even living in the same house. They
knew that Rumi hated drinking, and that was the only thing that he would not
even consider acceptable, even if the drinker was Shams of Tabriz. So they developed a rumor that Shams is drinking wine regularly, and his teachings are not
divine and are even evil. After the rumor circulated in the town and became wide
spread, the plotters made a group of oldest, most religious and respected members of society to go and talk to Rumi, to convince him to stop following Shams,
and continue his own teachings in his school. They went to meet him, and

explained to him that Shams was an evil man, and he was a drinker, and if he did not stop associating with him, they will turn their back on Rumi, and they would announce to all the people, in monthly town gatherings to stop coming to you for learning. Rumi listened peacefully, then said I am certain that Shams who is a gift of god, is not a drinker, even if he was a drinker still doesn't change who he is and how he is. You are correct in believing that drinking intoxicates not only the body but also the mind and soul as well. And for an ordinary person whose heart is like a small pool, even one drop of wine will make his soul polluted. Similarly if you pour one drop of wine in a small pool, you can no longer wash your hands, legs before praying, or that water cannot be used for baptism. On the other hand a divine person like Shams' soul and heart is as big as an ocean, even if 1000 ships full of wine get drowned in the ocean, the ocean's water is still clean and can be used for pre-prayer hands wash, and baptism.

Shams' love for god and everyone else makes his heart so pure and vast that no wine can affect his state of consciousness and closeness to god. Therefore my answer is clear, please give up your plots and conspiracies, because nothing can pollute neither the purity of Shams love toward God, nor the purity of my love toward Shams.

The wisdom of the story is that the greatness of a person does not lie and depend on his social status. As we have seen, all the prophets have come in a time when there was a total lack of spiritual values in the society. They had acted in a totally unorthodox manner, and have rebelled against the existing structure. They always faced resistance and opposition from those who were benefitting from the status quo, and any change meant a loss for them. There have been many plots and conspiracies by the rulers of various times and places, to sabotage the spiritual movements. However as the history of many religions have demonstrated, the conspirators and enemies of truth have failed many times. They have failed because of the true faith, loyalty and love that many followers had toward their holy prophets. They loved and trusted them fully with their heart and soul, because they could sense and see the truth and love that were emancipating through him, they could see the god's attributes such as vibrancy and love glowing from his soul. True master, is a master that loves all, have a powerful presence, demonstrates respect for all, and is willing to serve all. This wisdom is very useful in our lives, because many often people may enter to our life, who are jealous of our loving relationships, and try to sabotage our lives by spreading lies and rumors. We all have experienced or heard about some other people's experience, of how their lives were ruined because of a foolish and invalid rumor. Therefore we should stand by the people we love, no matter what, and should not allow strangers who play no roles in our lives, to ruin our lives. If we hear any thing negative being said about our loved one, we should simply ignore it, because if we react then, we would plant the seed of doubt and suspicion in our heart, and it will drive us to become suspicious, angry and frustrated.

But instead decide to tell yourself, that I love her and I trust her hundred percent. And by the same token, we should also refrain from spreading rumors about other people. Even if you are certain that someone has done some thing wrong, you do not need to say it to everybody else. Remember what you send out, you will receive. If you talk behind some body's back, they will talk behind your back also.

Exercise: This week, keep this story in mind, and make a decision to be trustful and protective of your loved ones all the time, and do not allow anyone to talk behind their back. Even if you could not stop the spread of rumors, which is often impossible decide not to respond to those rumors, instead tell your self that I love her or him, and I am absolutely certain that she is a trust worthy person, and since I know her, better than anyone else, I should not listen to this invalid rumors. Also, by the same token decide to stop spreading rumors and talking behind other people's back. Be attentive and catch yourself, when you find yourself telling some thing negative about someone else, when you do so, immediately stop and either don't say any thing, or even better is if you say some thing positive thing about the person. Remember if you say, think and do good and positive things for others, they will also say good things about you, and you all win and benefit. And by the same token if you say bad and negative things behind others, they will also say negative things about you, and you both lose. So make a decision to say only good things about others, and if you don't find any good and positive thing to say about someone that you may, not particularly like, it is the wisest to remain quiet. In general, focus on goodness, send love and blessing for all, and as a result you will receive the same back in return but many fold. And never doubt your loved ones because of some body's comments and rumors. Doubt creates inner divisions and may damage and destroy your relationships. Instead choose to love, and trust whole heartedly, because what you send out, you receive, when you love and trust whole heartedly, your loved one will love and trust you whole heartedly also.

46. Can you rush enlightenment and self-development?

Once upon a time in China, lived a great master who was training twenty disciples to become the future senior monks in his Buddhist monastery. He had announced to them that there will be total of ten lessons to be learned. However he did not specifically tell them about how long each lesson will take. Since he had chosen the students carefully and attentively himself, all of them were highly intellectual and knowledgeable about Buddhist holy scriptures and discourses, and they all have been his disciples for more than five years. However, training to become a high-ranking monk was much different from regular mentor ships. He had also told them that he would pick only five people at the end of the lessons. And those are the five persons who have acquired the most of his teaching. All of them worked so hard and endured very difficult spiritual exercises such as fasting, meditation, not sleeping for many days and many hard physical works and activities, such as aimlessly cleaning the jungle and streets for days. About two long years passed, some of the students dropped out and gave up due to level of difficulty of the training, and when they successfully passed the ninth lesson, there were only six persons left. That meant one of them would be disqualified at the end and the other five would be appointed to the high council as senior monks.

One of those six young men, was the best student in terms of knowing the scripture and Buddhist theories and exercises, and he was certain that he will be the first one selected, so he was not worried at all about the final outcome, however he decided to study very hard, so when the time came for the selection, he would impress the master with his extensive and superior knowledge, so he would make sure he is easily selected. About six months passed and one day a messenger came to the tent where these six people were staying and meditating as part of their training, he informed them that the master was expecting them in the monastery to announce the final five people to become members of his high council.

They all got excited and were very happy to find out that the hard training days had finally come to an end.

They all went to the monastery the next morning, and they were directed to go to the main hall, where that master was going to greet them and announce the names of the five men. After a short wait, master arrived and greeted them, and as was the custom he would ask them to briefly explain their experience about those two and a half years of training, and then he would serve the tea himself and announce the chosen ones.

So he started asking the questions one by one, the first five people answered briefly about what they learned and how they felt about the exercises and lessons, and they were very happy and humble about being able to successfully finish and endure the hard training. The master served the tea for each one as they finished their statement.

Then it was the young man's turn to speak, so he started to explain that these exercises were too easy for him, and then he started giving long explanations and speeches from the Buddhist scripture that he had memorized and prepared in order to impress the master, however he went on and on, talking about his higher wisdom, knowledge and understanding of the Buddhist religion. Master gently got up as the student was still talking and picked up the pot of tea and a cup and approached him, The student realized that he must have talked too much and he stopped talking, Master handed him the cup, and started pouring the tea to his cup, but to every body's surprise the master did not stop pouring, he kept pouring the tea into his cup even after it was overflowing, he poured the whole pot of which most of the tea poured to the floor. The student said master I guess your mind is preoccupied! The master smiled and said no I am perfectly sane! You are the one who is too pre occupied and saturated with what you already know, you have focused too much on what you know, that your mind has no room for extra knowledge, because your mind is like this cup with a certain level of capacity, and the divine knowledge is like the tea in this pot even much greater. So when the mind is full, there is no use to add new knowledge because it will not be grasped, and it will bounce back and pour outside, just like the tea was overflown from your cup. Therefore, you are not ready to move to a higher level of consciousness yet. You need to become humble and consume and pass on your existing knowledge to others, and not to keep them all to yourself in order to gain precedence and advantages. Because love and knowledge are of those things that if you don't pass it on and don't share it with others it will become a heavy burden on your shoulders and heart.

The wisdom of the story is that we cannot push growth and spiritual unfold-ment by only our will power. Some times we get caught up in a competitive life style, where we try very hard to make it, and by the passage of time we master the art of finance by learning and applying certain business formulas that facilitates and quickens our success rate in making money. These formulas and strategies may include but not be limited to, goal setting, an action plan, which needs your dedication and will power to carry them through. This is how a road to material success is generally viewed. If you pay closer attention, you can see that we mostly rely on our conscious mind's will power, instead of god and our soul's creative power. We tend to search for an existing and working model or formula, and then we try to learn and copy it, and then put it into practice by our will power, and keep doing it persistently till we succeed. Of course this formula works for wide variety of situations and goals, however some times this type of attitude can negatively limit our lives and our selves. Our subconscious mind picks up this trend of thinking and behaving, and it will try to deal with all of life's situations in the same way. However the problem is some challenges and situations are not and cannot be resolved by will power alone. For example if your partner feels neglected, you cannot simply create a mental formula, such as taking her out every Wednesday and Saturday, buying her a gift every month, and flowers every week.

It may work for a while, but since relationships are usually spiritual in nature, since two souls connect together in many different levels which also includes mentally and physically. Therefore, just satisfying your partners' physical and social needs will not fully satisfy her as a soul. Doors of soul open inwardly, not outwardly. Our soul which is part of god, and therefore is omnipresent and omniscience is not fooled by gifts and dates that are not truly from heart. All the real things in life, like compassion, love, charity, wisdom, understanding, creativ-ity and enlightenment, have their source from our soul and god. And our soul is attuned to universal divine laws. In a spiritual realm, there is no rush toward any goal, because life is not about reaching anywhere, because for a spiritual being time and space has no meaning, because soul is boundless and infinite and has always been living and will always be existing, it has all the time ("What we call time") to experience any thing he wishes for which is necessary for its spiritual unfoldment. Only our mind is in a hurry, because it has too many illusional goals, and believes that it has limited time, because it views physical death as ter-mination of its experience. On the other hand our soul is not focused on reaching any where, but is concerned about its state of being. Closer we are to our core and real self which are our soul, and closer we are to god and his attributes such as happiness, beauty, love, wisdom, charity and creativity, better and more empowered we will feel. Therefore one should not rush the process of learning or reaching, because our soul knows and sees the big picture and is not limited like our mind which only seeks reward, outcomes and pleasure regardless of considering the spiritual and emotional values that may be lost in the process of rushing. Our soul puts us in many different situations, to give us the opportunity to learn more about ourselves and god, and this was the whole purpose of the creation and descending of souls to physical planes anyway, so we shouldn't miss out this opportunity to be self-realized and god realized, which is only possible, by walking on the road of life in a flowing and spontaneous manner, and with a peaceful, confident, satisfied and passionate heart. Of course I am not implying that the use of will power and purpose ful living should be abandoned all together, what is suggested here is that one should have his real passion, mission and purpose be focused on positive and heavenly attributes of god, and live according to the divine laws. We do not need to follow ant specific religion or philosophy to be liberated, because god loves us regardless. There has been many human beings who had lived on this planet and probably else where, before the emergence of any of today's religion, still god took care of, loved and protected all.

One should focus on a filling his life at this exact moment with peace, love, growth, wisdom, charity and creativity, regardless of one's life style, religion, race, age, gender, background. This focus will attune us to god consciousness, and will lead us to enlightenment and spiritual freedom, however we must not rush or hurry, we must just live in this moment. For our soul there is only nowness, future and past is nonexistent. So decide to be happy, healthy, peaceful, content and loving today, and you are happy every single day, then all of the days of your life will also be filled with joy, peace and happiness also.

Decide to be and live "now", instead of trying to become something later. Remember tomorrow never comes, there is only today and now. Past and future are products of the mind and unreal, but now is the reality, now is the only time that real change and unfoldment can happen, so stick to now and be happy.

Exercise: This week, keep this story in mind, and evaluate your goals in life. With this exercise, you want to focus on the situations where you some how are attaching too much importance to a material, academic, relationship or any other type of project. Write these goals and projects in your workbook, and go back in your memory line, and check to see how you felt in the beginning, when you initially set the goal? Next see how you feel about the goal right now? Most often when we decide to do some thing new, we get very excited and motivated, and we continually think about it, setting plans and also taking some actions toward that goal. But after a short while, all of a sudden a sense of helplessness, doubt and lack of interest and energy overwhelm us, and some type of inner voice and force is not letting us carry through the necessary actions that will get us to our goal. But what is that inner voice? Why is it sabotaging our success? The answer contains both mental and spiritual reasons. First let's focus on the mental part. Our subconscious mind's primary job is to protect us from getting hurt, and making our life easier. Our subconscious mind has created many established habits based on our previous belief systems, these habits are created and designed to facilitate our daily lives and to save us time. Our subconscious mind views sameness and habitual and automatic actions as easy and comfortable. And by the same token, any "change" to these habitual behavioral trends will be considered a threat to our comfort level and easiness of our life. Therefore our subconscious mind uses all its resources to stick to the status quo, and to avoid change. This often creates the inner self-talks and conflicts, where our conscious mind wants a positive change, but our subconscious mind wants to stick to the previous negative programs. Of course this is also true for the opposite, meaning if we consciously try to develop an unhealthy and negative habit, and our existing subconscious programs and habits are positive, again our subconscious mind won't allow or resist the change. Our subconscious mind is against the change whether positive or negative.

And our subconscious mind will resist if we push for change or if you try to add any new program, this is called the law of reversed effects, which means more the conscious effort, less the subconscious response. Our subconscious mind accepts suggestions only, when it is repeated in a calm and peaceful manner.

Of course there are ways to change our belief system, and as a result our behaviors and subconscious trends will also change, which has been discussed in details else where in this book. In this exercise we will focus on the spiritual aspect of growth and change.

If we evaluate the matter in spiritual perspective, we yet come to another point of view. Our soul which is part of god, and is omniscience and omnipresent.

Meaning our soul is aware of every thing that is happening in the universe, and it sees the whole picture or the bigger picture. Our mind is limited, because it has access only to a limited source of knowledge, which consists of its direct and indirect learning materials and experiences.

Our mind, is focused only to maximize pleasure and minimize pain, and is not necessarily concern about what is best for us. The problem arises from a wrong archetypal cultural belief. This belief has programed our mind to view our selves as a physical, emotional and mental being. Therefore our minds try its best to maximize our physical, emotional and mental pleasures and avoid any pain. Of course this is one of the positive functions of the mind, however the major component of our beings is missing the equation, and that is our soul. The correct belief system is that we are a multifaceted being, our soul is major and deciding factor, and we also have the other parts of us which are really created to help our soul's experiences and manifestation in this world, these are our emotional, physical, mental selves. If we consider ourselves as a multifaceted being, then when we are trying to set goals, we should make sure that the new goal is congruent with all of our aspects, if one part is neglected or dismissed then it will start to use its resources to sabotage our success in achieving the new goals. Each and every one of our different selves, needs energy to stay healthy and balanced, and they get their needed energy from our caring, attention, love and mental focus. This analogy will facilitate the understanding of this phenomenon. Imagine our collective self is a family, whenever they want to make a major decision, like moving to another city because of a job offer, there should be a family meeting, where all members examine and voice their concerns and needs. Usually even though the parents make the final decisions, however if they fail to successfully and emotionally satisfy and convince their teenage children, who may have emotional bonds with their existing class mates and friends, it will cause major problems later. For instance the children, may become rebels, and not study, or become depressed or violent. As we can see no part should be neglected, if we want to have a harmonious and positive results. Similarly when we are setting a goal, whether it is studying a new subject, moving to another city or country, marriage, or any other changes in our lifestyle settings we need to consult with all parts of our being, and to make sure the new change is mutually and collectively beneficial and satisfactory for all aspects of our being. For instance if a new setting like moving to another country, means more money, but you may lose your loving relationship, or lose your social status and recognition, friends and family, even though mentally and financially this move feels right and attractive, however when we consider the ecology or the bigger picture of the situation, we can see that making the decision is not that easy. We need to add and accommodate either our other aspects and needs into this new plan, or we should not go and wait for, another, more proper opportunity. Therefore spiritually speaking, that is the reason why sometimes our goals that we have mentally set based on our limited resources, get stuck or is not accomplished. Even though we may have felt frustrated or sad that why a certain plan of you failed, just to find out later that it was a blessing, that it didn't happen, because you got to somewhere much better in life.

47. If you just give up lying, you will be transformed to a noble man

Once upon a time in Persia lived a young man who was addicted to gambling. In order to support his uncontrollable and horrible habit of gambling he had also became a thief and burglar, because as we all know that gamblers lose most of the time to the hosting dealers. And being a married man, he was forced to lie to his wife about his personal life and the way that he was making money, and he used to tell her that he is a merchant involved in export and export with foreign merchants mainly the Greeks. So his one destructive habit of gambling had transformed him to an unemployed thief and a big liar. One day he stole a big sum of money, from a rich man's jewelry store, so that night he decided to gamble all of that money, with the hope of doubling that money. So that night he dressed up pretty elegantly and being an expert in lying, he introduced himself as the prince, because he knew they would credit the prince as much as he desired, just in case if he lost. He figured he would continue playing until he wins, he figured it was a win-win situation, and there was no way for him to lose, and since he had lots of gold coins and money which he had stolen from the jewelry store they would not become suspicious of him lying, so they would credit him if he lost all his money. He once again lost all his money, and he acted as if he wants to get up and leave, and as he had predicted, the owner of the gambling place approached him and offered him to stay and continue and he said that he would credit him as much as he wanted, since he was the prince. He agreed with a serious look on his face, but he was laughing in his heart that he was successful to fool them and his plan had worked. But it was not his day, he lost three times more than what he had stolen, and it was the time to close the gambling place. The owner told him that, he will come with him to the palace so he can collect his money, but the young man told him that it is too late, you can come tomorrow, because my father may get upset with you and punish you, since he doesn't want any visitor's at midnight. But the owner said your father is a good friend of mine, and he would even be happy to

174

meet me, since I have not seen him for about three years. The young man even though was terrified inside, because probably the king would have him killed the same night if he found out that somebody was acting as his son and successor, and endangering the royal's popularity and legitimacy. But he kept his exposure and said, sure let's go, he figured he can find a way to escape before they arrived to the palace.

However he could not even attempt to escape, because he was accompanied by the owner and two of his humongous body guards, and they made him sit between those two body guards, and when he tried to sit at the corner in order to escape, the owner told him no, because he was responsible for the prince's safety and if any thing happened to him, his father would kill all of his family. So they got to the palace, and the messenger told the king that his son who is usually residing in a far province of Persia, is in the palace now, making an unexpected visit. So the king got prepared and came to the main hall to see his son that he had missed a lot, but when he got there, he saw a total stranger with a royal suit which matched the exact suit of his royalty. He asked for explanation, the owner of the gambling place talked to the king about what happened that night, the king who was a very wise man decided not to say any thing to the owner of the gambling place, he acted as if the man was really his son and embraced him and welcomed him back home, he did that because he didn't want the whole town to know, how easy it is to temper with the royal family and the king, and he decided to deal with this young man after the owner of the gambling place leaves. So the king asked the owner, how much do we owe you now? He stated the amount, and the king ordered his treasurer to pay him in full, plus a generous reward for his extra services to the prince. By this time the young man thought he was really losing his mind, or maybe he was dreaming all this. Shortly after the owner received his money, he asked permission to leave, and left happily. At this moment the young man started to feel the chill in his spine, but he decided for the first time and probably the last time to tell the truth.

When everybody else had left the hall, the king showed his frustration and concern with this young man, and told him how dare, could you impersonate my beloved son, who is a respected prince that one day would become the next king of the great Persian empire? The young man started telling his story, he said I am a compulsive gambler, I am a thief and I am a liar, and I deserve to be punished. As a matter of fact it is the first time in my life that I have told the truth. My life is full of problems, I don't mine being killed tonight, because there is no hope for me to make an honest, healthy living because no body will hire me with my previous terrible reputation, and one day or another I will eventually be caught and punished. I am at least happy that my sufferings will come to an end by the king. This time he was really talking from the heart and was crying like a little child. King who was a very wise, kind and generous man, offered him a last chance for change. But the young man said no thanks, because no one will hire me, so I have to steal to survive and gamble, because there is no way on earth that I would give up gambling. The king smiled and said it is your lucky day, I will hire you as my personal guard, and your duty will be to guard the palace, specially the safe, I will even give you the special key to the safe. But in return for all this, I want you to give up at least one of your bad habits of gambling, stealing or lying. He told the king that he had no doubt in his mind that he could not quit gambling, and in order to continue gambling he had to steal if he ran out of money so honestly speaking he couldn't give up stealing neither. So he asked the king to forget about the job offer and kill him, because there was no way for him to be fixed. But the king said what about lying, can you at least give up lying. The young man said sure that is the easiest. So they agreed and the young man was hired as a personal guard of the king and the palace. King became found of this young man and they became very good friends. The young man would inform the king about every little things that had happened in the palace, since he was obliged by his promise not to lie to anyone. Every thing was going great and even though he was still gambling and stealing outside of the palace, his life had improved a lot, until one day again, he decided to go back to the same gambling place that he went years ago and asked for credit, he figured he can ask for credit again and try his chance again. He went to the place and asked for credit, the owner recognized him and gave him a lot of credit, and again he lost all of that. This time the owner trusted him, when he said let me go to the palace and bring you the money, since he had seen it with his own eyes that he is really the prince so he let him go.

As he was going back to the palace, he decided to take twenty gold coins, from the safe. He figured that with those gods, he could pay back his debt, and also to try his chance again, and try to, win what he has lost, so he could put the coins back to the safe the same night, so the king would not even find out about it. Late that night, after he waited for everyone to go to sleep, he used his keys and opened the safe. Right at that moment, the king who hadn't been able to sleep that night, witnessed what was happening, but he decided to not intervene and simply watched him from a distance. The young man took twenty gold coins and without seeing the king, he left the palace, to go to the gambling place with a hope to win his money back. The king, who was very upset and disappointed with this young man whom he really liked and trusted, and since he could not sleep, he continued to walk around the palace. Then again, he noticed that his treasurer who also had the keys to the safe, came and opened the safe. He started counting the coins, and when he realized that twenty coins are missing, he decided to take all of the coins which were total of 5000 golden coins. He figured, that he will put the blame on the young guard who also had the keys. Again the king decided not to intervene, and wait till tomorrow to resolve the problem. Mean while the young man paid his debt to the gambler that night, and won back his money. So he came back to the palace, and put the golden coins back to the safe, and went to sleep, without noticing that all of the golden coins are stolen.

The next day, the king asked both the young man and the treasurer to appear in his private room. Then he acted as if he does not know what had happened, and told them that, the safe was robbed last night. Which one of you, is responsible for this robbery? The treasurer started, by saying that last night when he came to check the safe, he saw the young guard emptying and stealing all of the golden coins, but since it was to late, and I was alone I decided, not to intervene and let you know and have him arrested today. Next the king asked the young man to respond to these accusations. The young man said, our majesty, I have promised you that I will never lie again, therefore I will tell you the truth. Last night, after I lost my money in the gambling place, I came back to the palace and took twenty golden coins in a hope to win my money back. I just borrowed the coins, only to put them back the same night. My intention was never to steal them, and to take off. Because if it was so, then I would take all of the coins, and would never come back to the palace. Furthermore, I put the twenty coins back to the safe, early this morning. But I can assure you that, I did not take all of the coins. The king, thanked the young man for his honesty, and then told them that he had actually witnessed what really happened last night. Then he ordered to his guards to arrest the treasurer for his lying and stealing. And he decided to appoint this young man, as the new treasurer. This meant that now, his salary was ten times more than before. This position, not only changed his financial situation and social status, it also made him stronger within. As he felt richer and more trusted, respected and loved by the king, he dropped the habit of gambling and stealing, altogether. Because he no longer felt insecure financially, so he wasn't feeling the need to gamble in order to provide a better life for his family. And since he quitted gambling, automatically his habit of stealing was also eliminated. As a result of simply giving up lying, his whole life was transformed, and became one of the most noble and righteous man in the whole kingdom.

The wisdom of the story is that usually any bad habit and deed will lead to other similar and bad and immoral behaviors and actions. In a way one negative thought, emotions or actions will have a domino effect on our life, by forming a trend and behavioral pattern which tends to be developed subconsciously, and if do not consciously decide to stop the bad and negative thoughts, words and actions they will take root in our subconscious mind and becomes a permanent imprint in our mind's memory. And Lying is the mother of all evils. Because a liar is capable of any act. Because a person who does not believe and respect the truth, his subconscious mind develops a belief and as a result a pattern that not doing the right thing is okay and acceptable, in regard to any situation in life, because it figures a lie can cover that bad action and make the person to get away without facing any punishment. Therefore if we manage to stop lying and being truthful all the time, all of our other negative behavioral trends will also be eliminated.

Exercise: This week, keep this story in mind, and be attentive to catch yourself whenever you are being untruthful, or exaggerating. Be honest to yourself. All most all human beings lie, unfortunately it has become a social and global trend. And most people believe that their lies are okay and justified, because it was beneficial for the listener, and the truth would hurt him. If you are faced with a similar situation, if you are certain that you may really cause harm to the person by telling the truth, instead of lying be silent and don't say anything.

Yet most people believe their lies are small lies, and small lies are okay, or some believe they lie to joke around with their friends. However it is not okay to lie, even if you believe your lie is meant as a joke.

Because our subconscious mind operates like an automatic and nonjudgmental machines like computers, if it records that lying is funny and okay with you, it will make it a mental habit and program to lie all the time, because it believes lying makes you and others happier. Therefore this week decide to stop lying, however little it may seem consciously, because to our subconscious mind a lie is a lie regardless of its circumstance, nature or magnitude. Write every time you catch yourself when you attempt saying any thing untruthful, and write the correct and truth answer in front of the lie that you wanted to talk about. Then ask yourself, why should I feel the need to lie? What are my benefits when I lie? What is the possible harming if I tell the truth? When we answer these question we realize that there are in most cases no dangers or harm in telling the truth, and there are no benefits in lying. Usually the reason we lie is not logical in nature, but it is emotional. It is usually a trend picked up from the childhood. The children who were punished repeatedly when they did some thing wrong, somewhere in time they develop a mental strategy not say the truth if they did some thing wrong, like breaking the dishes on the table with a ball. They found out that by saying something like, oh mom I am sorry I was trying to clean up the table and wash the dishes to help you out, but I accidentally dropped the dishes and broke them. Usually in these cases the punishment was much softer or even zero. That is when the child learned to lie, in order to avoid getting hurt. Later in life this becomes a subconscious and automatic mental strategy, whenever the going gets tough, and there is a possibility of loss and punishment the adult lies automatically and effortlessly.

As we learned earlier a subconscious program remains active, until it is replaced by another program. So from this week on, decide to catch, record and eventually stop lying forever. Your whole life will be harmonized and you will develop an inner peace that you have never thought as possible.

48. What makes a person successful?

Once upon a time in London, a young lawyer who was a new graduate was getting prepared for his first day at his new job, which was in a very large pharmaceutical company. He was so nervous and excited, because his employment was not guaranteed yet. He was to go through a probation period of three months, in which if his performance was acceptable he would only then get hired. He had heard and read so many things about how becoming successful in your first day of the job. And some how all that knowledge was making him more worried than confident. Because there were so many aspects and details that he had to consider and keep in mind. For example importance of knowledge, look and proper uses of legal and professional language. That evening as he was going over his final notes that he had prepared for his initial day of work, the phone rang, it was his uncle asking him if he wanted to join him for dinner. His uncle lived in another town, and he was visiting London for some important business engagement. He happily accepted his offer, he figured it will be good to get out of the house and focus his mind on some thing other than his job. He also thought maybe god has sent his uncle who is a very successful business man and Harvard graduate to give him some powerful insights that will help him for his first day at the job. So they met that night, and when the uncle asked him about his job, he explained his dilemma and confusion. His uncle smiled and said don't worry I have the answer for your question, because I faced the exact same situation when I was graduated and wanted to join a firm. Then he started telling his story to his young nephew. "When I went for my first day at the job, I was supposed to join the advising committee which had senior staff meeting in one of those humongous conference rooms, in which 25 old, serious and professional members of that company were sitting at the table and reviewing their notes for that meeting. What a day to start your job! Any ways as I was entering, I decided to go with my gut feelings, and since the immediate attentions were not on me, I could move almost freely in the room before the meeting was to start. So first my heart told me to find a young, good looking and sharply dressed person and sit beside him, because I figured a person who is young, energetic and well dressed is a kind of person who takes care of his business as well as he is taking care of himself. As we all sat down, the first session of the meeting started and as the meeting progressed, I noticed that a gentleman in the other side of the table is very knowledgeable and he talks and presents his arguments in a very professional and confident manner. And I decided to sit beside that man and learn some thing from him, because the first sharply dressed man did not even say a word. The second session started, and as it progressed the meeting reached to a point that a decision had to be made, then I noticed that a very old man who was very quiet up to that point, announced the best final option which was finally decided by the board of directors. As the day ended, I wish I would sit beside that old man and got acquainted with him, so I could learn and benefit from his amazing wisdom.

That night as I was thinking about my first day at work, suddenly an inner voice told me that a successful person is a combination of all those three people that you met today, meaning you should pay attention to your physical appearance, you should also do your research and become an expert in your profession, and you should also empower yourself internally and spiritually to gain inner wisdom and confidence so you can make brave and wise decisions when they are called for." Saying that the uncle finished his story, and told his young nephew that the wisdom of his story is that one should develop and grow multi dimensionally and in a harmonious way, in order to be successful. That means you should be physically, emotionally, socially, professionally, mentally and spiritually appealing and competent, if you want to be successful in not only your job but life in general.

The wisdom of the story is that we should understand that in order to be successful in any aspects and fields in life we need to grow multi dimensionally in all of our various aspects. If we compare ourselves to a house, each room represents one aspect of our being. For instance our financial aspect is one room, our physical aspect is one room, our emotional and relationship aspect is one room, our intellectual aspect is one room, our social self is one room and our spiritual aspect is another room, and so on. If we focus only on one aspect of ourselves and neglect and ignore the other aspects, it is like cleaning only one room every day, and not cleaning the other rooms. For sure the other rooms will get dirty and uncomfortable. And These rooms will not be cleaned by themselves, they need to be cared for and cleaned by us. This looks so obvious, but we usually fail to comprehend and apply this fact. We usually sacrifice other aspects to improve one particular aspect of our life based on our mental priorities and goals of that time.

For example if we need money, we may focus a hundred percent of our attention on working. And by over working our financial status and situation do change, however our other aspects such as health are negatively affected, because we have not dedicated any time and energy to exercise and to follow a healthy diet, similarly our relationships and love life will be negatively affected, if we ignore or neglect it. All of our aspects need attention and maintenance to remain clean and vibrant. But we mistakenly believe that since we do better than most people in one aspect of our lives, lets say finance, then we are all set and we can be justified to neglect our other aspects. Then we try to buy our way through for a while, for example we don't put enough time and caring in our relationship and try to fix it by buying expensive gifts, we don't put time to exercise but we buy the most expensive exercise machines to fix our problem but we never actually do it because we don't have time and working and making money is more important than exercise or spending some time with loved ones. Our constant focus on one aspect of our lives, and attaching too much importance to it, programs our sub-conscious mind to view all other aspects as unimportant, and therefore it is okay to neglect them. Remember nothing is fixed, until you decide to fix it.

So decide to view yourself as what you truly are, which is a multifaceted being and live a harmonious and balanced life style, which serves and satisfies all of your different aspects and needs. It should include all your physical, emotional, social, intellectual, professional, financial and spiritual aspects. Because if any aspect of your being is not balanced, it will cause imbalances in all different areas. You are a soul, living in a multiple room house, and for your soul to be balanced, you need to go to every room on daily basis, and if any of these rooms are dirty, imbalanced, frustrated, sad and un cared for, your soul will suffer. So decide to find out how many rooms your soul's house, which is actually reflecting the different aspects, of your life has, and take care of them.

Exercise: This week, keep this story in mind and make a descriptive list of your different aspects in your work book. It should include and cover all of your aspects, like your physical health, emotional and relationship, financial, intellectual, social and spiritual aspect. Feel free to add any aspects of your life that you feel should be accounted for. Then make an honest assessment of the quality and shape of each aspect at the present moment. Write down and record any short comings that you find in each and every aspect of your life, which has been caused by your lack of attention and care to it. Once you have done that, make a practical plan to balance and rejuvenate the unattended and weak aspects. For example if you find yourself over weight and unfit, make a plan to be more attentive to your physical habit, change them to more active one, include a healthy diet and exercise plan in your life. And get help if you need support in any of your needs. Keep a daily and weekly performance chart in your workbook, and record every single detail. This way you can monitor your success and break through, and this will give you the motivation and mental stamina to continue with your plan.

Continue until you have reached your desired level, which is a totally harmonious and balanced level.

You may also want to do this mental and spiritual exercise to keep yourself motivated and energized during and through your plans. Find a quiet place where you would not be disturbed for 15-20 minutes, lie down or sit in an upright position, take five deep breaths, and attend to your breathing for 2-3 minutes that allows your mind and body to relax, then visualize your self as a soul with a vibrant white and golden energy field around it, then imagine your life and reality is appearing to you as a very large house or temple, and each one of the rooms has a sign on it, indicating one aspect of your life. Imagine walking into each room and visualize it as you wanted to be, for example if you are entering your relationship room see it as if it is the exact same way you wish it to be. You see your lover is happily waiting for you, giving you flowers and her lovely smile, she embraces you and tells you I love you with all my heart, and you see yourself also sending her love and giving her flowers, while you are in the room you make a promise to yourself to visit this room often, and make sure it is cared for and it is always full of love and happiness. Bless the room by sending your love and divine energy and leave that room. Similarly you need to visit every different room, financial, physical, intellectual and spiritual, and in the same way make a promise to your self that you would continually and on a regular basis would visit each and every room and make sure every thing is in order and is balanced. Send your love and blessing to all of your rooms which actually represent different aspects of you. Each of these rooms has a life of their own, and if they are not taken care of, they will be imbalanced, and as a result, our whole being will be irritated and imbalanced.

As you finish your tour, tell yourself that you will come back to every room in an equal and balanced way, and will take care of it and send your love and attention to all of them. This way you are blessing your life, by being present in all of its aspects in a harmonious and balanced way. And then on the count of three open your eyes feeling energized, happy and motivated to take the necessary steps to balance your life.

Remember our life has many different aspects, and if we want to live a healthy, happy and fruitful life we need to take care of all these aspects, by being attentive to them and taking care of each and every one of them.

49. How Important is our social status in spiritual terms?

Once upon time in Canada, at the beginning of a first year physics class in the university, a Professor who was not only very knowledgeable in the subject of physics, he was also a very spiritual and wise man. He was famous in the way he was teaching physics, of which he was combining it with different spiritual philosophies to make it very attractive and memorable. On the first day of the class, he started by asking for volunteers to tell their intentions and motives in attending the university. One of the students raised his hand and volunteered. The professor asked him to give his reasons and motives for studying. The student said, I want to study and become a member of the intellectual, elite and rich part of the society. I want to enjoy life, and being able to do and to buy whatever I or my loved ones wish for. The professor said very well and thanked him for his comments.

He then without asking anyone else, said let's now watch a short movie, which is my favorite one. Then we will continue by asking the other volunteers to respond if they still wish to do so. Then shortly after he turned off the classroom's lights and started the movie projector. The movie showed a very handsome and young man in his early 30's driving a very expensive brand new Mercedes Benz convertible, well dressed in a $3000 suit with fancy ray ban glasses on his eyes. At this point a question flashes on the screen asking "Is this man successful and significant?" At this point the professor stopped the movie and asked the students to answer, And everybody unanimously said yes of course he is. Then he started the movie again, the young rich man was introduced as a brain surgeon living in Beverly hills, California and after a short while he arrived to his gated mansion, the house looked like a castle, he would park his car, and walk to his yard where there is a beautiful pool and five beautiful and young ladies are waiting for him, as he goes to take a shower. The professor stops the movie again and asks the students again, Is he significant and successful? Everybody would say oh, yes. Then the professor allows the movie to run again, Now he returns to the pool side and one of the ladies bring him a cold icy lemonade and another one was rubbing his

shoulders, at this point the movie stops and becomes like a motionless picture
and question is asked again, Is he significant? Every on said yes. Then the view
and angle are changed, and he is shown from 50 meters above his house, Now all
of his beautiful house, pool and vast yard is clearly visible, Again the movie
becomes motionless and question is asked, Is he still significant? Everybody says
yes, Next the camera moves 200 meters up, and the house is still visible, but the
man is not, the question is asked again, Is he still significant? At this point some
students started mumbling and saying well almost, I think. Then the camera was
moved 1000 meters up, the city was visible but his house wasn't, let alone himself!, The question was asked again, Is he still significant? Most of the students
said not really.

Then the camera was moved 10,000 meters above his house, then all of the
American continent looked as small as a dot. Then the camera was moved to
outer space, where the earth looked as big as a golf ball, and the same question
was asked again, Is he still significant? Everybody said with loud and affirmative
voice, no, not at all.

Then the camera would go even further and higher, so our solar system looks
as big as a small tiny dot. Then the same question is asked, Is he important? Then
the camera moves even further, so the milky way galaxy which is the galaxy that
we are in, looks like a dot, question is asked again, Is he still significant?, At this
point all students were confused and dumfounded and simply shook their hand
as sign of a no. And finally the camera moves so high that nothing can be seen
anymore. And the question is asked for the last time, Is he significant and successful? At this point the professor turns on the light, and explains to the students
that if you want and consider success only in terms of materialism, it will boost
your ego only. The most successful of you would, become only as significant of
this gentleman in the movie, however if we growth multi dimensionally, and specially spiritually we can be as significant of the whole universe. Because a person
who, is not limited to his ego, has access to the whole universe. One who develops sense of love, charity, wisdom, understanding and cooperation will have
access to all of god's blessing, love and protection.

The wisdom of the story is that we should always remember that we are a
divine being. The correct spiritual belief should be that we are all equal, no matter how differently socially, financially, and physically we are, we all have a soul
which is our divine self and is a part of god. The truth is that we are all interconnected by invisible webs of divine energies consisted of light and sound. That
mean we are a building block of the whole, not separate from the whole. Our

wrong belief which is created by western orthodox religions is that we are a separate entity from god. This wrong and limited belief causes us to see ourselves separate from each other and god. And as a result of this, we develop the illusional idea of "I ness," which creates separation and competition among us. This creates the belief that "I am better and more significant than anyone else," and this false beliefs, causes us to be in constant battles and competitions. Almost all of the world's problems, conflicts and wars are stemmed and are caused by this wrong belief. If everyone believes he is the best, and since he is the best, everybody else should follow what he likes, or believes to be a right way of living, then conflict is eminent. Since all of us have developed different values, beliefs and priorities based on our environment, parents, teachers and nationality, if we all think unidimensionally that our way is the best way and should be the only way, then war and disaster will be the only outcome. That is how millions of people have lost their lives due to this single wrong spiritual belief that "I am better than others, So my way of thinking and living is the best way and everyone else should follow it." This belief has created our egoistic or selfish self, which views ourselves as a separate entity which has to be competitive, aggressive, dictator and selfish. But the correct belief is that we are all the same in essence. And our true essence is soul. We just look different, because we each represent a different aspect of the total reality or god. This example will clarify this principal: If we put an elephant in a dark room, and then ask five people to enter the room and by only using their sense of touch to describe to us what is in the room. They should be allowed to touch any thing only once and then exit the room. So the first person who touches the elephant's leg, exits the room and reports as thinking there is a pillar in that room, the second may touch the elephant's ivory, and when he got out of the room reports that there is a baseball batt hanging from the wall. The third person touches the ears, and reports as thinking there are curtains or sheets in the room. The fourth person touches the body and believes that he has touched a large stone. And the last person touches the elephants tail, and thinks there is a rope hanging from the wall. You see, the same object caused five people to imagine it as some thing totally different, because they were not equipped with the necessary tool, which was vision to see the truth. Similarly due to our limited beliefs, habits and way of thinking we are usually blinded to this simple universal truth, that we are all the same in essence, only our experiences vary. Eastern religions like Hinduism and Buddhism had realized that, and call this truth "Unity in diversity." Because if we see ourselves as separate entity, then no matter how successful and big our egoistic self is, we are still a very small dot in relation to the total existence. But if we see ourselves as a part of the whole and from the whole,

then we become as powerful and big as the whole. As the Persian poet Shah
Nematollah has put it beautifully: if a person walks alone in life is only a drop,
but if he walks with god then he is an ocean. So decide to choose to be an ocean
instead of a drop.

Exercise: This week keep this story in mind, and decide that you will change
this wrong archetypal belief that you are a separate entity from others and god,
and also to change the subconscious belief that you are better than anyone else.
Decide to replace those beliefs with the positive and correct ones. Which are," I
am an equal part of the whole, and I am as good as anyone else. I love the whole
universe, including all people, animals, plants and even inanimate objects,
because every thing is created by god and are from god. And since I am part of
the whole which is god, then every thing in this existence is interconnected.
"Decide to respect every body's uniqueness, as you expect them to respect yours.
Love and respect others as you expect them to do the same thing. Do not push or
force your beliefs and values on others, just the way you don't want others to
push you with theirs. You can also do this mental and spiritual exercise to make it
easier to feel and see the true nature of reality which is, we are all interconnected
by the invisible web of light and sound and love.

Find a quiet place where you would not be disturbed for 15-20 minutes, lie
down on your back, close your eyes, take five deep breaths, attend to your breathing for 2-3 minutes, this will allow your mind and body to relax.

Put your attention on the gravity that is pulling your body downward toward
the ground, feel your arms and legs and gradually your whole body that relaxes
and becomes heavy. As the gravity is pulling your body downward, imagine that
your consciousness and soul move upward, until you can see your body lying
down on the floor. Tell yourself that your body is perfectly safe and it is protected
by god's divine shield and no thing will happen to it, next imagine and visualize
yourself as a soul surrounded by a vibrant white and golden energy field. Then
visualize your loved ones and all other people, animals, plants, planets, stars, galaxies and every thing else in existence in a similar energy field. Then imagine that
there are infinite number of beautiful and colorful webs, which are connecting
every thing together in a harmonious and happy way. Imagine as you become
aware of each different wave that is coming toward your energy field, you feel
livelier and happier, then imagine more and more things are entering into your
soul's energy field, and simultaneously lot of love and energy is sent from your
soul to the rest of the universe. Then visualize that this trade of love and energy
empowers, enriches your life. More you send love and energy, more you receive,

and stronger and happier you become. Love and energy follow the universal rule which is no love or energy should be kept solely for personal use, it has to be shared and traded in a regular basis, otherwise it will not be recharged and it will darken the energy field and will be even harmful to its holder. Similarly when the water does not move, and remains stagnant, once fresh waters turn into a swamp, on the other hand a moving and sharing water like a river remains fresh and full of life.

So it is logical to decide to choose to be like a river, instead of a swamp. As you experience the vibrancy and love which is resulting because of the collective networking of consciousness and love, tell yourself that you chose to attune to this new way of looking at reality, and you can access this state any time you say the term universal love, or unity in diversity, or any other terms you like. This makes it easier for your subconscious mind, to help you remember and get back to this state of consciousness. Then send love to all, and receive it back and at the count of three, open your eyes feeling empowered, happy, healthy and full of love.

50. The joy of making others happy

Once upon a time in America, two men both seriously ill, occupied the same hospital room. One man was allowed to sit up in his bed for an hour each afternoon to help drain the fluid from his lungs. His bed was next to the room's only window. The other man had to spend all his time flat on his back and could not move. The men talked for hours every day. They spoke of their wives and families, their homes, their jobs, their involvement in the military service, and where they had been on their vacations. Every afternoon when the man in the bed by the window could sit up, he would pass the time by describing to his room mate all the things he could see outside the window. The man in the other bed began to live for those one-hour periods where his world would be broadened and enlivened by all the activity and color of the world outside. The window overlooked a park with a lovely lake. Ducks and swans played on the water while children sailed their model boats. Every color and a fine view of the city skyline could be seen in the distance. As the man by the window described all this in exquisite detail, the man on the other side would close his eyes and imagine the picturesque scene. One warm afternoon the man by the window described a parade passing by. Although the other man could not hear the band, he could see it. In his mind's eye as the gentleman by the window portrayed it beautifully with descriptive and colorful words. Days and weeks passed. One morning, the day nurse arrived to bring water for their baths, only to find out the lifeless body of the man by the window, who had died peacefully in his sleep. She was saddened and called the hospital attendants to take the body away. As soon as it seemed appropriate, the other man asked if he could be moved to the bed next to the window. The nurse was happy to make the switch, and after making sure he was comfortable, she left him alone. Slowly, painfully, he propped himself up on the elbow to take his first look at the real world outside after almost three months. He strained to slowly turn to look out the window beside the bed. It faced a blanked wall!. The man asked the nurse what could have compelled his deceased room mate to describe such wonderful things outside this window, whereas there is nothing but a blank wall. The nurse responded that the man was blind and could not have seen the wall or any thing else.

Perhaps he just wanted to encourage you and make your days happier and more joyful.

The wisdom of the story is that, there is a tremendous happiness in making others happy, despite our own situations. If we share our happiness with others, then our happiness is doubled. If you want to feel rich and happy, just count all the things that already have and is given to you by god for free, that money can't buy.

Remember today is a gift that is why it is called "present." Therefore we should appreciate and be thankful to god for all the blessings that he has provided us with, and share our gifts, blessings and happiness whenever we can. Some times a simple gift, a word of encouragement or simply a smile can transform and empower another person's life. Therefore, give the gift of happiness and love to others freely without expecting any thing in return. Do not worry, god will return your rewards for your good deeds and intentions in multiple folds. As we stated before what we send out to others, we get back from the universe. So send love and happiness to all the people you meet, and watch your life transform to a more peaceful, harmonious and happier life.

Exercise: This week, keep this story in mind, and make a decision to encourage, support and make every person that you meet in your life happy. Remember gifts should not be limited to material gifts and money, it can be a smile, a verbal encouragement, or giving your time to help the person in need physically, emotionally, mentally and spiritually. Because in most of the times just being there for someone who is going through tough emotional times, such as loss of a family member, or a break up in the relationship, will be enough to help them to get passed by these challenging times. Secondly keep in mind that you are offering your services, companionship and support freely and without any expectation of rewards. You must tell yourself, before, during and after your support of the others that, you are doing these out of love for that person, and out of the love you have for god and all of his creations. Because this will help to make your intentions clear in your subconscious mind.

Do every thing you do for others, or even for yourself, in the name of and for the sake of love and god and watch your life become more harmonious, loving and progressive. Because you will develop an incomparable peace of mind and inner peace, and also the quality of your relationships will improve tremendously. That in turn will lead to improvement in all the aspects of your life.

51. Are the events we view as bad luck, really bad for us?

Once upon a time in India lived a farmer who had a young son who was helping him in his farm. He also had a cow that was used to pull the plows, to make the ground even, and ready for the plantation. One day the heavy plow, which was not tied properly, broke lose and broke the cow's leg. The cow could no longer be useful and died shortly after. Now the son had to pull the heavy plow himself. The neighboring farmers came to visit this farmer, and told him, oh you have such a bad luck! Now that you lost your cow you won't be able to prepare your land properly, and you will not be able to produce as much crops as last year. The farmer who was also a wise and spiritual man, and knew that these fellow farmers are not really feeling sorry for him, and just trying to bring his moral down, calmly smiled and said bad luck, good luck who knows, only god knows. After about three months later, his son's leg also broke the same way, and he had to stop with only preparing half of the field for the production, and he also had to send his only son to a hospital where he had to stay for one month. So the farmers came to see him again and said, oh my god this time you are really finished, you are just having bad luck this year, first your cow died, now your son's leg is broken. The farmer smiled again and said, good luck, bad luck who knows, only god knows. Few days later, war broke out, and the government authorities came to this farm land and whole nation, to recruit soldiers and also to take some of the farmer's crops for free, because it was customary that during national emergencies such as a war, serving in the army and giving of your agricultural food was mandatory. So the authorities took all of the farmer's sons, and also took three quarters of their crops. But when they came to the wise farmer's farm, since they saw only little crop, they did not take any, and since his son was in the hospital, he was automatically exempted from serving the army. All of the farmer's sons were slaughtered in the bloody war, and the farmers paid a visit to this wise farmer again, and told him that this time you were lucky your son's leg was broken and he did not have to join the army and as a result, he was not killed. He smiled and said he even got married with a beautiful nurse whom he fell in love with, in the hospital. The other farmers said your luck is changing, you are having lots of good luck these days. The farmer smiled and said Good luck, bad luck, who knows, only god knows.

The wisdom of the story is that we should not prematurely make a judgement and emotionally react when some thing happens in our lives that are not to our likings. We should look at the bigger picture, that god loves us and an apparently unpleasant event or accident in the present, even though maybe very painful in short terms, but in long terms it will be evident to us, that incident had actually caused and led you to transform your life for better.

For example a friend of mine, graduated from law school in Canada about two years ago, when he was out of school and passed his BAR exam, he tried wholeheartedly to find a job in one of the big law firms. He literally sent 200 resumes by fax and mail. However none of them were hiring, at that moment for the salary that he was expecting. The fair salary rate for a newly graduated lawyer was $75,000 plus, annually. But the few answers he got from some smaller firms, offered him only a salary of $50,000 a year, which he refused to accept, because he believed that he deserved to get at least the average salary. After spending three more months looking for a job, one night when he was really frustrated, because he was newly wed and he needed money urgently, and also he felt cheated by the system because he studied for nearly 10 years in the university to study political science and law, and they had promised him a good level of income and life style upon graduation, but now he thought he has wasted 10 best years of his life. He decided to pray for guidance and help that night.

He prayed all night for a message from god that would give him a solution. He fell sleep praying. The next morning he was awakened by a phone call from his classmate and friend from law school. He was facing the same dilemma, and couldn't have found a job yet. He offered him to join him as a partner and to open a new firm. His friend advised him that since you are from the Iranian community, we can specialize in immigration law, and offer our multilingual services to your community and other ethnic groups. He agreed, and thanked god for his immediate and effective solution, and they immediately started. The process was so smooth that he was surprised as why he didn't think about it before. Their business loan was approved in less than two weeks, they placed few ads in the local Persian newspapers and their business took off like an air plane. They attracted many clients, and made twenty thousand dollars the first month, and in three months they got so busy that they had to hire a secretary and legal assistance full time. And in six months they moved to a bigger office almost three times bigger than the first one. Now they are comfortably making three times more than the average lawyers in the market. The point is what he viewed as a disaster, turned out to be blessing for him in long terms. If he was hired by a firm, he would remain an underdog, and subject to restrictions and strict disciplines of the major firms, and he would also be financially less successful. Remember the god's ways are mysterious and if a new good thing is about to happen in our lives, first a destructive or limiting habit, belief, and life style pattern should be gotten rid of.

Exercise: This week, keep this story in mind, and decide not to immediately react when some thing is not going our way. We need to learn to discipline our thoughts, language and behaviors. We need to stop making any negative comments about our lives. Because comments such as "I am a failure, I just have bad luck, That's it I am finished, There is no hope, I am doomed for life" are very destructive to our lives, since using these lingual patterns continuously, makes them become a subconscious imprint, and consequently form our belief system and point of view about the world. And these beliefs are directly responsible for controlling and shaping our behaviors. In summary limited and negative words will lead to negative beliefs and values, and negative beliefs will form negative behavioral trends and habits, and negative mental habits leads to negative and limited actions and behaviors. And consequently this chain reaction will destroy our life and make it as we just said it ourselves. That is, we will really be doomed for life and would always have bad luck in our lives.

Therefore if you ever catch yourself using such destructive and negative language, stop it instantly and change it with a positive comment such as these following comments. "I am certain that things will change for better, I have to and I do trust in god, and I am sure there are valuable spiritual lessons in what just what happened. And like any thing else I know that these conditions will pass, and once again I will be happy and successful."

You can also do this mental exercise to facilitate the process of getting over the emotional difficulties you may experience as a result of a loss. Find a quiet place where you would not be disturbed for 15 minutes, lie down and take five deep breath, then take 2-3 minutes to attend to your breathing that helps both your mind and body to relax. Then imagine yourself as a soul which has glowing white and golden energy field around it, then imagine you are sitting beside a river that is very wide and has very strong and fast current. Imagine that you can see the past events and memories are floating in the river, and are approaching the point where you are currently sitting it includes both your good and bad memories.

Then see how they arrive where you are sitting, but quickly going way by the strong currents of the river. Now imagine this new and recent event that is causing you emotional pain, then watch it getting away from you and being pushed away by the strong current of the river, keep looking at the memory until it goes too far that you can't see it anymore, and it finally disappears. This river is life, and life's nature is constant change and moving on. And the movement and current of river shows the passage of time in our life. As time passes by, we naturally forget and adapt to the negative and disturbing emotional effects of the bothering and unpleasant experience. We like all other things, follow the laws of nature. However we have the mental and spiritual ability, to fasten the process, and ease our pain. In this exercise you can visualize the bothering condition, feel its emotional intensity within, you must allow yourself to completely and deeply express your feelings, feel free to cry and mourn because it will help to discharge the emotional attachment from the experience. After feeling the experience, then in your mind using your imagination faculty, increase the speed of the current in that river and see the event traveling from the past and passes where you sit, which is actually the present moment and finally gets away from you very fast and disappears. More you do it, less negative and disturbing emotions will be remained attached to your experience. Instead of waiting three months to get over a negative event, such as death of a loved one, you can overcome it faster and easier.

And you don't have to feel guilty about, not mourning for a long time after a loved one dies. Because now, you have a greater understanding about the god's rules. You know every thing happens for the best reason, and you know that, god loves all of his creation, and death is simply a transformation of consciousness, and it is always to a higher level and closer to godly worlds. And choose to pray for their soul happily, instead of crying and being discontent. Remember god loves all, and every thing happens at the right time and place, and it is necessary for our spiritual unfoldment.

52. It is all in your hand

Once upon a time in America, there was a very famous old professor and lecturer at Harvard University. He was so popular, because of his style of teaching and also because he was so knowledgeable, he had a prompt and correct answer to any question that any student may have. There has not been a single time that he had failed to answer a question while he was on the podium giving a lecture or speech. All the students and staff used to enjoy his lectures so much that, the faculty had decided to always appoint him as the main speaker and announcer of the university, and of course this position meant a lot of extra income for this old professor. His popularity and higher level of income caused the other professors and lectures to become jealous of him, and they decided to team up against him. They agreed to meet one evening after their teaching hours, to think of a strategy to, either to come up with a better subject or a better way of presenting a lecture, which would be superior to this old man's lectures and speeches. About ten of these professors showed up that evening, but none of them could come up with a convincing strategy to underscore the old man at the next lecture day, which was to be held next week before the end of midterm. When they were about to give up and disperse, one young professor who looked so ambitious and greedy, said: Wait I have an idea. Everybody stopped, and became silent. He said it is not an idea for lecture, but it is a plan to embarrass the professor in front of students. Before he starts the lecture, in this way he would lose composure and concentration and cannot continue giving his lecture, or at least the quality of his lecture will be dramatically lowered, and consequently he will lose his popularity and there will be opportunity for other lecturers like us to have a chance for future lecture positions.

Even though the other professors felt, it was unethical to try such a thing on a co-worker, but they decided to give it a try any ways because, they knew if they didn't do any thing about it, they will never be able to get a chance of becoming a leading speaker for the university. So he started explaining his plan, Right before the commencement of the old man lecture, I would hold a little live bird in my right hand, I would get to the podium and challenge him to answer my question, Then I would ask him what am I holding in my hands old man? Most likely he won't be able to know, but even if he could guess correctly, I would continue by asking him, Is It alive?, Or is it dead?

At this point the old man has only two choices to make as an answer, if he says yes it is alive, then I squeeze and kill the bird, then I open my hand and I prove him to be wrong, on the other hand, if he chooses to say that the bird is dead, then I would not kill the bird, and then open my hand and let the bird fly, and again I would prove him to be wrong. He said, as you can see there is no way for him to become the winner this time. They all agreed on this plan, and they decided to do it at the midterm ceremony where all students and teaching staff were attending.

So as they planned, right before the old man was to start, the young professor got on the podium, and used one of the two microphones which was on a table, and said ladies and gentlemen we would like to start the lecture with a challeng-ing question to day, of course if our main lecturer agrees and looked at the old man for his answer. The old man calmly and confidently said yes of course, that would be my pleasure. So the young man said thank you for accepting, now here is the question, I am holding some thing in my hand, can you guess what it is? The old man who was a very intuitive and spiritual person, smiled and said you are holding a little bird in your hand. The young man was shocked by him know-ing the answer, but he did not show his surprise and continued, Okay very good, correct answer, but the harder part of the question is, Is the bird alive or dead?

And as he finished asking the question, he smiled victoriously being absolutely sure that this time the old man could not answer the question. The old man smiled again and calmly said it is all in your hand, if you want it to be alive it will live, if you want it dead, you can destroy it. He continued, it is similar to our time, our lives, our relationship, our health, our finances, our development and every other aspect of our lives, god has given us the choice and control to choose what we want to do about any circumstances, to be destructive or constructive.

And always having a choice is what is meant by true freedom that god has given to all human beings.

The young man felt ashamed of himself for trying to embarrass this divine man with such a high level of awareness, he opened his hands and allowed the bird to fly away, and said I choose to be constructive and positive, and later he confessed and apologized to this old man for plotting such an unfair plan against him.

The wisdom of the story is that the quality of our lives is in our hand. Most often we believe that we have no control over our lives, and we are simply the victims of life's circumstances and unexpected events. This limited belief has been programmed into our mind during our early stages of life. Our parents, teachers, and religious clergy men have contributed in the creation of this limited belief, that we have absolutely no control over what will happen to us in our lives. Most orthodox religions believe and insist that our fate and destiny have been pre-written and one should simply flow and accept the existing conditions, where we are born into. However some powerful philosophies and religions like, Hinduism, Buddhism, Shamanism view human beings as co-creators with god. They believe god, which is an ocean of mercy, has given human beings the power and freedom to create their own reality by their imagination faculty. In this way, everyone is constantly creating his or her own reality by imagining and thinking about different things and circumstances. God has given us the freedom of choice. Whatever we choose to mentally focus on, would manifest externally in our lives. We can choose to focus on the positiveness, love, beauty, happiness, peace, heaven, abundance, health, creativity and god, and consequently be attracted to the circumstances that contain these attributes.

Or by the same token we may choose consciously or subconsciously to focus on the negativeness, hate, ugliness, sadness, war, hell, poverty, illness, destruction and evil, and consequently be attracted to the circumstances that contain these type of negative attributes. We always have a choice in every single situation in life. Even though we cannot control the event itself, but we can control and choose the way that we react to that event. For instance, if someone you love is acting hostile toward you, instead of fighting back which would create, even greater level of bitterness and hostility, you can choose to focus on the love instead. You can offer her help and support, And by showing her your selflessness and readiness, she will also calm down and change her behavior for better. In this way we are not defeated by negative force, but we have defeated the negative force by our positivity. Remember since we always move toward the direction of our dominant thoughts, we must choose to focus on our godly nature and start growing in all different aspects of our lives. Because we are the co-creators, and god has given us the privilege of being the creator of our own life, therefore use this amazing power which has always been within you, to create a new you, and a new life. This new self will be empowered, happy, successful, loving and creative, and his life will be full of blessings and love. I wish the stories, wisdom, and exercises in this book will help you to construct a new empowered self and to create a happy, healthy and successful life.

Exercise: This week, keep this story in mind and decide to truly take charge over your life. By now you should have all the necessary tools, such as positive and empowering beliefs, habits and priorities. You have also learned many mental and spiritual techniques which will help you in all the aspects of your life. However you need to be reminded that, the direction and quality of your life are all in your hands. You are the only one in this universe that can choose to change for better. God has given every thing you need, but he will not walk the path for you. He wants us as free souls, to choose our own path in life, and also we are the only one that can walk the path that we have chosen.

To live a balanced and fruitful life, we need to live according to the highest divine attributes and values. It doesn't mean that you have to become fanatically religious. I believe you should fit spirituality to your daily lives, not the other way around. If you simply apply these positive divine qualities into your life. Your whole being will be transformed for the better, and these inner transformations will create a better and happier life in all aspects. These attributes are easily incorporated into your life, and do not need any complicated rituals or ceremonies, all you need is an open heart, some effortless focus and applying these natural attributes in your daily life. For instance applying moderation to all the aspects of your life will transform you beyond your imaginations. Remember, we need to have discipline in the way we think, talk and behave. Because as we think, talk and act, we are actually creating our destiny and our next destination in our lives.

Therefore if we discipline our thoughts, spoken words, and actions and use only positive, loving and empowering words, thoughts and actions then our next destination in life will be a positive place, full of love and prosperity. Therefore make a general plan for each and every aspect of your life, like you physical, emotional, mental and spiritual aspects, and make sure that you apply the positive and divine rules within your daily life. The more frequent you apply these positive attributes, sooner and more efficiently they will become part of you and your life. In conclusion, if you focus and live by god's values and attributes, you will become a godly person, and your life will be full of blessing, happiness and love. It is all in your hand. Instead of killing and destroying your life by focusing on negative and destructive things, decide to choose to let your life flourish and grow to reach its true potential which is self-realization and god realization.

0-595-29829-X

Made in the USA
Lexington, KY
03 December 2014